Behold the State I'm In

A Novel By B. Graham Simpson

Beta Logos Books, LLC
Fort Washington, Maryland

Cover Design by Mark A. Richards
Cover Photos by Beta Logos Books, LLC
Edited by Linda Frommer

Library of Congress Control Number: 2004096779
ISBN: 0-9668517-1-4

Beta Logos Books, LLC
Fort Washington, Maryland 20744
www.BeholdBooks.com
E-mail: Author@BeholdBooks.com

PRINTED IN THE UNITED STATES OF AMERICA

To my mother, Susie Mae Adams Graham,
whose memories about life in the South
were the initial inspiration for this novel.

Most Sincere Appreciation ...

My interpretation of foundational Biblical principles as taught at From the Heart Church Ministries and the valued consultation on characterization and plot development that was provided by the following people, as well as the encouragement and support of family, friends, and acquaintances during the course of this project, contributed greatly to this book's content and its becoming a reality.

Consultants:
Eugene C. Simpson, Sr.
Elder Margaret Crosby
Sandra E. Fryar
Rosie A. Wilson
Lynda K. Wright
Reverend Willette O. Wright
Linda Frommer, Editor

Members of Gospel Book Fellowship:
Owilda D. Fields
Julie D. Long
Lois G. Long
Claudette E. Pride

To God be the glory!

Foreword

Behold the State I'm In chronicles the lives of the Christianson family—how the young people in the family leave the poverty and lack of opportunity of rural life in the South and head for the new opportunities and dangers of urban life in the North. For the sisters and brother of the Christianson family, their successive moves out of The Sticks emerge as the only possible recourse in response to the event that opens the book: the death of their mother, Heart Christianson, and her replacement with the less-than-genuine stepmother, Mumzy. In truth, this death takes the heart out of the family; without it, its individual members are lost. The first quarter of *Behold the State I'm In* tells of how each child of the Christianson family gropes toward life—or the promise of it—again. In all cases, the hope for life—no matter what form that hope takes—beckons them away from the Christianson farm to migration north and to dispersal—a dispersal that is both physical and moral.

This is the framework for the central character of the novel, Patience, and it is mostly through her eyes and through the prism of her struggle that we see the story of the family. From the first moments, as Patience describes her vigil at her mother's deathbed, the tensions between her extreme vulnerability and her fortitude bring her alive to the reader. We are filled with an anxiety for her and her sister that at every moment compels us to turn the page, as Patience decides to leave her father's home, head north, and seek a college education, meeting temptations and difficulties at every point on the way. We briefly feel secure, believing that all is well with her marriage to Will B. Done, until catastrophe, unjustly and irrationally, lashes out and strikes Patience with her gravest challenge yet.

It is a story well told. Many African-Americans in the United States know this story firsthand or as related to them by parents and grandparents. It is not unfamiliar terrain for many American readers.

What sets this novel apart is the telling of Patience's spiritual journey. For Patience, life's events are secondary to her primary concern: her relationship with God, beginning with her dying mother's loving words to her, "Baby, don't leave God." Patience's struggle to follow the Word toward God, and toward the only peace possible within herself, is the true subject of *Behold the State I'm In*. The road signs are Second Peter 1:5–8: "And beside this, giving all diligence, add to your faith virtue; and to virtue knowledge; and knowledge temperance; and to temperance patience; and to patience godliness; and to godliness brotherly kindness; and to brotherly kindness charity. For if these things be in you and abound, they make you that ye shall neither be barren nor unfruitful in the knowledge of our Lord Jesus Christ."

God's presence in the book through His Word and through Patience's fight to cleave to Him opens new territory in the story of the migration of many African-Americans northward over the course of the last century. The unfolding of Patience's life—from her grim determination to escape the evil of Mumzy to the flowering of her love of God in marriage with Will to her confrontation with injustice and cruelty—becomes both a spiritual parable and a profound and enriching glimpse into a human soul.

Linda Frommer
Writer and Editor

"Not that I speak in respect of want: for I have learned, in whatsoever state I am, therewith to be content."
Philippians 4:11

Not That I Speak ...

Behold the State I'm In

1951

She was hot … she was cold. Mama's shallow breaths tickled Temperance's ear. Mama shivered, Mama shook. It was a noisy kind of shaking, my sister Temperance must have thought—a dull rumbling deep inside Mama's chest. Temperance must have felt special getting all of Mama's attention that day, despite her wondering about the rumbling in Mama's chest and the shivering, and the warm perspiration that dripped onto her little face when she looked up at Mama. She searched for answers and assurance. She was afraid, and young enough not to care who knew it.

Mama held Temperance with all her remaining strength. More coughing, more rumbling in her chest as she breathed. More shaking. Mama's chest was filled to its capacity with fluid.

"Baby, don't ever leave God," Mama said. Her voice was weak, her throat raw from coughing so much for so long. Her arms gripped her little girl.

"You going to have beautiful children one day," Mama said. "… The Lord liveth and blessed be my rock … you my baby … my baby … hold on. … No comfort in sin … no comfort … sin. … In His Body are many members … you the hair, baby, don't mean you suppose to be on the head … you still the hair. … Where you supposed to be? … Know your purpose … find your place. … No comfort in sin. … Do the right thing."

Paw went over to where Mama was lying, pried Temperance away from her grasp, and gave her to me.

"Patience, take this gal," Paw said. "Five years old and your mama acting like she still a baby." I thought I saw him dab a tear from under his eye, but no. Paw crying? No.

3

"Heart been talking out of her head too long," Paw said.

"Can I help, Paw?" I asked. I looked around, found a comb on the floor behind me, and started to undo Temperance's braids so I could comb her hair.

"Nothing you can do, baby girl," Paw said, "except keep them damp rags on your mama's head." At Paw's suggestion, I dropped the comb, got up, almost knocking Temperance to the floor, and went to the kitchen for water to fill the wash pan. Temperance followed me.

As I poured water into the pan, I remembered when I was the baby in the family.

"You know you my knee-baby," Mama said, "and your Paw's too. There ain't nothing that's going to change that." Paw sat in the wingback chair, his favorite place in the house, carving a piece of wood into a walking stick. He winked at Mama, which always made her laugh with her mouth closed, pushing air through her nose. "I love your old Paw, and me and him think the world of y'all children. But you special, and we know it. If anybody in this family is going to make it, maybe get a college education, maybe even Up North, you the one."

I remembered feeling a pressure within me that I was too young to describe or explain. It made me proud that my parents thought of me that way, and I promised myself I would always give whatever I did my best effort. With conflicting emotions welling up in me like the spring that was our source of water, I hugged my mother's neck and kissed her on the cheek.

Paw—worried, helpless, and vulnerable—had always been so big and strong, especially when he was behind a team of mules out in the field plowing.

"I don't know. I just don't know," Paw said. He paced the floor. "I done sent for Doctor Partial, but he taking his time coming to see about Heart."

Being sick usually didn't stop us when there was work to be done. It was February, and there wasn't much work to do in the dead of winter when you're sharecroppers like we were. When it got cold, Paw went hunting for rabbits or deer with my big brother Soldier, or they'd go fishing. Because we didn't have a refrigerator, whatever they shot or caught, we shared with other sharecroppers so the meat wouldn't spoil.

When Mama's coughing became so intense that she no longer had the strength to get out of bed, Paw didn't complain. After all, she had done her share all during the planting and harvesting seasons. In addition to working some of the time in the field alongside Paw, she was a homemaker in all respects. Throughout the winter we ate the fruit and vegetables she had canned that summer— peaches, tomatoes, blackberries, figs, and whatever else was edible that grew in our part of The Sticks. She deserved a little time off to be sick if she wanted to, Paw had said. That was the only time anyone in our family could rest. It was almost Scriptural, based on the Twenty-third Psalm: "He maketh me to lie down in green pastures." I thought God was making Mama lie down, because she wouldn't take time to rest.

When one of the children got sick, all of us got sick. We slept in the larger of the two bedrooms. Bedrooms. We didn't have beds; we slept on pallets spread out in no particular order all over the floor. With no heater in our room, we kept warm at night until we fell asleep by heating large rocks or bricks on the kitchen stove, wrapping them in heavy rags, and positioning them at our feet or wherever we wanted to keep warm.

Before bedtime, we huddled together in the front room on the ragged couch that Miss Grace and Mister Mercy, the owners of the house we lived in and the land we sharecropped, gave us. They also gave us a wood table and seven wooden chairs with bottoms woven with straw; these graced our cozy eat-in kitchen. Ernest and Heart Christianson were never too proud to receive from Miss Grace and Mister Mercy. With thankfulness we received, and all that they gave—whether food, clothing, books, furniture, or advice—they gave with love.

We sharecropped Miss Grace and Mister Mercy's land using the halves system, which meant that Paw turned over half the proceeds to Mr. Mercy, and Mr. Mercy provided all the essential equipment, the farm animals necessary for transporting and tilling, and the seeds needed to plant the cotton crops that Paw raised.

During summer in The Sticks, the unforgiving heat from our wood-burning cook stove shooed us away like bothersome flies at an outdoor dinner during August Meeting at New Mount Saint Bethel Holy Church. (For years we attended church almost every Sunday, but our attendance eventually dwindled away to our going to service only on Christmas, Easter, and Mother's Day.) In the frigid winter, the same heat, repentant from its midyear cruelty, summoned the family to join together in silent communion as we consumed hot biscuits and blackstrap molasses around the stove on a typical Saturday morning. With only space in front of the stove to stand and cook, and space on both sides for wood and a small table, every evening after supper I staked my claim on the corner beside the back door, sat Temperance on my lap, and whispered the alphabet song close to her ear until she fell asleep.

From sunup to sundown, Paw carried out his unwritten mission: to labor in Mr. Mercy's field so Mr. Mercy made a profit and, as Paw put it, "Maybe give us a little extra piece a money if everything turned out good." Soldier and Mama worked alongside Paw. Goody, Sister, Temperance, and I helped by carrying burlap sheets and sacks for the harvest, hoeing the ground, dropping seeds, loading the wagon, or carrying buckets of water from the spring.

No one worked the day the doctor came to see Mama. Goody (short for Goodness), in deep thought beneath the front-room window, sat hugging her knees to her chest listening to the wind whistling through the cracks in our old house. She was my oldest sister, ten, a year older than I. Nevertheless, she asked for my advice on such subjects as boys.

"Is it okay to let a boy rub your shoulder?" Goody asked.

"What for?" I asked. "Why would a boy worry about rubbing your shoulder?"

"I didn't say it was *my* shoulder," Goody said. "And how would I know what for? That's why I'm asking you. I saw a boy doing that to a girl, that's all."

"It doesn't make sense. Was something on her dress? Dirt? Lint? Was her shoulder hurting or something? That's it. Her shoulder was hurting, right?"

"You read the Bible a lot. Is there anything in there about not letting a boy rub a girl's ... shoulder?"

Goody's question had caught me by surprise. She had a genuine interest in my opinion, but I knew nothing about what the Bible said about boys rubbing girls' shoulders. I read the same Scriptures every day, over and over. Otherwise I read the Bible at the place where I happened to open it. In fact, I read every printed word I could, whether in the Bible or a discarded newspaper. I dreamed of someday going to college like Mama said I would.

"Uh-oh," I said. A light came on in my head. "Goody Christianson, you're talking about Noppa, aren't you? You know better than to be bothered with him. Don't you let him near you, Goody, you hear? You don't need to read it in the Bible to know he's bad."

"It didn't ... look bad," Goody said. She giggled, smiled, and looked down to the ground.

"Everything that doesn't ... look bad doesn't mean it's good, either. Don't you let him touch you and don't you touch him. That's all I have to say."

Noppa's real name was Inopportune, a name that, because of its length and uncommonness, most people, even his family, shortened to Noppa. He was thirteen, Soldier's age. Noppa was often truant from school, wasting his time with dropouts who gambled. Sometimes he worked to earn money to support his gambling habit by helping Paw and other area sharecroppers bring in their crops. He also helped himself to the oftentimes innocent and naive sharecroppers' daughters. Once Paw caught him in the back twenty acres with a young girl and ran them both off. After that incident, Paw didn't use Noppa's help again.

"I've got too many daughters to have the likes of Noppa sniffing around here like a hound dog in heat," Paw said.

Noppa was tall for his age and could have easily passed for at least sixteen. He was handsome, and he knew it, and had been known to court girls as young as twelve and as old as twenty.

Mama began to wheeze when I placed the cool damp cloths on her forehead. I folded back one of the three patchwork quilts that covered her, and she peered from under the cover with red eyes and a forced smile.

In the front room, I loosened the rest of Temperance's braids and continued combing her hair.

"You're hurting me, you old nasty," Temperance said. A burst of laughter was Sister's reaction to Temperance whenever she was being a brat. This encouraged Temperance further. Sister was a middle child and was either competing with Temperance or was her accomplice in mischief.

"You old nasty goose head," Temperance continued. More howls from Sister.

"I'm not old or nasty, and stop calling me names," I said. "I'm trying to tame this stuff on top of your head and you and Sister keep cutting up. Sister, you're next. When was the last time I got hold of your head?" Mama usually combed Sister's hair. Mama. Our thoughts drifted back to Mama, almost at once, and Temperance shivered.

"I'm cold," she said.

Sister opened the heater door and heaved another piece of firewood onto the fire. It crackled and sparked, then became silent when Sister shut the heater door.

Usually I was slow and gentle when combing out Temperance's thick, tightly curled, neck-length hair so as not to break the ends. But that day I couldn't concentrate because of Mama.

"Y'all getting on my nerves, now," Paw said. He got up from his chair and looked out the window again for the doctor. "It's bad enough with your mama sick as she is without all you in here keeping up noise. Now go on in your room, you hear?"

We all heard, but only Goody got up and left the room. Her shoes, which she had outgrown and had cut out the backs, clip-clopped as she walked away barely picking up her feet. I held Temperance in a strong grip between my thighs so she couldn't move and began to comb out her hair and braid it in cornrows. She squirmed trying to loose herself from my control.

"I'm going in the room with Goody," she said.

"No, let's wait, the doctor's coming," I said. Temperance's untamed curiosity caused her to settle down. The door swung open, and Doctor Partial entered. Paw pointed to Mama's room, and he went in to examine Mama.

"I'm cold again," Temperance said. The fire in the heater had gone out when Doctor Partial came out of Mama's room and whispered to Paw. But I could hear, and the others could, too.

"Ernest," Doctor Partial swallowed and shook his head, "there's not much I can do. How long did you say Heart has been like this?"

"She been coughing up yellow and orange cold for nigh on to two weeks, and been having hot and cold sweats too. She won't eat neither, says nothing taste right, but I been forcing her to eat buttermilk and cornbread, and drink some cider now and then. She—we both—thought it was just a bad cold, doctor. She don't usually complain, and we didn't want to bother nobody about it. But I thought I better get hold of you when the fever made her start seeing things and talking out of her head."

Paw's expression was a montage of fear, and pain, and shock, and guilt, all framed with a helpless anticipation of the news he was about to hear.

"I wish you had called me before now," Doctor Partial said. "We have medicine to take care of the pneumonia these days."

"Pneumonia," Paw said, a little louder than he wanted to. We all knew the word. It was a word like diphtheria, like polio, like the plague. And although we didn't know the full ramifications of the word, we knew it was a word that made us wonder. We probably couldn't spell it, but we knew it could spell death.

"You can heal it, can't you? Can't you do something for her?"

"Calm down, Ernest, now. I'll see to getting some medicine for her. We can't take her to the hospital, she being Colored and all, but, well, I already gave her two aspirins to bring down the fever. Here—here's the bottle. You got to make her drink plenty water."

"Yes sir, lots of water. I'll have the young'uns fetch more from the spring down the road."

"Send for me if she gets worse," Doctor Partial said. "You know how to reach me. I'll check on her day after tomorrow." Doctor Partial looked over his glasses at Soldier and then at Paw. "Heart is a strong woman, Ernest, so don't you worry."

Doctor Partial spanned the room again, looking over at me, at Temperance, and at Sister. A slight, fleeting smile brightened his face, and at that moment the beauty of his smile gave me hope. But then he looked down. Why did he have to look down? I knew what that meant, and Paw did, too. We all did.

Doctor Partial came back to see Mama the day after next as he said he would. Paw sat in the front room with all of us children when Doctor Partial came out of the bedroom. He slid on his jacket and straightened his tie. I

11

noticed that he slumped more now than he had when he arrived.

"Heart is gone," Doctor Partial said. He departed to join his family, I imagined. It had been less than a week since Paw first called him to check on Mama.

After Mama died, I all but adopted Temperance. I wouldn't allow anyone else to dress her, comb her hair, put alcohol on a scraped knee, or attend to any of the many little demands of a five-year-old. She was mine, and I promised God that I would always nurture her and ensure that she was safe and sound. After Mama died, Paw didn't volunteer, that often, to do anything for Temperance or any of us. It was almost as if when Mama died, a part of him died also, the part that all of us children adored and needed so badly.

After Mama died, no longer did we scramble on the floor for Paw's roasted peanuts after all the field work was done. Paw would sit in his wingback chair, and Temperance would stand behind him sandwiched between him and the chair's back. The smell of peanuts, dark-roasted in their shells and right out of the oven of our hot woodstove, which warmed most of our cozy little house on a cold winter's evening, would fill the house and seep out where the frigid wind seeped in. All would be well in our household, when we scrambled for peanuts. Paw would grab a handful of the warm nuts, sort of shake them around, and then cast them to the hardwood floor. Goody and Soldier's heads sometimes would bump together hard, and the nuts sometimes would crack as they hit the floor hard as we all tried to grab as many as we could.

With her spittle, Temperance would anoint Paw's balding head and rub it in well. From his cup Paw would drink coffee or cider or something else, closing his eyes, savoring the taste, or the warmth, or both. Temperance would be in charge of Paw, and she relished every minute of it—probably hugging his neck not realizing that Paw wasn't given to displays of affection, howbeit he had plenty of it bottled up inside him. Maybe she had let the excitement of the moment conveniently rob her memory of hard work and hot days in the field—although she was too young to do any real work—rob her memory of scant tables bearing pinto beans and cornbread—although to her the cornbread was cake—or rob her memory of nights when Mama and Paw were too tired to give us the attention we needed.

The mood would be cheerful, yet eerie—a happy, serious tone. Whether it would be Sunday or Thursday, I don't remember, nor do I recall whether Mama and Paw would be even getting along well. They were given to bouts of arguing, as many parents are. But when we children would scramble for Paw's peanuts on the floor, all was right in our little world. Our hard life was a good life.

When we would scramble for Paw's peanuts on the floor, we would laugh and joke, and at no one's expense, while Mama would make herself comfortable to the side in her straw-bottom mate's chair, adding the finishing touches to a daughter's petticoat, a son's topcoat, a sheet, a shirt, or her latest sewing notion. Scrambling for peanuts would make us forget about the overriding hard times and be thankful we had a family—a Mama and Paw in the same house, and siblings we could choose to fight or hug, as the mood struck us. We were content, in that little house, on Miss Grace and Mr. Mercy's land.

1953

It was Wednesday, a typical hot July evening in The Sticks. Mama had been dead for two years, and my sisters, brother, and I hadn't seen Paw since Friday morning. His going missing on the weekends had become a regular occurrence for about a month.

I will never forget that particular Wednesday evening. I was resting in the front room with Temperance after picking cotton all day. Because of Paw's absences, Soldier had to pick more than double his normal weight of cotton to make up for Paw's lost share. We girls helped as best we could, but were unaccustomed to picking more than a total of a hundred to a hundred and fifty pounds a day.

That Wednesday, Paw burst into the front room with excitement in his eyes and a woman on his arm. From the first moment I saw the woman with Paw, I knew that life as a Christianson was about to change.

She was the most beautiful woman—Colored woman—I had ever seen. She and Paw made a striking couple. Paw was thirty-nine, so she must have been no older than thirty-five. Paw's tall stature; his high cheekbones; his large, wide nose; his dark-brown skin; his thick, black eyebrows and mustache; his short, tightly curled black hair with specks of premature gray; all played against, yet complemented the woman's features: Her tan skin, her medium-length, straightened, and loosely curled hair tucked to the sides by two blue combs that picked up the blue in her flowered, cotton dress; her little mouth with her full, bright red lipstick-smeared lips; her smile that acted like it would break if prolonged; and her almond-shaped, searching, looking, observing, contentious, spying eyes, slightly slanted—eyes that revealed something evil, if you were brave enough not to look away. Angry, upset, disgusted—that was my first impression of the woman Paw brought home. When Paw looked at her, though, his eyes gleamed like a hungry baby looking at its mother's breast in expectation of timely nourishment.

I gazed at the woman and watched Paw as he gawked at the woman. Temperance and I resembled Paw more than the other children—we were dark-skinned. In those days, to be so dark-skinned was to be deemed ugly. Therefore, I, too, looked like I didn't belong in the same room with the woman. My dress didn't have bright flowers on it, but was made from sun-bleached potato sacks.

When the woman noticed my gaze, she shook her head a couple of times, making her curls dance on either side of her head. Before I could give it much thought, I shook my head, causing an old comb, which held in place a thick plait at the top of my head, to come loose and fall to the floor. The woman snorted a snicker as I picked up the comb and covered my embarrassment by using it to undo the plait, which resulted in a ball of bushy hair. At that, the woman chuckled, and I ran outside. Temperance joined me on the step.

"Your hair needs fixing," I could almost hear Mama say. Fixing.

"Temperance, don't you ever be embarrassed about your hair," I said. "It's just as good as anybody else's. It's what God gave you."

I was embarrassed, but not of my hair, not of its being called nappy or kinky, for which its natural, tightly curled state had come to be known. I was ashamed of allowing the woman to push a button I didn't know I had. Since I could remember, Mama and I had struggled over to-straighten-or-not-to-straighten. She would heat a metal

15

dime-store straightening comb to straighten us girls' hair and a huge nail, which she found in the field, to curl it. She either wouldn't let my hair dry thoroughly, which generated hot steam when the hot comb touched it, or she would apply to the hair too much grease, which would drip off the straightening comb or nail onto my skin. Sometimes she would just place the comb or nail too close to my scalp, and when I didn't relax and jerked in fear of the heat, Mama sometimes would accidentally burn my scalp, neck, or face, which didn't do too much to assuage my fear. Out of defiance or because I was born in April, but at the first rain after Mama straightened my hair, I would walk outside and it would revert to its natural, God-given, indigenous state. So, to protect her blood pressure and nerves, Mama gave up and resorted to only washing and braiding it.

"I said okay, I won't be ashamed," Temperance assured me. She leaned in front of me and waved her hand in front of my face as if checking to see if I saw and heard her.

"Who is that coming down the road?" I asked.

Temperance blocked the glare of the sun with her hand to get a better view. It was Able Short, a little boy from New Mount Saint Bethel that occasionally visited Temperance. I read Scriptures to him hoping his reading skills and his ability to learn and memorize facts would improve as a result.

"Hey Patience, hey Temperance," he said, and sat down on the step.

"Hey, Able. You'd better go on back home," I said. "We've got company today."

"Okay," Able said. He stood up and started walking back down the road. "Oh, Elder Rector said if you're going to be reading to me, for you to read me the Bible verse about children obeying their parents."

"I will, just come back Saturday," I said.

"Patience, you and Temperance get on back in here," Paw called out to us. We obeyed and found the woman sitting in Paw's big chair. Paw went through the kitchen and called out the back door for the other children to come in.

Soldier entered wiping sweat from his forehead beneath the brim of his hat with the back of his sleeve and crossed the room to sit with Temperance and me on the couch. Then Sister came in. Last through the door, removing a wide straw hat, was Goody.

"Children, this is—"

"All y'all can call me Mumzy," the woman said.

Mumzy looked around at us with those eyes and caught a glimpse of herself in the cracked, framed mirror on the front-room wall. She dabbed under her bottom lip with her finger, correcting a bit of out-of-place red lipstick.

"She ain't no mama of mine," Goody scoffed under her breath, but loudly enough to make sure we, especially Mumzy, heard.

"Shut up, gal," Paw said, and jerked up his hand as if to give Goody a back-hand slap. "You respect your elders, you hear? This here is my wife."

Paw had never raised his hands to threaten us before. He would get Old Tickler, his thick leather strap that he whipped us with. Usually, our punishment was justifiable: A smart remark from Goody would summon Old Tickler, or a bad report from a neighbor about one of us who happened to be with the wrong crowd doing the wrong thing. Once Soldier stole a honey bun from the trading-post store. Paw learned about it and whipped him with Old

Tickler. Soldier never stole again.

"Yes, sir," Goody said. She backed to the wall, just as surprised as I was to see Paw's hand go up.

Mumzy got the message; Goody had a bad attitude toward her, our newest family member. She looked Goody up and down, wrinkled up her nose, and then looked away, dismissing any importance anyone could have placed in Goody's comment.

"I didn't say 'mama' anyway, I said 'Mumzy.'"

We had called our real mother "Mama." And I'm sure my sisters and brother felt as I did—no one could ever take Mama's place, certainly not Mumzy.

We didn't go to school much after Mama died, not even our customary two or three times a week. Even so, every day before bedtime, I read Mama's Bible out loud to Temperance.

"*The Lord is my shepherd. I shall not want,*" I read. "Temperance, that means no matter wherever you go, and whatever you do, just be good, and the Lord will take care of you. *'He maketh me to lie down in green pastures: he leadeth me beside the still waters.'* You see, Temperance, that proves that God will see after us. We all are like sheep, you know. And the Good Shepherd won't let anything bad happen to His little sheep." By the time I got to *"and I will dwell in the house of the Lord forever,"* Temperance would be sound asleep. "Sleep tight, Temp," I said. And as if she had the same yearnings as I, each night I affirmed over her: "We're going to be somebody one day. You and me. Just like Miss Grace said. ... Just like Mama said."

Mumzy operated a laundry business, and after moving in she continued to make a living hand-washing, starching, and pressing laundry for the well-to-do White families in The Sticks—such as the Hardies, the Prides, and the Knockses. Each day before sunup she and Paw made their rounds into town picking up and delivering laundry. They'd be back, though, by the time Temperance and I, and the other children woke up. After they returned, a bang of the screen door closing signaled Paw and Soldier's leaving the house to commence their duties in the field, our signal to get up and eat breakfast. Goody prepared homemade buttermilk biscuits to go with the blackstrap molasses. During late fall and winter, all of us except Soldier walked to the school-house. However, after Mumzy moved in, we stopped going to school altogether, because unlike raising cotton, the laundry business wasn't seasonal.

"Ernest, those gals need to help me with my laundry," she told Paw.

"All right, y'all heard Mumzy," Paw said, without thought or hesitation. "Mumzy been doing too much work around here, I have to agree." He turned toward the broken mirror on the front-room wall and saw his reflection. For countless moments, he stared at himself. "Don't want nothing ever to happen to Mumzy," he said still looking at his reflection, finally blinking, quietly shaking his head. Then he looked at Temperance and me. "Go get them buckets and start toting water." Turning to Mumzy, he said, "You lookin' kind of tired. Go on in yonder and lay down."

"Okay, Ernest," Mumzy quickly acquiesced. She walked into their room and shot a grin over her shoulder at us— everything had transpired exactly the way she had planned.

Mumzy's laundry business became the family business. Because Paw stopped working in the field, the family had to move out of Miss Grace and Mr. Mercy's house and into a two-room shack Paw found even farther from town. He sold the wagon and mule to get the money needed to move in. All day, Paw, Soldier, Goody, Sister, Temperance and I, and sometimes Mumzy, chopped wood for the fire, boiled laundry, scrubbed laundry, flat-ironed laundry, and walked to town to deliver it to Mumzy's customers. Soldier continued to work Mr. Mercy's land in order to make extra money for the family and earn spending money of his own.

Mumzy was good—good at getting her way with Paw and making us children do all the work. And because of us, the business grew. Mr. Knocks and his three sons changed shirts every day. They also changed their sheets every day, which totaled twenty-eight shirts and sheets a week from that family alone. We laundered nearly a hundred shirts a week, plus bed and table linen and various women's articles of clothing.

"Mumzy, can I have two pennies," Goody or I would ask. It didn't matter what we wanted the money for—a cold drink from Mr. Mercy's Storehouse, or just to see if she had grown any kinder since the last time we asked. She'd always make an excuse such as, "Gal, I ain't got no money. I got bills to pay." Or she'd say, "I have to pay on my bank loan." Goody and I never questioned her further about what she did with all of her money. We only knew that we didn't live like a family with a household income of fifty dollars a week, which was a relatively good living for a Colored family in the fifties.

"Where you been?" Mumzy asked. She hunched up her shoulder and then grabbed it with the opposite hand, as if she were in pain.

"Up to Miss Grace's," I replied. I didn't look Mumzy in the eyes, fearing that she would misconstrue what I said. I lowered my eyes and my head, and put my hand in my apron pocket, feeling the lace-trimmed handkerchief that Miss Grace had given me, being careful not to fiddle with it too much—Mumzy might take it.

"She needed my help ... with something," I said.

"Well, I need your help around here, too. And don't you forget it.

"Yes, Mumzy," I said.

Only Temperance knew about the odd jobs I did, everything from picking blackberries and selling them to Miss Grace, to picking cotton for Mr. Mercy. Miss Grace had detained me that day to show me books from her college years and the lessons she had prepared for her reading students when she used to teach.

"Do they really have colleges for people like me?" I asked her. She didn't answer, but kept thumbing through her lesson books. From my experience with Miss Grace, I knew that when she ignored a question that I asked, it meant either that I should know the answer for myself without asking or that it was a silly question, although she would never say that it was silly.

"Do you think I could really go to college some day?" I asked her, hoping that I had phrased it just right to get an answer from her. As I handled Miss Grace's old reading lessons, a bit of paper crumbled in my hand. She noticed it, too, but didn't make a fuss about it.

"You can do anything you set your mind to do, Patience," she said. "I have a gift for you." She turned, reached into the silk purse that lay on top of the bureau behind her and pulled out a white lace-trimmed handker-chief. "Every young lady aspiring to become educated needs one of these," she said.

Almost trembling, I was filled with excited curiosity as I took the handkerchief from Miss Grace. I had never owned anything so pretty, so strange to the world I knew, yet so ... sufficient for its purpose.

For two years we worked Mumzy's laundry business. Every day, seven days a week, we went through the same routine, from morning until night, carrying water in sometimes leaky buckets from the spring to the black, grand wash pots in our backyard. Before a load dried on the clothes lines, we started the cycle again.

1955

Like seasons that never change, ice that never melts, and midnights that never give way to the dawn of a new day, life with Mumzy was dark, cold, and monotonous. My siblings and I suspected that she couldn't read, or at least not that well, and we took pride in the fact that all us were good readers. Without effort, we absorbed all the old books, newspapers, and magazines that Miss Grace gave us. By candlelight, way into the late hours, every night, we read, joyfully, willingly, without grumbling. We did it for Mama—who had instilled in us, no, preached to us until it became a part of our being, the importance of reading—and not merely to flaunt our literacy in Mumzy's face in retali-ation for her sometimes cruel acts.

That summer, Sister escaped Mumzy's cruelty. She

begged Paw to spend a summer with Aunt Wits, Mama's half sister, in The Motor City, and he and Mumzy agreed to let her go.

"Now you don't have to worry about Sister," Aunt Wits said. She sat down next to Paw on the step of our splinter-ridden front porch, fanned herself with her open hand, and crossed her legs. Her gray store-bought gathered dress flowed amply down to her ankles, and out of modesty, she tucked the cloth under her thighs and legs making sure she wouldn't be exposed inadvertently by the wind that was a bit strong that day. "I'll take good care of Sister, just like she was my own daughter." Aunt Wits wasn't married and didn't have any children, so the idea of company gave her genuine joy.

Temperance and I stood wide-eyed in front of them staring at Aunt Wits, believing that everyone who lived in places such as The Motor City was rich, and then we ran between Paw and Aunt Wits into the house to see what Sister was doing. She had finished packing before we got there and was ready to go.

"You'd better write me," I told Sister.

"Write me, too," Temperance said.

"I'll write everybody," Sister said. She patted Temperance on the behind and pinched her cheek. "Where's Goody? I didn't tell her goodbye."

"She's at church doing some work for Elder Rector," I said. "I'm supposed to help him organize the summer Bible school, and he also wants me to take charge of the five-year-olds this year. I'm late, but I don't care. Be good, Sister."

"You, too, Patience," she said. "Aunt Wits said she'll bring me back in September."

"Come on, Sister, we don't want to miss our train,"

Aunt Wits said. Sister and Aunt Wits got in a long automobile with the word "Taxi" written on its side. With her thumb in her mouth, something she hadn't done since Mama's funeral, Temperance watched the taxi until it was out of sight. Paw, Soldier, Temperance, and I were speechless, transfixed by the sight of another of the Christiansons departing to a world unknown to all of us, to a new life. First Mama went to Heaven. Now Sister was gone to The Motor City.

"One less mouth eating up all my food around here," Mumzy said, and walked around to the backyard, bringing what was left of my family back to the reality of our world.

Without Sister, life in our family was devoid of what integrated its soul and character. Without Sister, we were doomed to become a group of strangers, drifting through life without any kind of bond that mattered. Sister was too young to realize her impact on us all. Her way of laughing at the jokes Temperance made at my expense somehow closed the four-year gap in Temperance's and my ages, drawing us closer together. When Goody's hands were blistered from scrubbing laundry and my feet were raw from walking barefoot to and from the spring for water to fill the wash pots, Sister made a simple suggestion: "Why don't you two just switch jobs for a while? You be Goody's hands, and, Goody, you be Patience's feet." That suggestion helped Goody and me realize how important we were to each other and that we could trust each other. It was Sister who ran and got Soldier when a rabid dog chased me into the chicken coop. Soldier shot the dog with Paw's shotgun, and from that time forward, Soldier protected me as a big brother should—naturally, without being asked. And similar cases could be made for all of the one-to-one relationships in the Christianson family, be it Goody and Temperance,

Temperance and Soldier ... or Paw and me. Sister and Heart Christianson were gone, and Mumzy was systematically driving a wedge between all our established relationships.

Sister and Aunt Wits bonded so well that, instead of bringing her home as she promised, Aunt Wits enrolled her in The Motor City school system that fall. Sister wrote me as she promised and told us about her new life.

Dear Patience,

I've never been so many places and done so many things. Aunt Wits takes me everywhere. She took me to the circus, under a huge tent, with elephants and clowns. And we went to the museum to see paintings and statues, I mean sculptures. Aunt Wits buys me a lot of pretty dresses, and she's letting me take piano lessons, too. Her house is so nice. She says she's not rich, but she makes a lot of money as the—I want to make sure I get this right—Executive Housekeeper at the Cosmopolitan Club. I'm pretty sure that's what she said. I have to go now. Aunt Wits is drawing my bath water. We're going to eat in a restaurant tonight. Tell everyone hello for me.

Always yours,
Sister

"I'm tired of working for Mumzy for nothing," Soldier said. "I'm leaving." And with a thud, the burlap sack containing all his earthly belongings hit the porch as he straightened the collar of one of the white shirts he had received from Mr. Mercy via Miss Grace. He had found his birth certificate to prove he was seventeen and a citizen of this country. A hard worker, big and strong, he had no trouble meeting the physical requirements for enlistment in the Corps.

"But why do you have to leave?" I asked, crying. I picked up his bag and pushed it behind me. The announcement of his leaving strangely tore at my heart. "Can't you just work for somebody else? Mr. Mercy. Can't you work for him?"

"I can do more good for the family and make more money in the Corps, Patience," he said.

"But why do you have to leave? Stay! Please! Please!"

"I'm proud of you," Goody said, taking Soldier's bag from me. I calmed myself, becoming resigned to the idea of his leaving and gave him a hug, as did Goody. We didn't hug him, we didn't hold him close so he felt our souls, we didn't linger in his space. We only gave him a hug, and we patted him on the back. Soldier did the same to us.

"Goody, Patience, Temperance," Soldier said. The reality of what he was doing slapped him in the face, and I could see his eyes glass over from the painful thought of leaving his family. Whatever he was about to say, he didn't say it, though. I imagined that he was going to say that he loved us. The Christiansons didn't say such things. We felt it, sometimes deeply. But we didn't say it.

"I have to leave, or I'm afraid I might do something I'll be sorry for the rest of my life," he said. "I'll see you when the War's over." And down the dirt road he journeyed on foot, with his sack slung over his shoulder. We stood looking at him until he was out of sight. Temperance waved, although Soldier was too far down the road to see her, and went into the house. Goody and I cried—we wept. I mourned.

"What's happening to our family?" I asked.

Goody straightened.

"Mumzy," Goody said. "Mumzy is what's happening to this family."

"It's a letter, everyone," Temperance said. The screen door slammed hard behind her, as she stormed into the front room waving an envelope over her head, startling Paw who had settled in his chair after Saturday-morning breakfast. "It's a letter from Soldier. Can I read it, can I read it, Paw?" Hearing the commotion, Mumzy came in from the kitchen, followed by Goody from our room.

"Go ahead and read it, gal, before you bust," Paw said.

"Pronounce any hard words slowly, sounding out each letter," I said.

"I know, you don't have to tell me," Temperance said. "I'm nine years old, you know." She tore the envelope down the right side and pulled out the sheet of cream-colored paper. She read loudly and clearly, without missing one word.

August 17, 1955

Dear Family,

How are you all? I am doing fine. The Corps is really different from anyplace I've ever been. It's hard, but I'm getting used to everything.

I arrived here at Preparation Island for boot camp on a green school bus. The bus stopped and someone got on and yelled "GET OFF THE BUS, GET ON THE YELLOW FOOTPRINTS." There were actual footprints painted on the ground. This was the way they got us into formation. After that, we went to Receiving Barracks and declared everything we had. I was surprised to see that people had brought along knives and guns. All I had besides my clothes was some chewing gum. They confiscated the knives and guns and shipped everything else back home.

They gave us little red rule books, and whenever we

got into formation and had to wait, say, to let another platoon march in front of us, we had to hold the red rule book in front of our faces, as if we were studying the rules. I doubt if anybody ever read the book, but still we had to hold them in front of our faces, in our left hands, not talking, until the drill sergeant told us to "PUT THE BOOK AWAY." After chow, we marched back to the Receiving Barracks. The drill sergeant yelled "CLOSE IT UP, SIT DOWN, GO TO SLEEP." And we did just that. Still in our civilian clothes, we stood facing in the same direction. We got as close together as we could and then sat down with our legs spread apart. We each leaned on the back of the person in front of us, and that's where and how we slept our first night here. What in the world had I gotten myself into?

The next morning, we marched to the Supply Building to get our uniforms. I think they purposely gave us all uniforms that were three sizes too large. "YOU'LL GROW INTO THEM," the drill sergeant said.

And about the haircuts. On the way to the barber's chair, we walked through mountains of hair on the floor. "If you have a mole on your scalp, put your finger on it," the barber told us. For those who had moles, the barber cut straight through them, and you should have see the blood running down the dudes' heads. If it wasn't for our eyebrows and eyelashes, we would have absolutely no hair on our heads, not even mustaches. I guess that was the Corps' way of making us all to look alike.

I kind of like it here, but I miss being home. I'll write when I can.

Love,
Soldier

1956

"Come on, Temperance," I said. "We got to get back to the house. Mumzy'll be awful mad at us if we're late. Come on here, girl. What are you looking for anyway?"

Paw and Mumzy had forgotten to take with them a load of the Knocks' clothes on their regular Saturday delivery, so Temperance and I had to deliver them. It was a seven-mile walk, but we took our time and tried to enjoy the sites on Ample Street—the neat, white houses, with expansive green yards, some with white picket fences.

A little girl in a pink dress played with a whole family of dolls in the shade of a tall magnolia tree by the side of her house. On the side of the road a black farm truck was parked. Temperance ran to it, heeding its call, and pushed a box near the truck to climb up.

"Patience," her voice echoed as she bent over the side of the truck's bed looking inside. "There's lots of stuff in here. Junk. Let's get in and see what we can find to keep."

"No, we won't. I'm not getting in trouble on account of you," I said. "Let's go."

Before I could say the word "go," she was rummaging through the truck's bed. Books, newspapers, rags, boxes, an old dress-maker's dummy, and all kinds of junk became airborne in Temperance's quest for hidden treasure.

"Oh, boy! I never saw so much stuff!" she said. "Do you think somebody's throwing this stuff away?"

Surrendering to her enthusiasm and becoming somewhat curious myself, I joined my impetuous sister in the truck. My eyes darted to a pair of objects in the corner—a tan suitcase and overnight case. Opening the larger piece of luggage, I saw that it was lined with tan satin. In the lid

29

and on the sides were compartments for hiding precious possessions, and satin straps were attached inside to hold clothes in place.

Struggling, I lifted the luggage over the side of the truck's bed. I was engrossed in inspecting them when Temperance called from within the bed.

"Patience! Look what I found!"

Standing on boxes she held up a pair of black patent leather shoes.

"They're nice. Try them on." I had plunged myself deeply in the spirit of the adventure.

We never wore shoes in the summer. By summer, the heels of our winter shoes (if we were "lucky" enough to own a pair) were run-over, and the soles were well worn through. When we worked in the fields in the summer, we cut up old tires and strapped them to our feet. And in the winter we wrapped our feet in rags or plastic to guard them from the cold weather if our shoes just didn't last or if we outgrew them. Temperance had never owned a pair of real shoes that had not first belonged to an older sibling. And although these shoes were apparently not new, sliding on the black shiny wonders caused her face to light up like a kerosene lamp.

Just then, we noticed the little girl in the pink dress watching us.

"Hey," I said. "My name is Patience, and this is my little sister, Temperance. Do these things belong to you and your folks?"

"Hey. My name is Tolerance," she answered, speaking very fast. Folding her arms, she continued. "My mother is doing spring cleaning, they're throwing away everything we don't want anymore, they found them old suitcases in the woods in the back of the house, this is my uncle's truck, and he's going to haul away everything in it, so I reckon you shouldn't be in it when he comes, or he'll just haul you away too, what kind of name is Patience anyway?"

That was a good question. Why had Mama named me Patience—Temperance was so much prettier. What a name to live up to, being steadfast, never complaining, at least that was my interpretation of the word's meaning. Plus, the Bible says tribulations make you patient.

"Do you think your maw and paw would mind if we took these things?" I pointed to the luggage and the shoes on Temperance's feet.

"I expect not," Tolerance said. She took in a deep breath, and I predicted that Temperance and I were in for another ear-whipping.

"My mama and daddy have been looking at y'all out here for a while now, Daddy already saw y'all out here on this truck, I told him I would go and run you off, we see your mama and daddy up and down this road every day, and we expect that you all are toting washing up to the folks in the city, go ahead and take those old suitcases and my sister's old shoes, we don't care." Finally, the answer to my question. Tolerance hadn't unfolded her arms since we'd been talking.

The suitcases. Had they always been so discolored, stained—maybe coffee stains—and dirty? I had just then noticed. And Temperance's newfound, shiny shoes. While wearable, the heels were run-over, and they looked as though they had been dragged through thorny ground cover.

But even more so I noticed the striking contrast between Tolerance and myself. Being slightly younger than Temperance, she stood a little more than chest high to me. While handfuls of her golden hair draped over each shoulder and down her back, my hair retreated in neat, convenient plaits and found sanctuary wrapped in an old piece of soiled rag. While Tolerance's early-morning iron-crisp pink summer dress befitted a ten-year-old whose folks, though of modest means, delighted in dressing her, I donned a pinkish dress, however, faded from many, many washings, torn at the right hemline, and oversized because it had once belonged to Miss Grace. Tolerance's eyes shone with blue innocent excitement. My deep, dark brown eyes reflected an innocence that had an intimate relationship with the knowledge that my beloved mother was dead, which had resulted in my father's deader heart. I had to stop myself— here I was again comparing myself with somebody.

I am me. I am the only me God has ever created.

As we approached the house about a half mile away, we could see Mumzy watching us. Still excited from our rummaging, I was sure she mistook us to be children from a happy home. Two people, she must have thought, the taller carrying two objects, coming her way. Closer we came to the house—oh, it was Patience, she must have thought, carrying suitcases? Where was Patience going? Or, where was Patience coming from? And where did she get those … those suitcases. She must have been thinking these things, because when we got there, she acted as if someone had replaced the Mumzy we knew with her evil twin, if it's possible for someone to be more evil than Mumzy.

"Where did you get those suitcases from, gal?" Mumzy wanted to know. Her words came at me like a growl from a jackal.

Silence. I knew better than to speak to her when she was in this condition. I had seen her like this only once before. It was when she accused Soldier of taking money from her purse. It was the week before he joined the Corps.

"Where is the money, boy?" Mumzy asked, her bloodshot eyes glistening beneath a furrowed brow.

"I don't know what you're talking about," Soldier said. He took off his hat and put it on the table beside the kitchen stove. Temperance and I hid in the front room behind Paw's chair. Soldier was as tall as Mumzy and was stronger than Paw. But that didn't stop Mumzy, who got right in his face, so close, I thought it looked like she would kiss him.

"Where is my money? I know you took it," she said. "You've been going through my things, and I know it." She stepped even closer to Soldier.

"You've got a problem, Mumzy," Soldier said. "You're my Paw's wife. I told you before and I'll tell you again, I don't want you or anything that belongs to you. So get off my back." Mumzy spat in his face. Soldier raised his clenched fist. After approximately ten seconds, he opened his fist, wiped off Mumzy's spittle, and left the house through the back door.

"Don't you walk out on me," she shouted at the top of her voice through the back door. "Come back here. Nobody walk out on me. You'll be sorry!"

"I said where did you get those suitcases from? Did you hear me, gal?"

With Mumzy, one's first instinct was always to apologize—her words, voice, mannerisms were always accusative.

"Mumzy, we were walking home and there was a truck with lots of stuff in it. The girl at the house said her paw said we could have these things."

"You're lying, gal. And I'm going to tell your Paw

that you stole them. He'll whip your behinds right good."

Mumzy spotted the black patent leather shoes on Temperance's feet.

"And you, take them-there shoes off your little rusty feet. You ain't got no business wearing shoes in the middle of the summer. Kick 'em off, you little—!"

"No, they're mine! The girl said I could have them!" Temperance cried.

"I said take 'em off!"

"She will not take them off," I said. I stepped between Mumzy and Temperance with my hands on my hips. "What makes you so mean? It's uncalled for. Nobody's done anything to you, but try to get along. Since Paw brought you home, you've done nothing but lie on us and make Paw give us whippings. And you can do it again."

Although I was apprehensive about what I was saying, I was determined to say it. Temperance stood close by with a look of wonder and curiosity; she had never seen me so emboldened.

"No, Mumzy. It's Paw that's going to take these things from us if they're going to be taken. Not you. I'm sick of it. And if we get a whipping because of your lies, then God have mercy on your soul, because we're innocent. I read the Bible, and it says that offenses might come, but woe to the person they come by." I pointed my finger at her. "Woe unto you, Mumzy, woe unto you, you're a liar, you're nothing but a liar." I was shouting now, and in tears.

My words struck her like an anvil on a spike. Her eyes moved as if searching, as if watching a scene no one else could see. She became confused, because for a moment she looked as if she felt bad about everything, as if she felt our pain.

"Daddy," Mumzy said. She looked straight into

Temperance's face. "Those gals of yours been talking sass to me. You need to go get Old Tickler. Daddy?"

I supposed it was our striking resemblance to Paw that confused her, that added to her anguish. It must have been as though he was standing in front of her, in duplicate. I pulled Temperance closer to me, holding her around her shoulders from behind.

"Daddy," Mumzy said, kneeling down and grabbing Temperance's hands.

"Leave her alone, Mumzy," I said.

"Who are you?" Mumzy asked. She tilted her head to the side. What was going on? She was looking straight at me, but she didn't know who I was?

"Are you okay, Mumzy?" I asked.

"What's wrong with her, what's wrong with Mumzy?" Temperance asked.

"Mumzy. Mumzy!" She was not responding, but her eyes kept searching, watching, from deep within her soul, some scene that the rest of us couldn't see.

"Go lay down, Mumzy," I said. I took her by the hand. "Temperance, grab her other hand. Help me get her to her room. Mumzy, Paw'll be back soon. You'll be okay."

1958

With the summer of 1958 in The Sticks came rising temperatures and escalating hormone levels. Goody was seventeen; I had just turned sixteen; and Temperance, approaching puberty, had many questions—some I could answer and some I chose not to address.

"How did Fasty get, you know, preg ... preg—" Temperance popped open a pea shell, and some of the peas flew up into her face and fell through the cracks between the porch planks onto soil as rich in nutrients as Miss Grace and Mr. Mercy was rich in kindness and sustenance, and as black as the old patent leather shoes she had long since worn out and forgotten.

"The word is pregnant, Temp," I said. "You're too young to know such things. And careful with those peas. I *will* tell you how to keep from getting pregnant. You don't speak to or even look at boys."

"That's not very friendly," Goody said. In front of us was a large silver tin foot-tub of corn that we had shucked, all but a few ears. Paw had given us permission to go to the church and help Elder Rector when we had finished our chores, which included shucking corn, shelling peas, and folding laundry. We both were anxious to get to church— Goody, because she would go anywhere to get away from the house, and I, because I had asked Elder Rector to explain how to apply for college grants and scholarship.

"That's the point. It's the friendly girls that end up like Fasty," I said.

The screen door snapped shut, startling the three of us, and the porch squeaked as Mumzy stepped out of the house and stood behind us.

"What y'all talking about out here?" Mumzy asked. "Y'all think y'all better than me, don't you? I bet you doing everything under the sun. It'll all come out in the wash. And don't expect me to take care of your young'uns when it do."

The hard clump of Paw's footsteps through the screen door onto the porch momentarily silenced Mumzy. But then, like molten lava from a volcano, it came spilling out.

"Daddy," Mumzy said. With that one word, she blasphemed fatherhood, parenthood, marriage—all that was good and pure and stable. "Goody been sneaking around seeing boys. Miss Knocks said so when I toted her washing to her. She said she saw Goody going in the bushes up there on Lead Mine Road with that Noppatune boy."

Mumzy baited Paw with her lies. Then she sat down on the porch and folded her legs under her to watch the fireworks.

"Paw, I haven't been sneaking into the bushes with anybody," Goody said.

Why did she say that? Why didn't she keep quiet and let Paw draw his own conclusions?

"Are you calling Mumzy a liar? Grown folks don't lie!"

Did Paw really believe that?

"We'll see how you like Old Tickler," he said, and went in the house.

I pulled Temperance closer to me, toppling the stack of soda pop lids she had constructed.

"Paw—no—I'm not seeing any boys! Paw—Paw!"

Too late. Paw was already beating Goody with all his strength. His long arm, together with the strap in his hand, seemed to reach to the porch cover and extend to the cloud that teased us with shade. Every second—one whack, one lick, one smack. Four—five. Goody, curled up on the porch in a ball, trying to protect her soft face and bosom—six—seven—eight—nine—ten—eleven—twelve—thirteen—fourteen—fifteen. Goody screamed, cried, but the hurt was deeper than her screams and cries could ever show. Sixteen—seventeen—eighteen—nineteen.

Through my tearing eyes I saw a look on Paw's face that frightened me—a merciless look.

Would he kill Goody? Does he hate Goody? Does he hate Temperance and me?

37

Paw's attitude, demeanor, face, actions testified that Goody deserved what she was getting, that she shouldn't have done anything to provoke Mumzy. On her head, her side, her backside, her legs, the blows landed where they landed—anywhere they happened to land.

This was not the first time Mumzy had lied to Paw about one of us, nor the first time Paw had beat one of us at Mumzy's request, whether that request was impishly implied or demonically demanded. She sat watching with crossed her legs, squirming where she sat, and closing her eyes as if relishing a good cup of tea. Then she did something she didn't do much. She smiled. Her little heart-shaped mouth for once showed life, howbeit perverted.

Goody lay whimpering, swollen, and bruised. Untouched by leather straps or splintered wood floors, Mumzy had a heart that was just as beaten and bruised. Her beauty faded in my eyes and mind like the cheap red dress she wore; her soulless hatefulness masked any physical appearances. I prayed that God would remove Temperance and me from that house, away from Mumzy—*and from Paw.*

Either Mumzy had been right about Goody, or Goody gave in to Noppa's advances out of spite. In either case, she and Noppa eloped a few weeks after her whipping. A year later, their daughter, Heartstring, my niece, was born. Times were hard for everybody, and Goody and Noppa were no different. To make ends meet, Goody moved back in with us, and Noppa joined a workgroup that operated out of state.

1959

"Don't do it, Temperance," I quietly demanded. "If Mumzy ever finds out that you're stealing soap for Goody, you know she'll tell Paw."

"Goody's got to wash that baby's diapers, doesn't she?"

Yes, but you know how Mumzy counts her things every night." Temperance ignored my demand.

"I know," Temperance said. "I'll just cut off a little piece for Goody. Mumzy'll never miss it." Temperance took a pocket knife from her apron pocket, opened it as she looked around for signs of Mumzy—shadows appearing and disappearing, doors closing, or small animals running in the opposite direction out of fear. From the block of Octagon soap, she sliced three small pieces, slipped them into her pocket, and resumed scrubbing laundry.

"She'll never know," Temperance assured me. "And I can always deny it and say that I used up the soap on the regular laundry."

"Lying and stealing, Temperance? You know better, you know better."

"It's not a real lie because Goody will be using it for washing, just not for Mumzy's laundry."

I couldn't bear the thought of Paw's yelling at Temperance or taking Old Tickler to Goody. The former would ring in my ears and hurt my heart for Temperance; the latter would deafen my ears and make hard my heart for Paw.

"Go get Goody right now and tell her to bring the diapers so we can boil them before Mumzy gets back from town," I said. I dropped the basket I was carrying and poured more water into the wash pot. "Now you've got me

39

tangled up in your schemes, Temperance. What am I going to do with you?"

One cool autumn evening, Paw, Temperance, and I sat out on the front porch step listening to the nighttime symphony of crickets, featuring an occasional hoot-owl solo, and watching God's star-sprinkled showcase in the blue-black sky. Paw began chewing tobacco a few months earlier when Mumzy brought him a pack from town. He whittled a walking stick that he planned to give to Mr. Mercy.

Goody had left home and didn't return. She and Noppa moved to The Big City, and I wanted to leave, too, to "get out of Dodge," but it wasn't my time. I had taken an advanced placement test, which Miss Grace had arranged, to attend The Big City University and had passed it—praise the Lord! I didn't hate living in The Sticks. I didn't hate Mumzy. I hated ignorance, whether in me or in others, ignorance that stemmed from the inability to read or the inability to love. I tutored Able Short, not so much for him, but to gain control over ignorance. My diligence in reading to Temperance was so she wouldn't fall prey to the ignorance I had witnessed in The Sticks. Ignorance had rid Mama and Paw of choices, forcing our family into sharecropping. Ignorance was powerful, but I was determined not to let it overtake me. Therefore, I greeted the mailman daily hoping to receive my acceptance letter to college. I had not told Paw about my plans to leave. Perhaps that evening I would break the news.

"Paw," I whispered.

"What is it, gal?"

"Do you miss your children?"

"What kind of man don't miss his own children?"

"Do you miss Mama?" Paw stopped his whittling, looking out into the semidarkness up the road beyond the big oak tree.

"Heart was my first love. Can't nobody or nothing take that away from her."

A screech made me turn to discover Mumzy standing inside the screen door, listening. She frowned in disapproval of Paw's last comment.

"Ernest," she interrupted. "You best come on in out of that night air now."

Paw pushed himself up on one hand, as if the other were sore, or tired. He looked old for a middle-aged man.

The next morning, before the cock had even arisen to crow, before the moon had given way to the sun, Paw stormed into Temperance and my room waking us up.

"Gal, Mumzy tells me you been sassing her."

Who was this? Was I still asleep, dreaming? Paw? In his nightshirt? What?

"Wake up. Get up. Both of you."

"What is it, Paw?" I asked, still groggy.

"What's happening, Patience?" Temperance asked. Lying on her stomach, she raised her head up from the folded blanket she used as her pillow and then let it fall again.

"Go back to sleep," I said.

"Mumzy said you been sassing her," Paw said. He was holding Old Tickler.

One of us had to remain calm, so I elected myself. I had seen Paw like this before, and if I didn't calm him down, it meant the strap for me.

"Paw, have you ever known me to sass you or any grown person in all my years?"

Excited and volatile, Paw paced the floor like a caged animal. "Mumzy said you did, and that's all I need to know."

"Paw!" He looked at me, rather looked through me, but didn't answer, as if he no longer cared to identify with the title. "Paw!" I said again and made sure we were making eye contact. "Paw! I matter—I matter!"

"What did you say, gal?" He was still agitated. He raised his hand holding Old Tickler. I was certain he would bring it down on me.

"I said I matter." Tears threatened to seep from my sleepy eyes. I held them back but couldn't squelch the hurt I started to feel. "I'm your daughter, and I matter."

Standing tall over my pallet on the floor, Paw looked down at me and slowly lowered his hand and the strap. Relieved that my words had somehow touched him, I reached up and clutched the other end of Old Tickler, my fingers barely meeting around it.

"I'm real. Temperance is real. We're your children. When you look at us, don't you see Mama? Don't you see yourself? We need you, Paw. Father ..." Releasing the strap, I stood up, careful not to catch my feet in my long gown. I dared to speak words that Paw had never heard from me, that I had always felt, but couldn't bring myself to say. We hadn't been brought up that way, and it's hard to change one's upbringing.

"I love you, Paw." I leaned against him, my arms slowly reaching up and making their way around his neck. Paw said nothing, but looked at me as if seeing me afresh, anew. He looked at me the way he had once looked at Mama after a day of crop harvesting—happy, proud. I squeezed my eyes closed and clenched my teeth, releasing restrained tears—tears of relief. I was finally embracing my father, and it was amazing. I needed him so to return my feelings, to

42

hold me back, but instead he held back, his tall stature growing stiff in my arms. I didn't let go, realizing how many times I had wanted to show affection toward my father, how many times I had needed my father to hold me in his arms. Paw's arms loosely tightened around my shoulders, and I opened my eyes. Temperance had woken up, seen us standing in the middle of the room, and from behind Paw, lifted and pulled his arms around me. I smiled at Temperance, and she lay back down. Paw tightened his embrace. I cried.

"Oh, Paw," I said. What wonderful joy filled my being. I felt secure, my face against his night shirt. Again I saw that Paw's expression had changed. He now looked at me the way he had looked at himself in our broken mirror in the front room. I saw self-loathing. I saw self-hatred.

"No ... no," he said, shaking his head. "Mumzy said you sassed her."

"Don't hit her, Paw!" Temperance shouted.

"Get out of here, Temperance!"

It's Time

August 12, 1960

Dear Paw,

It's time for me to leave. Mumzy has supplied the mortar for the huge wall that you've built up between yourself and your children, and I don't want Temperance in this situation anymore.

I've been earning money by doing odd jobs and running errands for Miss Grace. With some of that money, I will buy two one-way train tickets to The Big City. Goody wrote and told me she can help me if I needed help. And right now, it looks like I need her help.

You're probably thinking I'm running off with a man like Goody did, but I'm not. I'm going to start attending The Big City University. I hope you can be proud of me, because this is something that I've wanted to do for a long time.

I hope you don't mind, but I'm taking with me Mama's Bible and her little pink cut-glass pitcher. I've just about worn out the Bible anyway. And the pitcher, well, I think Mama would have wanted me to have it. I know it's after the fact but thank you for these things. I'll remember Mama when I use them, but I'll remember you too because you two were once one. I pray that one day I will be one with a man—my husband—the way you and Mama were one. And I pray that one day things will be different, and that the whole family will be able to come together, and things will be as they were when Mama was alive, you know, with the same spirit. I can't explain it.

Don't worry about Temperance. I've taken good care of her these seven years, and I'll continue to do the same in The Big City. We will stay with Goody until I get on my feet. Miss Grace helped me get a grant and a scholarship for college. And I'll get a part-time job too.

I said it last night, and I'll say it again, Paw. I love you.

> *Goodbye,*
> *Patience (and Temperance)*

I placed the letter on the cushion of Paw's wingback chair.

"Are we leaving Paw and Mumzy, Patience?" Temperance asked. "Are we going to The Big City?"

"Quiet, we don't want to wake them," I said, looking toward Paw and Mumzy's room. "Yes, we are. I can be content wherever I am, but I refuse to be complacent."

"What's complacent?"

"It's what you do when you fill your belly with blackberry jelly and bread," I said, poking her in the stomach with my finger. "And you lie down out there on the front porch and go to sleep waiting for someone to wake you up." We laughed. Then we became silent, without expression.

"Stop poking me you old nasty," Temperance said.

"Shhh. Let's go." I eased the front door open. Temperance and I, the last of the Christianson children, walked a path that had been trod by three other children before us, down the dirt road past the big oak tree.

"What did I tell you about calling me names?" We laughed. And then we were silent, without expression.

Behold the State I'm In

... In Respect
of Want ...

Behold the State I'm In

Patience: 1970

A merciless alarm clock jolted me to a fresh day from a night of dreams, which for the life of me I couldn't remember.

"Five o'clock." I sat up and stretched. "Good morning, Jesus. Thank you."

When Temperance and I moved into our two-bedroom apartment in the newly built Pathfinder Garden Apartments on East Grand Boulevard two years earlier, I threw out the old Salvation Army Thrift Store bed we once shared in Goody's apartment, although I continued to use my largest suitcase as a nightstand, standing it on its end and placing a thick piece of round glass on top. In that piece of luggage I kept Mama's pitcher and the rhinestone hair comb she gave me, hoping it would inspire me to keep my hair "pretty." In the satin side pocket, I tucked my hankie.

Today, firsts and newness awaited me—a new bed and a brand new mint-green 1970 Firebird. Buying them just seemed right since I had just landed a wonderful job with State University as assistant professor in the prestigious School of Education. I was the first Black female the university had ever hired.

The down-filled pillows and the lush comforter, with its matching percale sheets and bedskirt, constrained and shackled me with luxury, preventing me from the mission of the day: To carry out a God-inspired plan, whatever that plan was.

Usually in the morning I listened to WWJD's "Hour of Enlightenment," where the host read Scriptures and played inspirational music. But that day my schedule called for a full class load, so for a lighthearted atmosphere, I tuned in to the loud and obnoxious Tom Levity Show. On occasions, if I had to read students' class assignments or deal with department heads, I set the dial for the peaceful KING station that played classical music.

The night before, I read Jude 20 through 21: "But ye, beloved, building up yourselves on your most holy faith, praying in the Holy Ghost, keep yourselves in the love of God, looking for the mercy of our Lord Jesus Christ unto eternal life." Not fully aware of what the passage meant, I prayed my regular prayer.

"Thank you, Jesus, for another opportunity to serve You and to do Your will according to Your written Word, and for working with me all night. Thank You for a good life— thank you for blessing me. Thank you for giving me Temperance. Bless and keep her—and Goodness, Sister, Soldier, Paw … and Mumzy. Thank you for being … my best Friend. *Amen*. … Let your conversation be without covetousness …"

How did the rest of that verse go? I couldn't remember.

I rubbed my eyes. My thoughts became clear. Today I had been given a chance to help people, be they my coworkers or my Juniors Sunday School class. Because I had prayed for my family, I tried to think of ways to help them. Paw. Would my mind ever be silent concerning Paw? In Sister's letters, she often spoke of her and Aunt Wits' regular visits to see him. Although during each visit they stayed at a motel near town, Mumzy usually left the house whenever Aunt Wits was around.

"Thank you, God, that except for a bit of arthritis, Paw is in good health."

According to Sister, Paw still worked with Mumzy in her laundry business. With all the children gone, they hired teenagers and adults who didn't mind hard work for low wages. Mumzy was still stingy. I felt guilty that with school and work, I found it impossible to fit into my schedule visits back home to The Sticks. I was a different person than when I left, but I still missed a simpler, slower life— winter robins on the limbs of snow-covered trees, my family working together toward a common goal, watching Paw sitting on the front porch whittling.

"Get out of here, Temperance!"

My grant and scholarship covered my tuition, but not my books and certainly not room and board. During the day I worked in a laundry, and I took all my classes at night; sharecropping and laundry work had prepared me for that. And after struggling through undergraduate school, getting my master's degree was a breeze.

Raising Temperance had been a challenge, though, but her love for school and learning kept her out of mischief. Her elementary and junior high school years flew by like the train we rode to The Big City. On many occasions throughout her senior high school years, I had to leave her at home alone; I didn't have much choice in the matter.

Temperance and I had slept on pallets in the hallway in Goody and Noppa's apartment when we moved to The Big City ten years earlier. That was hard—not sleeping on the floor—but living with Goody and Noppa. Their hallway led nowhere; it was a dead end like their lifestyle. But on the floor in their hallway, without complaining, I studied and helped Temperance with her homework. I wanted to complain. I wanted to scream, to beat some sense into Goody's and Noppa's heads. On the floor in their hallway, I wrote Sister, somewhat envying where life had taken her. I cried, and I prayed for the day when I could, no, *would* move out. "Could" signified my ability, whereas "would" was more of a condition of my attitude. I was able to turn tail and flee as soon as I saw the state in which Goody lived. I could have called Miss Grace for help, and I knew she would have found a way. However, I would not leave. Temperance and I needed Goody's help, but even more so, she needed ours.

So I stacked my overnight case on my suitcase beside my pallet on the floor and called it home. An olive green vinyl footstool served as a desk for writing, a podium for reading the Scriptures to Temperance, a table for our meals, and an altar for praying. Goody gave me her Underwood typewriter, which sat on a small wobbly table in the hall. The hallway was wide enough, so eventually I purchased a single thrift-store bed, which Temperance and I slept on.

Our arrival at Goody's destroyed any preconceived notions I had that everyone who lived in The Big City led rich, glamorous lives.

"Aaayyhhh," Goody screamed when she opened her door and saw Temperance and me on the other side. "Oh, it's so good to see both of you, and just look how big Temperance has gotten. Come on in, come on in." Goody guided us inside her apartment and picked up my suitcases. "Noppa, they're here. Come see my sister."

"Be there in a minute," Noppa yelled from another room. "I think I can win this hand."

"You reneged, man!" someone shouted from the room Noppa was in.

"You're a lie, too!" Noppa shouted back.

"What's going on?" Temperance asked before I could collect myself enough to ask the question. I was without words, so it was good that Temperance voiced some of what I was thinking.

"We're having a little rent party. Nothing to worry about," Goody said.

"Hey, Goodtime," a man yelled from the kitchen. He sat at a table with three others. "You got any more beer?"

"Can you pay?" Goody yelled back.

"You better believe it," the man answered. "I just won a forty-dollar pot. Whoowhee!"

"All right, now," Goody said, snapping her finger.

My throat ached from the adrenaline building up inside me, making my voice sound low and scratchy.

"Where's Heartstring?" I asked. I coughed, trying to clear my throat.

"She's with a neighbor," Goody said. Temperance and I stood side by side, and Goody grasped both our necks and pulled us close to her in a group hug.

"Why did that man call you 'Goodtime,' Goody?" Temperance asked. She pulled away from Goody's grip and turned in every direction, trying to take in as much of this new experience as she could. "Goody is short for Goodness, not Goodtime."

"Not anymore, baby," Goody said. "I changed my name to Goodtime a long time ago."

"What would mama have thought about that?" I asked. I surveyed the room and was shocked to see dirty dishes, beer and liquor bottles on the card tables and the floor, a couple kissing in the corner, clothes on the floor and strewn over the furniture, and drunken men and women.

"Mama is dead," she said. She leaned into me with

53

one hand on her hip and the other against the rear wall, pinning me to it. "Besides, ain't nothing wrong with Goodtime." I turned my head to escape the smell of liquor on her breath.

"Hey," she shouted. "We need some music in this place. It's too dead in here." She snapped her fingers to a beat that only she could hear and staggered to the hi-fi.

"Hey, y'all," she announced. Most of the people at the party looked her way. "If I'm not around and the music stops, just flip over the stack of records for me please. I can't be your hostess and DJ and bartender and everything else."

"You got it," a man responded from yet another table of four near the stereo. Including the table in the bedroom where Noppa was, five tables of four had been set up all over the apartment.

Goody led us to our room. I half-heartedly waved at people as I passed. Most of them didn't notice us, being engrossed in their game. The sound of men's and women's laughter and conversation filled the apartment. Temperance nervously coughed as we passed through cigarette smoke intermixed with the smell of liquor. My sinuses began to clog from the smoke and dust that lay thick on the furniture. Loud and boisterous music invaded my ears and filled my head against my will. We walked, almost stumbling over stacks of magazines and books and a dead potted dieffenbachia, to Goody and Noppa's inner hallway—our room. Goody pointed to two pallets made up on the floor in the hallway.

"This is where y'all will be sleeping," she said. "Sorry about the party, and on your first night here, but the rent and car payment are due next week. We had to spend the rent money on a few expenses. Noppa bought us a new

TV-stereo console. Did I write and tell you we got a new car, too? A white Plymouth Fury convertible."

"You didn't write that often," I said.

"Never mind that. If you need anything, come and find me. Oh, sorry about the mess. I'll probably clean up tomorrow, or the day after."

"What's that game they're playing?" Temperance asked. She picked up a deck of cards that had been dropped on the floor by her pallet.

"Thanks, hon," Goody said, taking the deck from Temperance. "I've been looking for this. It's bid whist."

"Goodtime, somebody at the door," a man yelled from the living room. "Says he don't have the ten dollars to get in. Wants to know if he can come in and pay you when he wins his first hand."

"And suppose he doesn't win?" Goody yelled back. "Tell him to try again next Friday." Turning to us she said, "If it's who I think it is, he never brings his own liquor and mooches off everybody else. I don't need him turning my guests off."

"I never knew you to be interested in playing cards and parties and such, Goody," I said. I sat down on the pallet and pulled Temperance down beside me.

"Noppa has showed me a lot of sophisticated things country people wouldn't understand," Goody said. When she looked down at us, she resembled Mama, but the resemblance was distorted by a demeanor that reminded me of Mumzy. "Besides, it's fun. Don't you worry about anything. You're here, and you've got a roof over your head." She took a cigarette from a pack that she pulled from her pocket, struck a match and lit it, and inhaled so deeply that at least a quarter of an inch of the cigarette was consumed. "And thanks to these rent parties, me and Noppa still got one over ours," she said, smoke escaping through her mouth and nose with each word.

I walked around my apartment, rolled up window shades, and straightened up a bundle of clothes here or a stack of papers there. Although still dark outside, it was time to exercise. My tights resisted as I pulled them on, but my leotards were more agreeable. The living room was perfect for working out that early, far enough away from Temperance's room so I wouldn't wake her. I turned on the stereo in the combination television/record-player console to the Gospel station.

"Blessed be the Lord: for he hath showed me his marvellous kindness in a strong city. Psalms 31:21."

A strong city: a fitting description of the place where I've spent the last ten years of my life.

"Ooh, my favorite song." While singing along, I did twenty waist twists and twenty toe-touches.

"How I got over, how I got over, well, my soul looks back and wonders how I got o-o-o-over. My soul looks back and wonders, my soul looks back and wonders, well my soul looks back and wonders how I got o-o-o-over."

During a commercial announcing the opening of a new restaurant, I did more waist stretches and deep knee bends. As I exercised, my mind wandered to our old house in The Sticks on Miss Grace and Mr. Mercy's land.

"Thank you, God," I whispered.

"Looking for Mr. Right?" The feature article on the cover of the latest issue of *Quintessence Magazine* shouted at me from the chair in the hallway as I walked to the kitchen. A coworker gave me a gift subscription, but I didn't have time to read the magazines. Temperance enjoyed reading them and looking at the pictures, though.

"Are You Tired of Being Alone?" The subtitle taunt-

ed me—heckled me. But I permitted its seizing my attention, so what did I expect? Ignoring its taunts, I steadied my pace to the kitchen to prepare my lunch that I would eat in my office, where God had accomplished something in me that I couldn't have done on my own. He gave me the desire to bridle my tongue when silence was the most effective message. I shared an office with a fellow professor name Fool. Fool was tenured and had already earned his doctorate degree. He was supposed to be my mentor, as assigned by my department head. The first time he saw me reading the Bible during my lunch break, he called me on the carpet.

"Before you start preaching about the virtues of being born again, which zealous fanatics ... always find a way of working into every verbal exchange, the answer is 'No, I don't know the Lord.'" I was certain he had wanted to say "zealous fanatics like you." And when he said 'Lord,' he raised two fingers on each hand, indicating quotation marks. He reminded me of President Nixon making his victory sign.

"Furthermore, I don't care to be introduced," he added.

I let out a slow "O-kay," raised my eyebrows at him, succeeded at resisting the temptation to call him under my breath by his given name, and continued my lunch.

It was one thing to be named Fool, but must you be such an idiot? Oh, God, forgive me.

From that point, our mentor-protégé relationship was strained, to say the least. We, however, remained cordial and professional.

The clock on the wall let me know it was getting late. A Thermos of vegetable juice, a green salad, and some leftover grilled salmon fit neatly into my blue lunch sack, and I added a red rose from the vase on the kitchen table. It all reminded me of the Sunday school lesson I would teach on the Tabernacle of Moses. My lunch sack became the Ark of the Covenant, and its contents turned into the golden pot that contained manna, the Tables of the Covenant, and Aaron's rod that budded.

From the corner shelf, my Bible caught my eye, and I opened it and read the inscription: "To Heart from Grace." I pressed it to my bosom.

After putting away the extra lettuce and washing the dishes, I sat down at the dining room table and looked up one last Scripture for my Juniors class and read it out loud to remember it better:

"O fear the Lord, ye his saints: for there is no want to them that fear him. The young lions do lack and suffer hunger." *Oh, good, we talked about lions last month—I can tie that in.* "But they that seek the Lord shall not want any good thing."

I sprinted to the bathroom, and *Quintessence Magazine* gave me one last jeer from its cover: "How to Satisfy Your Man." I had had enough. I picked up the magazine and tossed it in the wastebasket.

"I thank you God, because your Word says they that seek the Lord shall not want any good thing."

My relationship with God was multifaceted. Sometimes I was His baby and needed Him to take care of me. Sometimes I was His mouthpiece, through which I taught His Word. At other times I was His friend, and I needed to know that He was pleased with me. God provided tender loving care for me in every aspect of my life. My relationship with God was very personal; I couldn't see Him, but I saw Him everywhere I looked. I knew that I hadn't been the best friend to Him nor the best child I could be, but I had an inner confidence that God could trust me, and that trust I never wanted to lose.

"Get moving, Temperance," I yelled on my way back to my room. "Are you going to sleep all morning, young lady? Get up. You'll miss your bus."

Temperance had grown into a beautiful woman. She was taller than I. Though some may describe her as lanky, she said that she was "definitively thin." Her size made it easy for her to wear and look good in anything. In ways, she looked older than her peers; field and laundry work had hardened both of us, but in a good way. Beneath our outward appearances lay wisdom, a work ethic, and a determination that a lot of city girls didn't possess.

"What time is it, anyway?" Temperance responded. Dragging her feet, she came out of her room and noticed the magazine in the wastebasket as she passed it.

"What's wrong with her?" she said. "A new magazine." She shook her head. "You'd rather read *Good Homes and Gardens*, wouldn't you," she shouted at me.

Her coal black, healthy hair, despite the weekly straightening that she insisted upon, was up in rollers. When she was a junior in high school she had convinced me to let her get her hair done every other week, or rather, she had worn me down by nagging me.

"All my friends go to the House of Curls to get their hair done," she insisted. "You burn me too much. Just look at that scar on my neck."

I had to admit that my hairdressing skills were minimal at best—Mama and I were harvested from that same row. After examining my budget, I decided we could afford the House of Curls.

"What next?" I teased her. "You want to lighten your

skin, too?" She had ignored that question.

How serious could she, should she, take me? My hair was just as stubborn and rebellious as I had been when I walked in the rain as a child. Summers were hot and humid in The Big City, and whether I walked in the rain or not, my hair always reverted to its natural state. I had not trained it with regular straightening. So, I not only had my hair straightened, I used chemicals to do the job. Getting a permanent was one of the first things I did after being offered the job at the university. I felt like a hypocrite; I felt like James Brown, singing "Say It Loud: I'm Black and I'm Proud," himself having straight, processed hair. I had asked myself what exactly did being Black mean. Though more than skin color and hair texture, being Black was at least those two things. Progressive Black men had stopped "processing" their hair in the sixties. We women were slower, I had surmised.

As for me, getting my hair done had said that I was old enough to make my own decisions. It had said that my hair could be as straight as anybody's. It said that I could be just as pretty as anybody. But lately I felt as if it was saying, "You're my slave. Maintain me, and pay a high price, or pay the price of being shunned." Temperance came into by room carrying the magazine.

"Look at your sister," I said, looking in the mirror. "She's escaped the drudgery of Mumzy's laundry. She's escaped the South where she partook in far fewer rights and opportunities than now. Yet her hair still holds her under bondage—her last bondage, a bondage for which she forges the chains every six weeks with toxic goo from a jar."

Temperance shook her head at me and left, as she always did whenever I started to wax deep.

I removed my curlers and combed my hair flat, and

pushed it up, freeing an abundance of curls.

Oh, well.

Shaking my head, I loosened the curls a bit more.

"All right, God," I said. "Help me, I'm running late. What outfit shall I wear today? Oh yes, my blue suit, and my yellow blouse."

Eight o'clock. Right on time.

With coat buttoned and briefcase and lunch bag in hand, I hesitated in the entryway, looked into the kitchen, the dining-room/living-room area, and down the short hall that led to the bedrooms and bath.

"Father God, as I leave, I'm taking You with me, and yet leaving You here. It's in You that I live, and it's in You that I move, and it's in You that I have my being. Let all that I do today represent You well. Let the people whom I come in contact with get a glimpse of You through the way I carry myself. Therefore, Father God, guide my thoughts, words, and actions. And God, it's all because of Jesus that I can have this relationship with You. Thank You for Jesus."

"See you tonight," I called out to Temperance.

"See you," she yelled back.

Outside, I took in a deep breath of air intermingled with a hint of auto exhaust fumes. My sinuses were as clear as my thoughts, and I had never seen a day in The Big City when the sky was as blue as this. Walking quickly to the bus stop a half block away, looking forward to the day I could drive my Firebird to work, I passed a gray-haired woman who stuffed purple knitted yarn into her shopping bag.

"Good morning," I said, smiling as I walked by.

The woman hesitantly spoke back, surprised at this rare courtesy. The look on her face reminded me that people were different in the city and reinforced my faith in the prayer I had prayed earlier—to glorify God in my actions.

By eight-twenty I boarded the bus, sat down on an empty seat and slid over to the window. As the big-city scenery moved in the opposite direction I was headed, I continued the devotion and meditation I had started at my front door. For me, to do nothing while riding the bus was to sit complacently, like so much mayonnaise in a jar waiting for someone to manipulate it, take from its contents, and consume it. So I read or meditated. I closed my eyes and mentally recited Scriptures committed to memory over the years.

If there be therefore any consolation in Christ, if any comfort of love, if any fellowship of the Spirit, if any bowels and mercies, fulfill ye my joy, that ye be like-minded, having the same love, being of one accord, of one mind. Let nothing be done through strife or vainglory; but in lowliness of mind let each esteem others better than themselves.

The bus came to a sudden stop, causing me to lunge forward in my seat. I opened my eyes as a man sat down beside me, the faint scent of aftershave fading after a moment. Around six-feet tall, he wore a navy blue business suit with a white shirt and a blue and red striped tie, and on his lap rested a black leather briefcase. His skin was dark, like Paw's, but his features weren't as pronounced. His hair was neatly and recently cut and edged; the tiny curl of it had been well-trained through diligent brushing to lie down in waves.

Ooh. Nice.

I closed my eyes again, retreating to a peaceful place in the Word of God.

Thou wilt keep him in perfect peace, whose mind is stayed on thee: because he trusteth in thee.

The bumpy ride, along with my meditation on God's Word, against my will transported me back to The Sticks to the time when New Mount Saint Bethel held its services in a little one-room house that the founding pastor (we called him Preacher Bird) had converted into a place of worship a few years after the Great Depression. Over the decade that followed, each new pastor with his members had enhanced the building, adding a baptism pool in the back, two additional rooms, a real pulpit where stacked crates had served before, and a used microphone and speaker system that one of The Sticks' more affluent Negro churches had donated.

As a young minister of the Gospel in his twenties, energetic and fresh out of Bible seminary, and youth pastor of New Mount Saint Bethel, Elder Rector had sponsored many church programs. When I was seven—when my family went to church before Mama died—I had joined in his Sunday School activities. We recited Bible verses, proud mothers and grandmothers applauded, and each child was given a small piece of hard candy as a reward. The children loved being on stage—as we called it—and we adored Elder Rector. After the programs, we gathered around him, hugging his slim waist.

Several years later, when I was a teenager, I often begged time away from Mumzy's laundry work to assist Elder Rector with putting on Christmas and Easter programs and with Summer Vacation Bible School.

"Easter comes but once a year," Elder Rector said. He had given up trying to teach Bible verses to little Able Short; Able couldn't remember any verse longer than "Jesus wept."

"Easter comes but once the year," Able repeated.

"That's once *a* year," Elder Rector corrected, emphasizing the word "a."

"That's once *a* year," Able repeated with the same

emphasis.

"No, son. The whole poem is 'Easter comes but once a year. Lots of fun so pull up a chair.'"

All the children laughed, but I thought the entire exercise to be asinine. To make an effort to teach Able such a poem that wasn't at all related to the Bible was a waste of his meager ability as well as of Elder Rector's time.

"Elder Rector," I interrupted. "I can teach Able a Bible verse for the program if you want me to. I taught my baby sister from the Psalms of David."

"Oh, you did? The Psalms of David, you say?"

I noticed a strange, unsettling look in his eyes.

Was he annoyed that I had interrupted him?

"Little Patience. This boy can't even learn John 3:16. You supposed to be a better teacher than me? I'll remind you that I've been through seminary, and I'll remind you, too, missy, that you don't disrespect grown people. Go ahead, recite me one of the Scriptures you know so well that you can teach somebody like Able."

"I didn't mean to disrespect you, Elder Rector. I'm sorry you took it that way. It's just that I read to my sister, Temperance, all the time, and she remembers and learns."

"Recite a Scripture like I told you, Patience."

The words mechanically churned from my lips with a conviction that startled Elder. He cocked his head to one side as I said the verse.

"That I may know Him," I recited, looking up at him, but thinking about Him. "And the power of His resurrection, and the fellowship of His sufferings, being made conformable unto His death. Philippians third chapter, tenth verse."

Studying me for a minute with his thumb and finger at his chin, he asked: "Now why would a teenage wash-girl want to memorize such an adult Scripture as that?"

"Why?" I pondered the one-word question for a moment. "I can't answer that. It's just that wherever I happen to open up the Bible is where I read. And one day it fell open in Philippians. So I read it, and it touched me."

"Touched you? How did it touch you?"

"It caused me to feeling, well, happy to read that I could even begin to get to know God. He's such a big God, Elder Rector." I raised my arms and made a circle that encompassed all. "In that verse I saw the word 'power,' and I saw 'fellowship.' And I asked myself how power was connected with fellowship. And since I didn't have the answer, the least I could do was to memorize and learn the verse— you know, get it in me." I patted my chest. "So I did. And it's here, in me so much now that when I recite the verse, I feel fellowship, with God, and a kind of power."

"You're just a Scripture-quoting smart-aleck," Elder Rector said. He smiled, but I was confused by his words. "Okay, children, you can go home now. Rehearsal is over."

"All right, I'll see you next week, Elder Rector?" I asked as I was leaving the sanctuary.

"Never mind, Patience, I won't be needing your help any longer for this program, thank you."

Something I had said or done must have made him angry with me. My heart was broken, and that evening I couldn't eat.

Despite my not being able to assist Elder Rector with his programs, for six months I tutored Able in reading the Bible and memorization. In the evening, he would wander over to our house, and I read to Temperance and him from the Bible. If they were successful in memorizing at least five words in their assigned verses and could build on the five words they had learned in the previous lesson, I rewarded them with Goody's homemade biscuits and blackberry jam.

Knowing Elder Rector's program and rehearsal pattern, that year a few weeks before Christmas I, with Able, showed up at his rehearsal.

"Elder Rector, listen to the verse I taught Able," I said, excited about showing off to this man whom I admired so much. "Go ahead, Able, just like you practiced."

Able cleared his throat and began to recite.

"For God has not given us the spirit of fear; but of power, and love, and a sound mind. ... And, ... and"

"Be not," I prompted.

"Right. And be not thou therefore ashamed of the testimony of our Lord, nor of me his prisoner: but be thou partaker of the 'flictions—"

"Afflictions," I corrected.

"'Flictions,' right, I got it, Patience," he said annoyed at my interruption. Able shook his head and started the phrase over. "But be thou partaker of the afflictions of the gospel according to the power of God; Who hath saved us, and ... and called us with an holy calling." He paused to take a deep breath. "Not 'cording ... according to our works, but according to his own purpose and grace, which was given us in Christ Jesus before the world began. Second Timothy, first chapter, seven through the ninth verses. See?" Able said, sticking out his chest in pride of his accomplishment. "Told you I got it."

"Now, what does that Scripture mean?" I asked him.

"It means that I don't have to be afraid of nothing or nobody," he answered, shaking his head from side to side.

"And what else?" I asked.

"And that ... and that ... oh, yeah. If Jesus ain't ashamed of me, I ain't ashamed of Jesus."

"Good, Able," I said, applauding his hard work.

"You can go on and play with the other children now."

"That's all right," Elder Rector said. "You're good. You should take up teaching."

"Really, Elder?" Teaching was a perfect profession for me. I was amazed I hadn't seriously considered teaching as a profession before.

"Surely. You'll have to go to college, you know," he said. "And college ain't easy, or cheap."

"I know, but God will provide."

"I have to admit," Elder Rector said, as he beamed with excitement, "I never thought you would be the first one in your family to make it to college. I told your father I didn't think you were strong enough to be college material."

Surprised at his comment, my voice rang out with a hint of my mother's stubbornness.

"Since I can remember, my mama and paw have always had faith in me."

"Well, I am pleased, truly pleased at your success with Able, I must say. Yes indeed. You have to let me take you to dinner to celebrate. The Lord is truly good. For He has truly been good to you and your family. Yes indeed."

"Thank you, Elder Rector. I'd be happy to have dinner with you. Can you tell me how college life is and what not, since you went to seminary?"

"I'll be glad to. Yes, indeed." He looked at his watch, which seemed as big as his hand and as bright as his gold tooth. "In fact, it's already past six. Let's leave now. We can go across town to a nice restaurant and have a nice meal. My car is right outside."

Having dinner with Elder Rector, a minister, and he was going to carry on a grown-up conversation with me—I was elated—yet not quite sure I was doing the right thing. I had known him since I was a child. We had almost grown up together, in a way, although he was over a decade older. In a short time, he had gained a lot of weight and was now close to three hundred pounds. When the children gathered around him to hug him, they had to join hands in groups of threes to encircle him.

What harm could it do?

"Sit right up front with me, Patience."

What did he think, that I was going to sit in the back seat like I was being chauffeured? Am I making a mistake?

"My car rides a little rough. I need to have the shocks replaced. But it's all right—don't be scared."

Scared of what? What does he mean?

After about a half mile, out of the sight of houses or field workers, or even a scurrying squirrel, Elder Rector pulled over to the side of the much-traveled road. Lush trees and greenery embellished the shady side of the dirt road. On the other side lay acre upon acre of cotton, which would be harvested within the month by local and migrant workers. A part of me missed harvest time; my family was never more united together than during the time of harvest.

"Where you supposed to be?"

"I need to check under the hood for something— make sure the radiator has enough water." He turned off the engine but didn't get out of the car.

"Elder Rector, what are you doing? ... I said, what are you doing? ... I think you had better take your hand off of me! ... You had better get your hand off me ... now!"

His hand rested on my thigh, and both of my hands curled into tight little fists. I raised them in front of me like a heavyweight boxer. I was sure I looked ridiculous, but Elder Rector wasn't willing to take any chances.

"Let's just go on to the restaurant."

"Yes, let's just go, ... you ... you ..." I wanted to call him a name but couldn't think of a word to describe what he was. So all that came out was: "... You, ... you nasty old man!"

What should I do now? My stubborn, vindictive side answered, *"You go in there and you order the most expensive thing on the menu. You make him pay for thinking he could take advantage of you."*

And that's what I did—I ordered the steak. And I didn't even like steak, but nothing would have tasted good to me that evening.

At first I told Temperance what happened, and then I told Paw. Paw confronted Elder Rector, who backed away laughing and ran out the back door of the church.

"I'm going to kill that preacher," Paw said when he returned home. But he soon calmed down, and the incident was forgotten.

Some years later, I discovered that Elder Rector had tried to touch Goody—right before Mama died.

Hurt, disgusted, disillusioned, I was certain the incident would jeopardize my Christian walk. What was the use in trying to do good? I trusted this supposed man of God. However, instead of turning from my faith, I considered it a valuable lesson. My hurt turned to self-admiration, because I discovered I didn't lack courage, nor did I lack power. I had stood up for myself. I was not a victim. I was Patience Christianson—woman of power.

Shaking my head hard, I scattered unwanted memories. Even so many years after the incident with Elder Rector, that day on the bus to work I could still feel an inkling of anger at him for invading my personal space. I replaced those thoughts with Scripture.

Be careful for nothing; but in every thing by prayer and supplication with thanksgiving let your requests be made known unto God. And the peace of God, which passeth all understanding, shall keep your hearts and minds through Christ Jesus.

"Hello. How are you doing?" the man beside me said.

"Fine. Thank you," I automatically replied.

More Scripture: *Finally, brethren, whatsoever things are true, whatsoever things are honest, whatsoever things are just, whatsoever things are pure, whatsoever things are lovely, whatsoever things are of good report; if there be any virtue, and if there be any praise, think on these things.*

"Oh, here's my stop. My name is Will."

He wants to know my name? People on the bus don't talk to each other. I don't talk to strange men. Why did he have to sit next to me?

"I'm Patience," I said.

"Patience," Will repeated. "What a beautiful name. And a beautiful yellow blouse."

I tugged at my collar and looked down.

"It reminds me of the sun," he said. "Have a nice day, Patience." This time when saying my name, it was not so much for me but so that he could enjoy the sound of it.

"Patience," he said again.

Why did I say anything to this man?

For the first time since he sat down, I gave my eyes permission to look into his.

"Thank you," were the words that found their way to my lips. He stood up, and I stood up with him thinking that it was my stop also. Something within Will's eyes—something strong, something peaceful—touched my heart and allowed me to smile.

Crash! The sound of metal against metal. The bus collided with another vehicle, its impact forcing me into Will's arms.

"What happened?" I asked.

"Are you all right?" Will asked. He held me around my shoulders; I was a little shaken. Nothing like this had ever happened to me before.

"Yes, I'm okay." The close proximity to Will stirred in me a nervous exhilaration.

"Is everyone okay?" the bus driver asked. "A car cut me off, and I hit it. The driver seems to be all right. He's getting out of the car. Not much damage to the car either. Good grief, there's a police officer already on the scene. Everyone, take your seats. We'll be on our way very shortly."

"What a mess," I said, looking out of the window and at the agitated people on the bus. "I'm glad no one was hurt."

"This is my stop anyway," Will said. "In any circumstance, it's a pleasure to have met you. Is this your regular morning bus."

"Yes, it is."

"I hope to see you tomorrow then—oh, here's the police officer."

The policeman stood in the bus's door on the steps and addressed us in a loud, official voice.

"I'll need a statement from some of you concerning the accident," the officer said. He pointed to several people.

"How about you, sir, and you, madam, and you, and you."

Then he pointed to Will and me.

"And you and your wife, sir," he said.

Will realized that he was still holding me, but it didn't feel at all unnatural or fleshy, just protective. And I hadn't felt protected in that way since Soldier shot the rabid dog. Will let me go and tried to explain to the officer.

"Oh, I'm not her husb—"

71

"I know you're not hurt," the officer interrupted him. "I just need a statement."

"No, I meant that we're not mar—"

"You have every reason to be mad. I'm sure this'll make you late for work and all," the officer said.

"I give up. What do you want to know?" Will asked.

We looked at each other and laughed. We answered questions and signed papers, and the bus was ready to resume its route.

"Have a good day," Will said.

The trees and cars and people continued to move away from me as I moved toward my destination, as the bus moved on, and as my meditation continued as if uninterrupted—as if I had not been distracted by a man in my past, and now this one in my present.

Will didn't get on the bus the next day, or the day after that—in my heart I hoped he would. He probably took a later bus, or I an earlier one.

So I meditated: *Those things, which ye have both learned, and received, and heard, and seen in me, do: and the God of peace shall be with you.*

And the peace of God shall be with me. God, my peace shall be with me. His peace is with me. Beside me is His peace. In me is His peace. I've learned, and received, and seen in Him, through Jesus Christ, love, joy, gentleness, goodness, meekness, temperance, faith, and long-suffering, and, yes God, peace. Thank you for Jesus, and thank you for peace.

My mind went to Will, and almost immediately it turned to the Cross. On it hung the Son, Jesus, Who had made the ultimate sacrifice so I could have a relationship with God. My mind lingered on the cross. It was the most awful, awesome sacrifice that I could ever imagine. My thoughts were turned from Will to Jesus. Soon I was recentered. Will was gone. My day lay ahead of me. Peace overwhelmed me.

Let your conversation be without covetousness; and be content with such things as ye have: for he hath said, I will never leave thee, nor forsake thee.

"Never leave me nor forsake me," I said out loud. The woman who sat next to me turned and looked at me.

Hebrews 13:5. Thank you, God.

Behold the State I'm In

... For I Have
Learned ...

Behold the State I'm In

Temperance: 1968

My relationship with Temperance developed into one of more than just siblings who loved each other. We were true confidants, sharing with each other every life experience, every new emotion, and every new illumination of God's Word. Either at the time they happened or later, we held nothing back from each other. Our thoughts were as if we shared one psyche. Without Temperance, I lacked the power to fully be me, and without me, Temperance had no reality of her purpose. When we were children we began to realize how deeply we were intertwined; we came to understand it, and now we accepted it as fact.

The sun peaked out about ten degrees over the eastern horizon. An unusually cold winter had delayed the blooming of May azaleas; only one or two blossoms dared to peak through the lush green hedges that lined the yards of the buildings on the road that led to Downtown Big City.

I slept in, but Temperance had to get out of the apartment on such a beautiful Saturday morning. She deserved it, having studied long and hard, passing all of her finals. She attended State University's Computer College on an academic scholarship. She hadn't wanted to attend college right out of high school, but I convinced her to take a few courses, which was all that she needed to rekindle her love for learning. That day, she asked our neighbor, Complacency, who lived in our building, to stroll downtown with her.

They walked for several blocks and entered a neighborhood with higher buildings and sparser trees and shrubbery than on our street. Clothing or towels dried and aired from some of the apartments' windows. Children were up and out already, getting an early start on their day of sidewalk hopscotch, jump rope, cops and robbers, or Star-Fleet officers and aliens. Men worked on their automobiles in oily black jumpsuits or casually sat on stoops laughing without a care. A woman in a loose, blue house dress with large yellow and brown sunflowers on it tossed something liquid from a wash basin out of her apartment's front door onto the pavement. On the avenue, the owners of storefronts not yet open for daily business busied themselves sweeping or picking up trash, getting ready for expected crowds.

Temperance and Complacency walked all day, window-shopping, and talking about the future and the past, and about mistakes and victories—all of which could be summarized into one topic—men. When darkness crept up on them, they bought dinner at Fast Food and left the restaurant with cups of frozen custard.

The trek home led them past The Grill, a little one-room house from which the proprietor sold sandwiches, chips, and soda pop, and where teenagers danced and socialized. Temperance didn't go to The Grill, considering it to be an unsophisticated establishment. As they walked by, one of two men in a parked car shouted, "Hey!" Temperance continued to walk, but Complacency slowed to a stop.

"Let's go see what they want," Complacency said.

"Girl, I know what they want, and it's dark out here," Temperance said. "I'm not trying to get myself mugged."

"Look at all these people," Complacency said. "Nothing's going to happen. Let's go back."

"You can go back if you want to, but I'm going home," Temperance said. "I'll see you later." Complacency reluctantly followed her. But before they had gotten a half a block away, the two men drove up beside them.

"You two look lost," one man said. "Do you need

directions?"

Temperance fixed her eyes on the speaker, annoyed at his assumption and at Complacency for placing her in this awkward situation.

"No, we don't need directions," she said. "Come on," she said to Complacency.

"Hey, not so fast," the man said. "We won't bite. My name is My Baby's Father, but everyone calls me M.B.F. And this is my chauffeur. No, seriously, this is my brother Jive." Jive smacked him over the head with his cap.

"I'm Complacency. Nice to meet you." She turned and looked Temperance straight in the eyes and said through clinched teeth: "Say something, girl. These guys are just too cute to let get away."

"Oh ... yes ... nice to meet you," Temperance said. "My Baby's Father, I've heard that name before. Do you go to State U?"

"I take a class now and then. I mostly do my own thing. But don't get me confused with somebody else—it's a common name."

The streetlight on the nearby corner flashed on.

Walk in the light, beautiful light. He's ever shining in my soul.

"Can we give you a lift?" Jive asked.

"Yes," Complacency said.

"No," Temperance rebutted.

"Which is it? Yes or no?" M.B.F. asked.

M.B.F. was the proverbial tall, tan, and tantalizing man that Temperance often dreamed of someday meeting. He reminded her of the models she had seen in *Quintessence*. But it was his eyes that got to her. They had a hazel-like hue, and his face exhibited a boyish innocence. She gave in.

"All right, why not."

Temperance and M.B.F. dated for about a month. She stopped seeing him because he liked to go to nightclubs and she didn't, although on two occasions she accompanied him. She liked to dance, but fervently disdained the smoking and drinking, which reminded her too much of living with Goody and Noppa. So, she spent most of her time studying. Plus, I insisted that she go to church with me, which she didn't mind, and even enjoyed fellowshipping and worshipping with other Christians.

Their backgrounds were totally different, too. M.B.F. was a native-born Big Cityan, as the people in The Big City liked to call themselves, and his father was a doctor with his own practice on the north side of the city. M.B.F. was a stranger to hard work. As the youngest of three children (his other two siblings were girls), his mother had spoiled him, because she had miscarried two babies before he was born.

When Temperance met him, she had dreamed of someday marrying him. But the more she became acquainted with M.B.F., the more she knew marriage was beyond the realm of workable possibilities.

At around eight o'clock, Temperance studied, leaning on the kitchen counter where she could spread out her books and notes. Boredom, brought on by hours of figuring calculus or topology, was her nemesis, against which she fought, wielding issues of *Black*, *Mahogany*, and *Sophisticate*, which she tucked neatly under her textbooks. It was time for a break, so she flipped through the pages in *Black*, which featured pictures of a famous couple who had been recently married. On a beach overlooking the blue Mediterranean

Sea in Nice, France, the couple took their vows, then embraced and kissed. They, along with family, friends, and well-wishers, danced in the grand ballroom of the Hotel Negresco on the Promenade des Anglais.

"Would you look at that wedding dress," Temperance said.

The bride in the picture wore a silver tiara of oval stones and small pearls. Pearl-like beads and sequins covered the entire bodice of her dress. The top layer of the skirt had a split front, with beads covering most of both sides, as well as covering her train. The back of the dress revealed a low V cut. Her veil was fingertip length, with several pearl beads sewn into the tulle.

A knock dissolved the image in her mind. Through the peephole, she saw M.B.F. holding a bag and two large paper cups of Coca-Cola. She opened the door without greeting him and led him to the kitchen.

"I thought you might be hungry," he said. "I hope you can use a little company tonight." Standing nearly a foot taller than Temperance, he bent and kissed her on the forehead. His eyes, twinkling under the bright kitchen lights, darted around the room as his lips rested on her forehead.

"Is this a good time?" he asked.

"What? Uh, I suppose."

"Hope you like steak-and-cheese," he said. "It's a foot-long, but it might not be enough for three people. I didn't have enough on me to get Patience a sandwich, too."

"She's out," Temperance said, still a little apprehensive about M.B.F.'s being there, but the smell of the greasy sandwich made her realize she hadn't eaten since five o'clock.

Time took wings as they ate and talked, and before she

realized it, it was ten o'clock, way past time for him to leave.

"Let's move to the sofa, Temp, and watch some TV."

"You should have called first," Temperance said.

"I know. I took a chance," he said. "It paid off, didn't it? You're home, aren't you?" He turned out the light in the kitchen on their way out. "It hurts my eyes," he explained. "You don't mind do you? Looking as cute as ever."

On their way through the dining room, Temperance turned on the light, but M.B.F. caught her hand at the switch and reversed her action, clicking it back off.

"No comfort in sin ..."

"What did you say?" Temperance asked. She looked around expecting to see someone ... a woman ... Mama?

"Did I say cute? I should have said beautiful. You're beautiful, Temp."

"I think it's time for you to go," Temperance said. "I'm expecting Patience at any moment."

He took her by the shoulders and pulled her toward him, and they kissed on the lips. M.B.F. had never kissed her that way before. She did not—could not—would not—resist. M.B.F. had exhausted all of her will power.

I am no longer a child. I am getting older. I am older. When I was a child I gave life little thought. My needs were met. What have I learned? When I was a child I learned how to pray. What's wrong with me? What am I thinking? Am I thinking? How can I be so gullible? Am I that lonely?

When I was a child, Patience taught me to pray.
All right. I said that before.
No, I don't play when I pray.
I didn't then and I don't now.
I'm all alone.
... How to hide... how to hurt back.
... How to build up walls.
Must protect myself.
Because I was hurt.

Who hurt me?
I'm fooling myself.
Patience kept me.
No, Miss Grace kept me.
Who hurt me?
How did he hurt me?
He assumed a lot.

I should know better.
I have learned ...
Learned ...
Learn ...

"You're not alone, because I Am *always with you.*
You've left Me for a little while, but you will come back.
I heal all hurts, because you learned how to pray.
I Am *the Wonderful Counselor."*

Oh, my God! What am I doing?

They got dressed.
"You'd better leave," Temperance said.
"I'll see you tomorrow?"

83

"I don't know."

"You do know that I love you, don't you?"

As if asking me that question would assure me that the "I love you" part of it is real. As if those three words make right the terrible wrong I've committed in God's face and in Patience's house. When we moved in here, I stood with Patience and declared with her: "As for me and my house, we will serve the Lord."

"I don't know," she said again.

Hurriedly, she straightened the living room and kitchen, drew a bath, and lay in the tub for what seemed to be hours, thinking about the events of the night, how I had taught her the difference between right and wrong, how I had preached to her all her life about waiting until she got married. Temperance's conscience whipped her worse than Old Tickler ever had.

This woman has sacrificed for me. She's given me everything I need to start making wise decisions. I've let her down.

Temperance wept.

When I arrived, the apartment reeked of grilled onions and lilac-scented bathwater.

Weeks passed before Temperance shared with me what had happened that night.

"Patience, I need to talk to you." She sat down at the table across from me.

"All right, let's talk." I continued to read and didn't look up immediately, but gave a half-hearted glance in her general direction.

"I really need to talk."

"You're serious—what's the matter?"

"I have to tell you something, and I know you're going to be upset with me."

"Temperance, did you wear my new dress?"

"No, I didn't wear your new dress." Temperance's eyes were red and swollen. She had been crying. I reached across the table and took her hands in mine.

"Baby, what's wrong?"

She couldn't hold back the tears any longer.

"I missed my period. I think I'm pregnant." The floodgates were now open.

"All right now. You just go ahead and cry. Cry enough for both of us." She must have wept for ten minutes before allowing herself to be consoled. When she calmed down, she told me what had happened.

A baby boy, Rock, was born in The Big City General Hospital on July 11, 1969. Goody and I remained by her side throughout twenty-two hours of labor. Sister traveled for a visit and also lent her support. In The Motor City, Sister was the head interior designer in a small company that she and a friend had founded. Some of her clients were rich and famous rock-and-roll singers, but Sister hadn't changed much. Though sophisticated, in her heart she was still just a country girl from The Sticks. She arrived wearing designer blue jeans, a plaid sleeveless shirt tied at her waist, and slides. In the waiting room, we caught up on each other's lives and learned that it wasn't as hard getting together as all of us had thought. Making just a few phone calls was all it took. Rock was already a blessing to us, providing the occasion to get all the Christianson sisters together.

Temperance decided on the name Rock, remembering what Mama had said to her just before she died: "Blessed be my rock." For a middle name, she honored Paw by naming his first grandson after him: Ernest. But she never dignified the fact, never called him Rock Ernest Christianson, preferring to use Rock E., which soon degenerated to Rocky.

A beautiful mother, Temperance lay in the hospital bed in the pink gown I bought her, with little Rocky lying on her breast. She gazed upon her creation, the smell of talcum and hospital disinfectant tickling her nose as she joyfully watched him be nourished by the liquid life oozing from her belabored body. With saddened eyes, she saw Rocky's striking resemblance to M.B.F. I didn't have to ask whether or not he had visited her and the baby yet. Her eyes revealed to a knowing sister that he hadn't.

"Listen, Temp," I said. "You know that I'll help you in any way I can. I pray that God will use this new birth for the good, for His glory."

"Thanks, Patience. Don't ever stop praying for me."

Praying for Temperance—I've been doing that all my life it seems.

"You and Rock will always have a home as long as there's breath in my body," I said. "It'll be rough at first, but we're no strangers to rough times, are we?"

"You got that right," she said.

That night in the hospital, concerns about her and Rock's future kept Temperance awake. She found the remote control and turned on the small television that was mounted on the wall in front of her bed. At three o'clock in the morning, most television channels made white noise. On one channel, a salesman sold spray paint for balding men. As a last resort, she watched the rerun of a well-known evangelist's crusade. The Reverend's calm, peaceful sermon on salvation almost put her to sleep, but then he asked a question that arrested her attention.

"If you died tonight, would you like Lazarus wake up in Heaven or would you open your eyes in hell? Give Jesus your life. Make Him Lord of your life. Invite Him in to save you."

As hundreds of people made their way to the altar, Temperance examined herself and came up lacking an acceptable answer to the Reverend's question. She wasn't sure she was saved. She had never said the words that the people on television were repeating after the Reverend. With a repentant and sorrowful heart, she accepted Jesus as her Savior and her Lord that night, on her son's birthday.

The next day, M.B.F. visited her in the hospital. Where she once saw in him a tall, tan, and tantalizing piece of manhood, now the tallness she saw slumped in spirit. She perceived a darkness in his eyes, through his eyes. An intelligent darkness. A calculating darkness. The handsomeness she once perceived wasn't validated by substance. His was a superficial handsomeness. It stopped at the surface. It went no deeper than his three-piece suit.

Being pregnant had delayed Temperance's graduation, pushing her back a year. After Rock was born, she continued with her college education and worked part-time at The University Bookstore where she met Riches, Vanity, and Pleasure. They worked side by side with Temperance, three times a week on various shifts. Riches even took a class with her—theology.

Pleasure had finished her shift and joined Riches, Vanity, and Temperance in the break room at two-thirty.

"Hey," Pleasure said. "Y'all want to go to out tonight, maybe to Dudes and Foxes? The paper said Rock and Roll will be there through Sunday." Pleasure found in her large purse a book of matches and lit a Thin Longs cigarette.

All three looked at Temperance for guidance, so she spoke up.

"Don't look at me. You know I don't go to clubs."

"What do you mean?" Pleasure asked.

"I mean just what I said. First of all, I have a son. Remember? And I have too much schoolwork to do when I get home." Temperance took a bite of the honey bun she had gotten from the vending machine.

"Tell the whole reason," Riches said. "Have you all noticed that Temperance don't work on Sundays? It's because she goes to church."

"So what's wrong with going to church?" Temperance asked. She took another large bite, trying to finish it before her break ended. "I've been going to church all my life."

"What did church ever do for you?" Vanity asked. She caught a glimpse of her reflection in the vending machine glass and rearranged her hair.

"Church doesn't have to do anything for me. Just like people don't have to do anything for me. What do you do for me, Vanity? I'm not even going to try to defend myself or the reason I go to church. Obviously some people wouldn't understand."

"No, I'm really interested," Riches said. She gulped her soda, and her gold bangles jingled like coins in a tin can. "Who knows, maybe I'll start going to church one day."

"Well, if you must know, it's about Jesus."

The three women's faces became contorted. They obviously had no idea who Temperance was talking about.

"No, hear me out. It's all about what The Wonderful Counselor did for me, what He did for all of us. He gave His life for us so we wouldn't have to die and go to Hell."

"So you believe in all that Heaven and Hell mumbo-jumbo?" Pleasure said. "I'm going to have my Heaven, but it's going to be right here on Earth. And Hell for me is standing around on my break trying to figure out why nobody wants to party with me tonight."

"That's all you think about," Riches said. "I agree with Temperance to a certain extent. She shouldn't have to defend herself or her beliefs. Just like I refuse to defend why I work so hard here and at school. I want to be a success in life, and nothing is going to stop me. I don't mean any harm, Temperance, but not even Jesus is going to get in my way."

"I believe you, I really do," Temperance said. "But let me tell you something. All the wealth and fame or whatever it is you want to accomplish in life won't mean anything without Him, Who by the way, *is* the Way."

"Okay, okay, I'll go to church with you Sunday," Vanity said. "We'll all go—won't we." She looked at the others for support. "But come on, Temperance, it's Friday night. You know, like that song says, put on your red dress and let's go strut our stuff."

"You don't get it. I don't think any of you do," Temperance said. She picked up her purse as if to leave. "I don't want to strut my stuff. I just want to do what I've got to do to raise my son, get my education, help out my sister, and live my life according to the Word of God the best I know how."

"Well, it's not like Jesus can see you or anything," Vanity said.

"Let me tell you something, Vanity," Temperance said. "I know for a fact that you can make your bed in Hell if you want to, and He is right there with you. Don't tell me He can't see me. He'll never leave me."

"My break is over," Pleasure said. She rushed to the

door. "I've gotta go. Bye."

"Why did she leave?" Vanity asked. "Why is everyone so upset? I just thought we could go out and, like, have
some fun with Pleasure, and, you know—"

"I know, Vanity, I know," Temperance said. "We'll
talk later. Okay?"

"You go to that big church in Cathedral Valley, don't
you?" Riches asked. "I heard they were doing big things,
like buying up hundreds of acres of land, and you all are on
TV, too, right?"

"Yes, Rugged Cross Ministry Broadcast,"
Temperance said.

"I might surprise you and visit you," Riches said.
"Look, Temperance, my roommate is supposed to be moving out at the end of the month. Are you interested in sharing an apartment with me?"

"No. I can't leave Patience. Besides, by living with
my sister, I can afford to keep Rocky in Rugged Cross's
Christian day care and school. Right now, I have to concentrate on him."

"I didn't think this day would ever get here," Temperance
said. She zipped her black graduation gown up to her neck,
slipped on her scarf, and tapped her cap in place.

"No, the tassel goes on the other side," I said, moving it, then flicking a piece of lint from her shoulder. "My
little sister, a college graduate. I'm so proud of you."

"Thank you. Where's Rocky? I have to get him
ready. I've got to have my baby there when I walk across
that stage."

"Relax. Rock's already dressed. I took him next
door. Experience wanted to see him all dressed up and give

him a toy." Experience was a neighbor in our building who proved to be invaluable when it came to providing a positive, godly role model for Rock.

"I don't know what I'd do if it wasn't for Experience," Temperance said. "Yesterday I caught him showing my baby how to tie a tie. I'm sure Rocky didn't have a clue what all that was about, but you never know what's going through a child's mind. Rocky's so precious—"

"And cute. ... I need tissue, you got any tissue?" Just thinking of him brought tears of joy. What a blessing to Temperance and me he had become.

"Yes, and cute. Don't start up already, leave the crying to me."

"I'll go get Rock." I left Temperance standing alone in the dining room. As I was knocking on Experience's door, M.B.F. came through the apartment's front entrance. We waved at each other, and he went into our apartment without knocking.

"Hey, Temperance," M.B.F. said. He leaned forward, intending to kiss her, but she dodged him. "You're looking good. Education becomes you. Turn around, let me look at you."

"I didn't know you were coming over today, but it's good that you did. Rocky's shoes are getting too small."

M.B.F. looked at his nails and rubbed them on his sleeve to shine them.

"How much?" M.B.F. asked.

"You know it's a shame you don't know how much shoes for your baby cost? Maybe if you bought him something now and then you'd know."

"So now you're supposed to know everything because you're graduating."

"I'm sorry. I shouldn't have even gone there." Temperance removed her cap. "This is a good day for me, it has been up until now, and it will continue to be."

"I hope so too. I don't wanta bring you or anybody else down. But every time I come over here, it's always about money. Money, money, money." He reached into his pants pockets and pulled them to the outside. "Look. I don't have any." Frustrated, he threw his hands in the air and opened the front door, but stopped in the doorway. "So?" he said after a while. "What do you think? Ten, twenty, twenty-five dollars?"

"I can't do this by myself, M.B.F." Temperance said.

"What do you want me to do?"

"I can't do this by myself," she repeated.

"What do you want from me?"

"Diapers, milk, baby food. Help in raising Rocky. For you to be a father. For you to show some responsibility. For you to be here when Rocky needs a man."

M.B.F., a man? I'd like to see that.

"I need help on a consistent basis for Rocky. Patience can't keep on footing the bill. Rocky's not just my baby—"

"Yeah, yeah, I know, he's my baby too."

Temperance picked up a pad and pen and scribbled some figures, then showed it to M.B.F.

"I want at least two hundred dollars from you every month, and believe me, you're getting off cheap. I know you have a good job. And we're not married, so it's none of my business what you do with your money. You're Rocky's father. I can't do this by myself. And why should I have to?"

Tears? Temperance didn't want him to see her cry. She didn't want him to make her cry.

I walked through the door holding Rock, followed

by Experience, as M.B.F. was walking back into the living room. He picked up an apple from the fruit bowl on the coffee table and took a bite.

"Oh, hi," I said. "I didn't know you were still here. Experience, have you met Rock's father?"

"No I haven't. Nice to meet you, man," Experience said. *There's that word again—man.*

"Experience has a graduation gift for you, girl," I said.

"Look here, Temperance. I'll talk to you later," M.B.F. said. "I'll do what I can, okay? I'll pick Rocky up next Tuesday and take him to get some shoes. Nice to meet you, Experience." He let the door slam on his way out.

To Temperance's surprise, on the first of June M.B.F. sent her a two-hundred-dollar money order through the mail. On the eighth of July he brought her a hundred and twenty in cash.

"I'll have the rest by the end of the next week," he promised.

And on the sixteenth of August, even that was cut in half—only sixty dollars in a card with a note that read: "I had to get some brakes for my car."

"I'm taking your behind to court," Temperance said.

1977

"Take me to the zoo, ma, today, will you, please?"

"Sure, I'll take you before the tiger exhibit leaves town. I promise."

Rocky's enthusiasm grew when he heard the word "promise," because he knew that Temperance only used it

93

when she knew she could follow through. But like many eight-year-olds, he was relentless when he wanted something.

"You know I was sick when my class went to the zoo on our field trip?"

"Yes, Rocky, I remember."

"And remember you told me when I got better you would take me—"

"My sweet little pest. Why do I love you so much? Didn't I say I'd take you to the zoo?"

"Let's go today, can we, Ma? It's sunny outside, and it's Saturday, you don't have to work, and I don't have to go to school, and Dad said he wasn't coming to get me 'til next Saturday."

Rocky's reference to M.B.F. caused an immediate change of mood in Temperance. In her mind, "Dad" had been transformed to "M.B.F," which made her want to flee, to escape from the very room that the word had been mentioned.

"All right, you win, my little nagger. Patience," she called out. "I'm taking Rocky to the zoo."

"Uh-oh, Ma, you called me that word," Rocky choked back a laugh.

"What word?" she asked, but then she caught on. "You're some kind of comedian. I said *nagger*. A nagger is one who nags—like you."

She grabbed a couple of grape sodas from the Frigidaire, and the two of them left to enjoy a day at the zoo, taking pleasure in the joy of the moment.

"Try to get back in time for my prayer team meeting," I said. My prayer team consisted of women from my church who participated with me in a two-prayer prayer chain at least once a week. I'd call the first person, and we would pray. Then that person would call the next person, and the two of them would pray, and so on until the last person called me again to pray. That way, each of us participated in two prayers. We prayed for each other, our family members, and about challenging issues.

"Sis, you really need to get out more. It's work and church, work and church. Now you're bringing church home. Where will it end?"

"Like you're any different?" I responded. "We're both getting old before our time. Besides, I like my job, and church is my life."

Temperance couldn't argue. She knew that if not for Rocky, she and I could be the same person.

"I'll try to make it back in time," Temperance said.

"Oh, Sister Wisdom is bringing over her grandson to play with Rock."

"Hurray! Come on, Ma, hurry up so we can get back." Rock put on his jacket upside down.

"At first you wanted to go, and now you can't wait to get back. Make up your mind, will you?"

"I just want to show my friend my new action figures Dad bought me."

"That's it." Temperance's button had been pushed, by her son, no less. "Let's get out of here before I change my mind."

Temperance chose to drive through the city instead of taking the freeway. She didn't want to waste such a beautiful day watching cement overpasses and yellow and white lane lines on roads. Instead she took in all of The Big City's sites. The bright blue sky chased away all of the dullness of the city. A hint of tree pollen in the air made it smell almost like The Sticks. She slowed when passing the quaint shops on the avenue and to look at the unusual hats in the window of her favorite hat shop. The smell of barbeque ribs, cooked on a half-barrel, makeshift grill by the side of the road, caused her to say, "Ah!" Out on a Saturday with her son was the good life, except that now her sinuses began to clog.

"Ma, look, over by that big grill. Isn't that Dad? Yes, it is. Stop, Ma, please, I want to say hi."

With one hand in his pocket, M.B.F. conversed with the man cooking as he waited for his order.

"No, Rocky, let's keep going. We don't want to miss those tigers, do we?"

"We won't miss them. Let's stop and say hi to Dad. Please?"

Temperance had to give in. She couldn't deprive Rocky of seeing his father, even though M.B.F. had deprived him of plenty during the eight years Rocky had been on this planet. She made a U-turn and parked. M.B.F. spotted the car right away, paid for his food, and took his time walking to Temperance's car. He poked his head through the window.

"Hey, Rocky, what's going on?"

"Hi, Dad, we're going to see the tigers at the zoo."

"Sounds good, champ," M.B.F. said.

"Doesn't Ma look pretty today, Dad?" Rocky asked.

"Your mother always looks pretty. How're you doing?"

"I'm okay," Temperance said. "How about yourself?"

"Can't complain."

"Dad's getting a new car, Ma, did he tell you? He told me. What kind will it be, Dad?"

"I'm thinking about a Grand Ville, champ."

"You like Grand Villes, don't you, Ma?"

"Rocky wanted to stop and say hello," Temperance said, ignoring Rocky's question. "We can't talk long. We're on a tight deadline. Patience has company coming over tonight."

"We got all day, Ma, we don't have to hurry."

"Anybody I know, Babe?"

"Don't call me Babe."

"I didn't mean any harm."

"He didn't mean no harm, Ma."

"He didn't mean any harm," Temperance corrected.

"Right, that's what I said, hey, Dad, you want to come over tonight?"

"I'm sure your father has better things to do."

"No, he doesn't, Ma."

"Really, champ. I do have things I need to be doing. I'll see you next Saturday. Take care. You too, Temperance."

"Yeah," Temperance said. "We had better be going. We'll talk later. This month's you-know-what is late ... again."

"Well, guess what" M.B.F. said, raising his voice. "It must be the Post Office's fault, because they started taking it directly out of my paycheck." M.B.F. sprinted to his car with no further goodbyes.

Good.

When Temperance and Rocky arrived at the zoo, Rocky moved more slowly than usual.

"Let's go see the elephants," Temperance said, trying to cheer him up. "Did you bring any peanuts to feed them? Elephants like peanuts."

"You know we're not allowed to feed the animals, Ma. Because it's a rule, and rules are made to protect us," Rocky said, and sat down on the bench in front of the sign that pointed to the lion exhibit.

Rocky had been listening to Temperance and me and learning after all.

"My friend says that rules are made to be broken," Rocky added.

"Don't believe everything your friends say. They can get you in a lot of trouble."

Rocky was up early the following Saturday morning anticipating M.B.F.'s arrival to take him who knows where and to do with him who knows what. Typically, when his dad came to see him, they would deposit themselves in front of the television set. But within an hour, M.B.F. would be watching what he wanted to watch.

Rock had determined that this day would be different. He woke up at five o'clock, excited and not even complaining to himself that he hadn't finished his dream. Today was his opportunity to be normal, like his friends who had fathers who lived with them.

He opened the refrigerator and spied the sausage links. Good. He could make that, and in the cupboard was instant oatmeal, something else he could make. He had seen Temperance make coffee, so he carefully measured out four scoops from the coffee can, put them into a coffee filter, and placed it in the filter pot. He filled the coffee pot with water from the sink, poured it into the coffeemaker, and flipped the On button.

What else would his dad like? A newspaper. Rocky raced to the front door and opened it, then remembered that we didn't have the daily paper delivered.

How about the TV Guide then? His dad enjoyed watching TV, so surely he would enjoy reading the TV Guide. Rock neatly placed it at the table where his father would sit.

It was time to begin. He had asked Temperance for permission to turn on the electric stove. She had made sure he knew to move anything flammable away from the heat.

Remembering her instructions, he shifted the dish towel from the counter near the stove to the sink's edge. Struggling with the heavy cast iron frying pan, he succeeded in placing it on the electric burner, turned on the burner, and spooned onto the pan two tablespoons of Crisco.

Eight links. That should be enough.

While the sausage was cooking, Rocky prepared oatmeal and toast. When everything was ready, he placed each dish in a separate container and covered them with aluminum foil.

Good. Oh, no. He needed to get dressed in case M.B.F. wanted to take him out.

Rocky rushed upstairs, pulled off his pajamas in three heartbeats, and jumped in the shower before it had a chance to warm.

"Whoa, this is cold," he said, shivering.

But he didn't care. He soaped up, rinsed, dried off, and put on clean underwear, jeans, and a new T-shirt.

He'd better brush his teeth, too. No, that could wait until after breakfast.

"What's going on? I smell coffee, and food. Are you up, Temperance?" I asked.

"Must be Rocky. I'm still in bed," Temperance answered from her room. "Be down soon."

"It's me, Big Ma. I cooked breakfast for us. Dad will be here soon."

"I'd better see what damage you've done to my kitchen," I said. Yawning, I tightened the belt around my robe. "And how many times have I asked you not to call me Big Ma? It's too much like *Grand* Ma." The sun through my kitchen window acted as a visual alarm to my senses, pushing from my body any residue of sleep.

"My goodness, Rock. The table is set and everything. I'm very impressed. Good job."

"Thanks, Big Ma. Oh, sorry, but I can't help it." Rocky hugged me around my waist, and I bent down and kissed him on the forehead.

"Are the knives and forks in the right places?" Rocky asked. He circled the table, straightening the juice glasses. "Dad should be getting here soon. What time is it?"

"You just hold your horses," I said, lassoing Rock with an imaginary rope and pretending to pull him closer. "It's still early, partner. What are you all going to do today anyway? Do you know?"

"No, I don't. It'll be a surprise. You know Dad."

Yes, sadly to say, I knew Dad.

"What time is he supposed to get here?"

"Ten o'clock. What time is it now?" Rock asked.

Poor Rock. He was so excited and nervous that he couldn't stand still. His eyes darted wildly. His head switched from watching the clock above the stove to peering through the dining room trying to see out of the living-room window.

"It's about ten," I said. "It'll be a late breakfast, so why don't we call it brunch?"

"Yeah, brunch, brunch is supposed to be good—better than breakfast, right?"

"'Yes,' not 'Yeah.' I don't know about better. Ah, here's your mother. Temperance, look what your son did."

Temperance came in showered and dressed in a royal-blue two-piece pants suit, smelling like Camay soap and mint mouthwash.

"Hmmh, there's nothing like the aroma of sausage cooking on a Saturday morning," she said. "Did you do this, sweetie?"

"Yes, ma'am," Rock said. He stuck out his chest proudly.

"We'd better eat before it gets cold then." Temperance pulled out her chair and sat down. "It looks good."

"No, we have to wait a little longer, until Dad gets here."

"Okay, we'll wait." Temperance looked at me with an expression bordering between frustration and anger. Rock looked to me for support. I smiled at him and cupped his chin in my hand. And we waited.

Minutes quickly turned to an hour. Rocky had knelt on the sofa in front of the window, the whole time anticipating his father's arrival, imagining how surprised and how proud he would be that he had cooked breakfast—no brunch. Two hours late. It was twelve o'clock, and Temperance had had enough.

"Listen, Rocky, why don't we go ahead and eat? Big Ma and I have already nibbled away half the sausages, and we had a cup of your coffee. It was dee-licious."

Rocky was close to tears.

"Ma, he said he would be here by ten," Rock said. "What happened?"

"Maybe he had a flat tire, or maybe he just over-slept. A hundred things could have happened."

Temperance wanted to believe her own explanation, but she knew better.

"We'll find out when he gets here," she said.

If he gets here. I'll kill him if he disappoints Rock again. Or at least he'll wish he were dead after my tongue-lashing.

"Come on. Let's eat. You must be starved," Temperance said.

Rocky suddenly perked up like a puppy hearing its master outside the door.

"He's here! He's here!" He jumped to his feet and

ran and opened the door.

M.B.F. was clean and pressed from head to toe, his cap was cocked to the side, and he strutted across the street with his hand in his pocket as he played with his loose change.

"Hey, everyone," M.B.F. said. "Sorry I'm late. Some kids had a car wash going on down the street so I stopped and got a car wash and a wax job. Can't drive around in a dirty car, you know. It's not cool."

I believe he actually expected everyone to be as pleased as he was for his accomplishment of attaining a clean car by the sweat of someone else's brow. The look on Rocky's face reminded me of a child who had just been told he had to stay after school. Temperance and I looked at each other in disbelief, but we dared not say anything just yet. Silence, save the clock on the wall ticking, reminded all of us, except M.B.F., of his tardiness.

"Rock cooked breakfast for all of us," I said. I rubbed Rock's head hard, trying to cheer him. "And we were just about to eat … or should I say, warm it up."

"Sorry, champ. Had to wash my car. So, what do you want to do today?"

"I don't want to do anything," Rock cried, as he stormed down the hall to his room, and slammed the door behind him.

"What's the matter with him?" M.B.F. put his hand back into his pocket and resumed jingling his loose change.

"You actually don't know, do you?" Temperance said. She threw up her hands. "That's the sad part about it. You tell your son that you're coming to see him, and give him a specific time—he can tell time, or didn't you know that? And then you come in here and all but tell him point-blank that your car is more important to you than the promise you made to him."

"It's not like that at all, and you know it," M.B.F. said. "Okay, I admit, I said the wrong thing—"

"*Said* the wrong thing? If you just *said* the wrong thing, that's almost forgivable. But you are wrong. You don't treat people like that, much less your eight-year-old son."

"There you go again." M.B.F. shook his finger at Temperance, then at me. "Whether you and your sister believe it or not, I love my son."

At that remark, I went into the kitchen and sat down.

"But y'all always trying to make me look bad in front of him." He leaned against the living room wall and jiggled his change some more, but this time he looked down and realized what he was doing and cut short his annoying habit. "Well, anyway, I do love him. And I'll make it up to him. I've got a friend who can get me a deal on a pair of Chuck Taylor's. Half price. Rocky likes red, doesn't he?"

"He doesn't need tennis shoes from you. He needs you." The more Temperance talked, the closer she drew to M.B.F., until she was talking almost nose to nose with him. "You can't buy your way out of this one," she said. "That child is hurt. And I have to come up with a lie to make him feel better."

"What do you mean, lie?"

"I'm going to have to talk you up. I can't tell him that his father is a selfish, self-centered, womanizer who—"

"Watch yourself, Temperance." He pointed his finger at her again.

"I think it's time for you to leave. I'll make up some excuse to tell Rocky."

M.B.F. turned toward the door, but remembered the

envelope in his inside jacket pocket, took it out, and put it on the coffee table.

"There's the money I was going to blow on Rocky today, but why don't you take? Money is all you want anyway."

"You just don't get it, do you?"

Rocky stood in his half-opened bedroom door. He had listened to the altercation between Temperance and M.B.F.

"Dad's right," he whispered.

Big Ma: 1982

April-showered springs exploded from frozen, wind-whipped winters, as year after year Rock and Temperance filled a void in my life. Goody never came for a visit, nor did Temperance and I drop in on Noppa and her. The Big City was amply named, and we all had our own lives to live—she and Noppa, a wild life of parties, gambling, and new toys; Temperance and I, a sober, Christian existence. Sister and I wrote each other, often mentioning getting the family together for a reunion of some kind. However, for more than twenty years this hadn't come to pass. Aunt Wits had so dominated Sister, had so possessed her, that even as an adult, Sister found it difficult to travel without her. Sister was my only contact with Paw. My desire was to visit, or at least call him (at Mumzy's insistence, he had a telephone installed in our old house), but for some reason my finger wouldn't dial the number Sister had given me. Something restrained me each time I picked up the telephone.

Soldier visited sporadically, but I dreaded his visits, because I knew my happiness would be only temporary; I couldn't afford temporary happiness; the sadness that would follow would be too great. When Soldier would leave, it would be as when he initially left The Sticks. So when Soldier came, Temperance and I usually left the house so he could accomplish some male bonding with Rock. He told Rock and his friends stories from the Corps or took Rock for motorcycle rides. Soldier owned three motorcycles, the first of which he bought as an inexpensive way to get around the bases where he was stationed. But after he made the rank of gunnery sergeant, he bought himself a Harley, and it was nothing but the best after that. After nearly thirty years in the Corps, he was promoted to the rank of chief warrant office, the highest enlisted rank, having earned his college degree while serving. He purchased a home Out West, his last assignment.

I felt only numbness when it came to Goodness, Sister, Soldier, and Paw's not being a real part of my life, and often joked about it to Temperance, saying that she and Rock were my only family. Was it a joke? Or was it really how I felt? I had to feel this way. Not even Soldier could protect me from the hurt inflicted on me by my past.

I sat folding clothes at the kitchen table pondering the state of my family, when Rock came out of his room, sat down beside me, and began to help with the folding. He typically managed to find all of his clothing, sheets, and towels and fold them first, shying away from his mother's and my unmentionables.

"What's up, Big Ma?" Rocky asked.

"Boy, how many times have I told you not to call me that? People will hear you and think I'm really old enough to be your grandmother. And what's up had better be your grade in Math."

"Sorry, Big Ma," Rocky apologized, laughing.

"You're asking for it, aren't you," I said and dumped the unfolded laundry in his lap.

"Come to think of it, you're the closest thing I've got to a real grandmother. Some of my friends have two grandmothers, so they get twice as many Christmas and birthday presents."

It was true. In ways I had become a mother as well as a grandmother to Rocky. Had I known years ago when I adopted Temperance that at my young age her son would be considering me as his grandmother, things might have been different. I looked around at my kitchen, and it was true: The potted African violets on the windowsill said grandmother. The lace doilies under my toaster and blender shouted grandmother. The tin canister set with the matching salt and pepper shakers all spoke the word to me that meant that I was getting old before my time—grandmother. I closed my eyes, no longer able to look at the evidence of what I had become—a forty-something-year-old surrogate grandmother.

"I might have known all this had to do with gifts." I folded a couple more pillowcases.

"No, seriously," Rock said. "Like I said, some of my friends have two grandmothers, and some of their dads live with them. And they have grandfathers, and brothers."

"When was the last time your father took you to see your grandfather?" I asked. I wanted to recant my words when I suddenly remembered that Rock had never even met Paw, who was also his grandfather.

Although Rocky straightened up and sat tall in his seat, the expression on his face sank.

"I don't know," he said. "Besides, Grandfather doesn't have much to say to me whenever Dad takes me. And he ignores me when I ask him anything. It used to hurt my feelings, but I'm used to it now."

I stopped folding so I could give Rock my undivided attention.

"It's kind of hard living with two women," he said.

"I know, and your mom understands that, too." How had Rock gotten so big? At twelve, he was almost as tall as Temperance.

"It's too bad Uncle Soldier lives so far away," he said. "I love it when he visits us. He looks so cool in his Corps uniform, shoes so shiny, you can almost see your face in them. And all those ribbons. Did he ever tell you if he's coming this Christmas?"

"No, not in his last letter. Maybe he'll call soon and you can talk to him on the phone."

"I hope so. I sure miss his stories about being in the Corps and all he went through. My favorite ones are about his drill sergeant named Hash-Mark."

"Old Hash-Mark," we said almost at the same time. I dabbed a tear from my eyes as I took in the joy Rock felt just thinking about his uncle. With his arm bent at the elbow and his index finger supporting his head, he looked at me, but he was seeing Soldier, out in front of our apartment building with himself and five or six of his friends gathered around listening to Soldier talk. He always started out by calling the little guys "men."

"Men. Gather 'round."

"Tell us another story," someone would always say after Soldier paused for moment. Without thinking too much about it, he would go into a story and didn't stop until he had told four or five of his tall—but true—tales.

"After about seven days into boot camp, we got our permanent drill instructor, old Hash-Mark. On Sundays, if you didn't go to chapel, you had to scrub everything down. So quite naturally, I went to chapel. We were coming back from service, in formation, of course, and had come to a stop after marching. Hash-Mark yelled 'PLATOON, HALT' to let another platoon march by. Now when we came to platoon halt, we were not supposed to move a muscle. But there were sand fleas everywhere, and one was nibbling on my left ear. I could see the drill instructor marching along side of us, but I didn't see Hash-Mark in the back. I flicked the flea off my ear, and before I could scratch it, old Hash-Mark whacked me so hard in the back of my head, I thought my eyes were going to pop out. Yeah, it hurt, and I couldn't help but cry. But the point was that if we had been in combat, by me moving, I had just given away our position. ...

"Because the War was still going on in full force, and so many Corpsmen had to be processed through and sent off to the war, and because we were the senior platoon, they had to move our unit into old buildings that hadn't been occupied for twenty years, since the war before. They were near a swamp. I don't know if they built them by the swamp or if the land became swampy over the years. But anyway, we had to get these buildings in shipshape and in a hurry. So we scrubbed the floors with hand brushes, and no matter how much we scrubbed, when they dried, they looked just as bad as when we started. We didn't have any wax or polish to make them look any better. We were content that they were clean. The next morning some one opened the back door, and in came a swarm of big black mosquitoes. You should have seen us scrambling to get out of there. But the damage was done. So we went to chow, and when we came back, I guess the drill instructors had sprayed DDT, because the mosquitoes were gone. ...

"Whenever Hash-Mark needed to give us all information, or pass out something, like our mail, he would yell, 'SCHOOL CIRCLE.' So when he yelled 'SCHOOL CIR-CLE,' that meant we were to drop what we were doing and gather around him in a circle. The trick was that we had to all get there at the same time. If everyone didn't get there at the same time, he would say 'GET BACK,' and we all went back to our bunks. He would do it again, yelling 'SCHOOL CIRCLE.' And he would do this until he was satisfied with our performance—that we got there at the same time. Then he would yell 'SIT,' and everyone sat on the floor, at the same time, but he would be in a chair. Then he would hand out our mail. He was trying to get us to act as a unit.

"But sometimes he carried that a little bit too far. Hash-Mark divided the squad bay into two sections: the port side and the starboard side. The head, or as you civilians call it, the bathroom facility, was only large enough to accommodate one section at a time. When Hash-Mark decided it was time for the platoon to use the head, he would yell, 'PORT SIDE IN THE HEAD,' or 'STAR-BOARD SIDE IN THE HEAD.' On this particular day, we were running late getting to the chow hall (each platoon had their allotted time to eat or you wouldn't get served). We were running late, but the port side was in the head. So Hash-Mark yelled out, 'BREAK IT OFF, CLEAR THE HEAD, PROMISE YOU MORE LATER.'...

"Smoke breaks were a riot. And, guys, this only happened once, just to show you what kind of man Hash-Mark was. Whenever he okayed a smoke break, he would yell, 'SMOKERS, LIGHT ONE.' That meant each smoker could smoke only one cigarette. One guy grabbed the bucket, which served as an ashtray, and all the smokers went outside and smoked. When it was time to come back in, Hash-

Mark yelled, 'SMOKE OUT.' Then he counted the butts. Thirteen smokers, there had better be only thirteen butts. Oops, there were fourteen. Hash-Mark yelled, 'WHO HAD TWO CIGARETTES?' Of course, he added a few choice words. The person who had two knew he had better confess or everyone would lose their smoking privileges. Hash-Mark let him smoke another one. The guilty party had to turn the bucket over his head and smoke inside the bucket. He was coughing and gagging and trying to keep his cool. Afterwards, he had to clean up the ashes and butts on the floor. Old grumpy Hash-Mark was trying to teach us to follow orders."

.

"I know it's hard on you sometimes, Rock, not having your dad around all the time."

"I wish I could talk to Ma about some things," Rocky said. "Ma, she tries her best, but it's not good enough. She never does what I want her to. It's like she always has to hold back, or prove something. Like the time when Hoodwink Purg and his big brother Disappointment started picking on me."

"Who? Why didn't you tell somebody?" This was news to me. "Why didn't you tell me? I would have—"

"You're not supposed to run to your Ma every time something happens to you," Rock said. "I need somebody to show me how to … defend myself." Rock got up and started boxing the air, pretending to fight. But then he got serious again and told me what happened shortly after school started. My heart went out to Rock as he told me his story.

It was the beginning of his seventh-grade year, and racial tension at his school was much like a civil war. The student population was about sixty percent White and forty percent Black. And everybody in the school was on the defensive. All the White kids sat on one side of the classroom and the Black kids on the other. They all talked and played within their own groups with no open conflict, but a clear battle line was drawn, which Rock had to cross.

Rock had felt compelled to join the Black side. After all, he had grown up in an all-Black community and had attended an all-Black elementary school. But he wanted to know more about the White children. He had never really known any Whites before—from a distance, all the kids looked the same to him. He had to get to know who they were saying his enemy was.

One day when the bell rang and the ground offensive began, he decided to sit in the middle row, the DMZ. He quickly discovered that straddling the fence was like going to another country to get out of being sent to fight in an unjustified war. Neither side respected his right to be neutral. The White camp didn't like or trust him, and because of his neutral position, his own group didn't accept him. He was an outcast and a fugitive during a time when he needed so badly to belong.

The henchman for the Black group was Hoodwink Purge. One day while in homeroom waiting for the teacher, Hoodwink pushed Rock's books off his desk and said in a loud voice, "I'm gonna kick yo' butt." Just then, the teacher walked in. Rock had been saved from a butt-kicking, at least until the class was over. He waited until all the kids, including Hoodwink, left before he went to his next class.

He knew Hoodwink wouldn't be in any of his other classes. Unfortunately, they had the same lunch period. Rock bought his lunch and sat on the White side of the battle line. It wasn't long before Hoodwink and his gang came over, and the first shots of an uncivilized war were fired. Rock had thought that they were supposed to be on the same side. Hoodwink knocked his lunch tray on the floor, and the battle commenced. Before the teacher could break up the fight, Rock delivered a few good shots—and gave Hoodwink a bloody nose. Victory! He looked at Hoodwink's wound and hoped he had gotten the message to leave him alone. Not so. Like all bullies, he had backup. Rock told me how as he walked home that day, he came **across** Hoodwink and his gang. This time they all jumped him. He fought hard, but lost the battle. He had a swollen lip and a cut over his eye.

"I thought about it a lot, Big Ma, and cried a lot too. But I decided that there must be some other guys at school with the same problem, that felt the same way I did."

"You needed some allies," I said.

He agreed. He told me that the next day, he began to talk to some other children. Not the White ones. He knew they wouldn't join with him. In their eyes he was just like Hoodwink. Over the next two weeks, he recruited eight boys. Their mission was clear. Whenever new boys came to the school (he said girls didn't seem to have a problem), they would befriend them.

"We would never fight," Rock said. "We all just needed a place to belong."

Rock pranced around the kitchen like he was the heavyweight champ, jabbing, punching, and flicking the side of his nose with his thumb. "One day I'm going to be

112

a hell of a—I mean a good father. ... Don't look at me like that, Big Ma. 'Hell' slipped out. Look, I'm floating like a butterfly, stinging like a bee."

"It can't slip out if it's not in you, my dear heavy-weight."

"I love you, Big Ma."

"Sure you do. You just better watch your mouth."

Behold the State I'm In

... In Whatsoever
State ...

Behold the State I'm In

Temperance and I sat down on the third pew at Rugged Cross a little early for the Friday night revival meeting. A guest minister whom neither of us had heard of was preaching. We didn't mind— as long as we were receiving the Word of God.

Prayer Band No. 3 was in charge of the devotional part of the service, which consisted of singing songs without the accompaniment of music, songs about dying, death, getting to heaven, going to heaven, hard work, and tribulation. Temperance usually read her Bible during the devotional; I sang along because the songs reminded me of church services in The Sticks. Intermixed with the songs were heart-wrenching prayers prayed by the deacons who knelt on one knee in front of the first pew.

Women gradually began to fill the church. Some wore wide-brimmed hats with feathers, flowers, or bows. Most wore work clothes or plain housedresses. The church trustees, deacons, and ministers, and husbands, sons, and other men mixed in with the women.

Prayer Band No. 3 started singing their fourth song when a procession of ministers, led by our pastor, Pastor Shepherd, entered the chancel area from a side office. A deacon added three more chairs to the chancel area for visiting ministers. Temperance and I knew all of the clergy who were church members, and many of the ones who visited for special services such as anniversaries, annual men and women's day, Good Friday service, or building-fund rallies. But a new face graced the chancel area.

Where had I seen him before?

"Will, from the bus," I said out loud. It had been more than ten years since I had last seen him.

He took his seat on the far left of the chancel area. As I stared at him, his head turned and his eyes met mine. He recognized me, and he winked at me. Out of surprise and embarrassment, I looked away, but when I looked up again, he was still looking at me and smiling. Then he threw his head back and almost laughed. I had never seen a man exhibit such life, with such joy emerging from such depth.

"I now turn this portion of the program over to the pulpit," the head deacon said.

A middle-aged minister in a gray pin-striped suit approached the pulpit.

"Can the church say 'Amen'?" he asked.

The congregation responded with a resounding "Amen."

"Can the church say 'Amen'?" he asked a second time, in an attempt to add excitement to the Friday-night program.

This time the "Amen" was louder.

"I said, can the church say 'Amen'?" he asked a third time.

"Amen," shouted the people, with some "Hallelujahs" and a few "Praise the Lords" thrown in.

"I would like to present to some and introduce to others a preacher who is sold out for the Lord. He hasn't preached here before, but I'm sure this won't be his last time. As you know, the minister who was supposed to preach tonight had an emergency and had to go out of town and could not be here. We asked this young man at the last minute, and, praise the Lord, he had a sermon in his pocket and a prayer on his lips. Let's give a hearty amen to Reverend Will B. Done. Let's hear it now. Come on, y'all can do better than that."

A preacher. I had no idea.

Will stepped in front of the microphone on the podium and began to speak. He spoke but I didn't hear. He said something about being glad to be here, and explained and apologized for not coming sooner. When I dared to look up, I found that he wasn't looking at me at all now. He gazed out in the congregation. I could see that he wasn't concentrating on particular faces or individual people, but on the message, on the words he delivered. Beautiful words. The Word of God.

In his message, the examples he gave were true to life, realistic, and applicable to our daily lives. He had us; we were captivated, entrapped, entangled in the words he spoke, which were straight from the Bible. His voice was calming, like the sound of crickets out in the backyard at the house in The Sticks on a warm summer night. The brief encounter of his eyes with mine was like the lightning bug's brief light that flickered off and you hoped would flicker on again, that you searched for until it flickered on again.

"Patience, what's wrong with you?" Temperance said. She poked me in my side with her elbow and whispered, "Sit up. You're sliding down in your seat."

I straightened up thankful that she was the only one who had noticed me. Will's amazing smile enthralled me, and I was sure many of the other women who were not deeply rooted in the Word of God, and some, like me, who dared to boast knowledge thereof, also noticed his smile.

Temperance took notes as Will spoke. I didn't take notes, I prayed. I prayed to God for forgiveness, because I was totally distracted. For years I had closed my mind and my eyes to men, and frankly was surprised that this particular man had so sidetracked me during this service.

At the end of Will's sermon, he asked that we all bow our heads and pray that those who needed Jesus would accept Him into their lives as their personal Savior. Three people stood and went to the front of the church—a married couple and their teenage son. Surprisingly enough it was the son who seemed truly repentant, with face wet with salty tears, with a cry of "Forgive me, God" on his lips. Will came from behind the pulpit and prayed for the three of them. As he prayed, Sister Substance could be heard speaking in tongues. She was the only person in Rugged Cross' membership to speak in an unknown tongue. Will kept praying, but after he said amen, he looked around, as if searching for the voice that had spoken.

This man was a man of God. I am falling in love with a real preacher of the Gospel. But how can I? I barely knew him. Why is God allowing me to have these feeling? Or is it me? Or could it be the devil?

I quickly ruled out the devil, because the devil would probably have me falling for someone who meant me no good.

Suppose this was the case with Will? Suppose he was not good for me either? Suppose no man was any good for me? Maybe I was meant to be alone, like Phoebe in the Bible. I've done fine by myself for forty-some odd years, just me, Temperance, and Rock. I can do just fine for forty more. I didn't need Mr. Will B. Done.

Temperance poked me again, interrupting the incoherently babblings of my mind.

"What?" I asked. It wasn't Temperance.

"Excuse me, sister," Will said. "Don't I know you?"

"Will," I said. I quickly pulled myself together and accommodated his outstretched hand to shake it. "It's so nice to see you again." My head was spinning from the excitement of talking to him again.

"This is my sister, Temperance."

"Pleased to meet you, sir," Temperance said, while giggling. I would have thought it impossible to giggle while talking, but Temperance did.

"Sir?" Will said. "You'd better call me Will."

We all laughed.

"Wasn't it an absolutely beautiful day today?" Will asked.

"Absolutely," I replied. "When we talked on the bus, you didn't mention that you were in the clergy."

"Well, it's not something I like to go around advertising. I'd rather live my life the best I can and try to let people see God through me."

"Reverend Done, I truly saw the Scriptures you used tonight in a new light," Temperance said.

"Thank you. God is good, isn't He?"

"That's the truth," Temperance said. Turning to me, she said, "Look, Patience, it's getting late, and I need to pick up Rocky."

"Can I give you two ladies a ride somewhere?" Will asked.

Will had made this day a gift to me. It was more than I could have prayed for and gotten in a decade of Christmases.

"No. Thank you, though," I said. "Yes, we'd better go."

"I'll see you out in the car, Patience," Temperance said. "I have to catch up with ... somebody ... oh, there you are," she said to someone whom I didn't see.

What was she up to?

By this time, the church had cleared out. A bright full moon glowed through the church's stained-glass window. We turned at the same time to notice the light.

121

"I'll walk you to your car," Will said. "Patience."

"Yes?"

"Oh, nothing."

Will's sermon had had such a spiritual impact on Pastor Shepherd and the entire board of deacons and elders that in their next board meeting, they voted unanimously to offer Will the job of assistant pastor of Rugged Cross Church. That position, though a paid one, had been vacant since Reverend Boomer died three years earlier. Will accepted and actively began to reform some of the church's antiquated traditions. He showed the board that observing Ash Wednesday was not Bible-based, and he introduced praise-and-worship music to the congregation. At first this new music was strange to us, but over time we grew accustomed to and rather enjoyed singing the Scriptures and clapping our hands on the beat instead of between the beats.

Will also actively courted me. After every Sunday service, Wednesday-night prayer meeting, and church event and activity that we both attended, he made a point of holding a conversation with me. We talked about everything from God's purpose for cockroaches to the different roles of God, the Father; God, the Son; and God, the Holy Ghost.

Although we didn't go out together or see each other in any way outside of church walls, the entire congregation thought of us as a couple, allowing us to talk whenever we were together without interruption. Even the children in my Juniors Sunday School class ceased from giggling when they saw Will and me talking.

My heart was softening toward this man, and God hadn't given me a clue to where this relationship was heading. At night at home I prayed for guidance—out loud; I had to get it out of me. But praying verbally was hard because during prayer, I cried easily. When it came to Will, I never knew exactly what to pray for.

"God, I'm open to whatever you have in store for my life. For years I've suppressed the thought of marriage, concentrating instead on my relationship with you, on Temperance and Rock, on my church work, and on the wonderful teaching job you've allowed me to have. ...Lord, I've fallen in love with Reverend Done. ... I have a spiritual perception by faith that You are Love. ... I patiently wait for Your Love to manifest itself ... in me ... through me. ... I give this situation with Will over to you. Let your will be done in my life."

For weeks, Will surprised me at my car with flowers; after Bible study with a chocolate kiss; or in the foyer after service—when the majority of the parishioners were having an early dinner or chatting in the Fellowship Hall—with an invitation to watch how the light sparkled through the replica of the Rose Window of Saint John the Divine over the front entryway.

"Sister Done," he said, turning to look into my eyes.

"Yes. *What?*" I asked. His question, along with the flecks of red and blue light that were reflected in his eyes, caught me off guard.

"I can't help it, Sister ... see, there I go again. It's just that to me you're Sister Done. Don't ask me why." He turned to face me, reaching for my hand. "May I?"

He took my hand in his and with the other hand pulled a ring box from his pocket.

"Forgive me for being presumptuous, Sister Done," he said. He released my hand and opened the box to show me the diamond ring inside. "But since the time you were thrown into my arms on the bus, every time I've seen your image in my thoughts, I've heard the words 'Sister Done.'" Will knelt down on one knee. "Patience. Will you make my dreams come true and be my wife?"

"Oh, God," I said. I shook with joy. "Oh, God, yes!" He slipped the ring on my finger.

Three months later after intense counseling with Pastor Shepherd, without much pomp or circumstance, in the pastor's study, with Temperance and Rock, Aunt Wits, and Sister as witnesses, we were married.

Our honeymoon was glorious—all that I could have imagined a honeymoon to be. We spent four nights at the Beautiful Lake Resort in Ontario. We took morning walks together on the shore, drank in beautiful sunsets while eating dinner at an outdoor café, canoed on the lake, fished for pickerel during the day and cleaned and cooked our catch in the evening, and ate on the cottage porch, listening to crickets, owls, and other woodland creatures. The best part was waking up every morning lying next to Will, holding him, him holding me as if we were found treasure that couldn't be spent. It all seemed like some strange dream; I was afraid to talk, to move, to blink, or I might wake up. Then I looked at the diamond on my finger, and I knew that it was real. Will was real. I had been blessed with a gift from God—a husband who loved the Lord and who loved me. A man whom I adored.

"Does it have to end, Sweetie?" I asked Will. I stretched my back and shoulders under the covers, waking Will who was still sleeping lightly.

"What has to end?" Will asked. He yawned and

stretched, and we kissed. "Good morning." He got up, put on his robe, and sat on the side of the bed.

"Our honeymoon, this vacation, this glorious time, why must it end?" I pushed my pillow against the head-board and sat up also.

"Life is full of beginnings and endings," he said. After having just waked up, Will became energized, ready for whatever the day had in store. "I have a better question for you. It's always bothered me." On the round table, Will found his study Bible.

"Why can't the baptism of the Holy Spirit with the evidence of speaking in tongues be for our time?"

One of Will's qualities that I adored was his passion for interpreting the Scripture correctly. We had started this discussion the day before. While we strolled on the beach, I asked him what he thought about the woman who spoke in tongues the day he preached at our church when we were reunited. Now, it was like he was no longer talking to me, but unearthing thoughts that he had kept buried.

"Do you want some coffee, honey?" I asked, but it was no use. He would not stop until he felt a release or got an answer.

"The Scriptures plainly say that after the Holy Ghost comes upon you, you will receive power, and it always says that the people spoke in other tongues."

"Come on, sweetheart, sit down. Stop pacing."

"If there's power, supernatural power, out there for God's people, I want it, I need it, to do what I believe God is calling me to do. We both need it."

We were newlyweds, and this was a grand opportunity to develop good habits, such as not debating an issue, which could lead to disagreements, or even worse, arguments.

"Let's look it up, then," I said.

We sat at the table and looked through the concordance of Will's Bible and read every Scripture on baptism, the Holy Ghost, the Holy Spirit, tongues, and power. Finally, Will had his answer. Anxiety on his countenance was replaced by anticipation.

"Sing with me, Babe," he said.

He rarely called me Babe, but when he did, I always turned to Jell-O. We held hands and sang.

"Lord prepare me to be a sanctuary, pure and holy, tried and true. And with thanksgiving, I'll be a living, sanctuary, Lord, for you."

The third time through, Will let go of my hands and raised his toward Heaven. I did the same. Then we rejoined hands, and Will prayed.

"Lord, I and my wife ask simply and directly to be baptized in Your Holy Spirit as Your Word promises. And, Lord, we desire to speak with other tongues. We confess that we don't know all that there is to know about it, but we've read it in Your Word, and we believe Your Word. So now Lord, we wait."

We stood there, Will, with his eyes closed, humming the tune to "Lord, Prepare Me," and I, looking at Will, thanking the Lord inwardly for such a wonderful man in my life, remembering Jesus' sacrifice on the Cross, thanking God for how far He had brought me.

"Why don't we just open our mouths and speak," Will said. He began to say syllables that I did not understand.

"Dah-tah-nee-toom. Da-ta-nee-toom."

His grip was intense, almost to the point of shaking, trembling, yet not so tight that it would hurt. I obeyed and opened my mouth and began to say syllables.

"Kee-mon-dee-fro-mee."

The more we spoke, the more confident we became in what we were saying, although we didn't understand each other or ourselves. We simultaneously dropped to our knees, still speaking.

"Dah-tah-nee-toom. Da-ta-nee-toom naree," Will said.

"Kee-too-mon-dee-fro," I said.

Will released my hands and took my face in his hands, still speaking his language, and me mine. He looked deeply into my eyes, and we were one in the Spirit. My thoughts were his thoughts, which were focused on Jesus. We both cried, then wept. It was too much to bear, we couldn't contain ourselves. We fell to the floor and lay there stretched out, head to head, face down, for what seemed liked hours, but in reality it had only been about fifteen minutes. And then we sat up with our backs against the bed.

"Let not your heart be troubled: ye believe in God, believe also in me. In my Father's house are many mansions: if it were not so, I would have told you. I go to prepare a place for you," Will said. "Those Scriptures were so clear in my mind, no, in my spirit as we were praying."

"Oh, Will."

"Come on, let's sing again."

"Thank you, Lord, thank you Lord. Thank you, Lord. I just want to thank you, Lord. You've been so good. You've been so good. You've been so good. I just want to thank you. Lord."

After our honeymoon, I moved into Will's house on the west side, bringing with me my bedroom set, which took the place of his because mine was a queen-size bed and his was only a full size. My television found a home in the guest bedroom where his old bedroom suite went, displacing boxes of stored papers and books. His beige sectional sofa occupied most of the wall space in the living room.

"No TV in the bedroom, honey, okay? The bedroom should be for sleeping."

"And the like," I said. He knew exactly what I was alluding to. He knew I loved him dearly.

"Patience ..."

In the short time we had known each other, Will had developed a habit of saying my name while entreating me to live by my name.

Why had Mama named me Patience—Temperance would have suited my personality better.

"Will, ..." I always responded spontaneously whenever he said "Patience" that way. It was like I was saying "I'll be patient, but I need will power."

About watching TV in the bedroom, I had to agree with him. After all, I always fell asleep before the first commercial came on.

My bigger suitcase faithfully stood on its end on my side of the bed, topped with a three-quarter-inch, round piece of glass to give it a touch of class, dutifully serving as my night stand.

"Wait, don't tell me. Sentimental value, right?" Will looked at it and shook his head in disbelief.

"Yes, sweetheart," I said. "Did I tell you how I found the suitcases?" Already in my nightgown, I went into our master bathroom to complete my nightly routine.

"You did, and I still can't believe you've kept them this long."

I reappeared in the bathroom doorway with soap on my face, and Will toppled over from laughter.

"Don't laugh at me, Will," I said, almost laughing myself.

Will was assistant vice president at the Commerce Bank, and I had long received tenure at the university. Will toiled over ledgers, and budgets, and bottom lines, and employee problems. Occasionally, he worked on Saturdays or in the evenings until midnight, especially when the quarterly reports were due. His truck was often the only vehicle in the bank's parking lot during those times.

We agreed that whoever got home first would start dinner. I did most of the cooking, but Will was a good cook also. When he got home first, he usually threw some chicken breasts in a baking pan with sliced potatoes and onions, and opened a can of whole kernel corn or peas. To add variety, sometimes he baked pork chops with potatoes and onions, and we ate canned or frozen green beans as a side dish. His specialty, though, was baked salmon marinated in Italian dressing, with rice and peas.

We often left home and returned at the same time. In order to spend more time together, sometimes Will dropped me off at work or I him. He taught me how to drive his truck, which had a stick shift.

"You might have to drive the Ram sometimes, for whatever reason, and I want you to know how," he told me. After a few lessons, I drove a four-speed like I'd done it all my life. Stopping on a hill was even easy. Will taught me how to set the hand brake, put the Ram in first gear, then slowly release the brake while releasing the clutch and pressing the gas.

"What can't you do, Mrs. Done?"

"I don't know. I haven't tried everything yet," I said.

During football season, I took pleasure in watching Will enjoying the games on television. After church, on a Sunday afternoon around two o'clock (the games usually started around three), off came tie and suit, high-heel shoes and dress, and on went the sweats or other comfortable clothes. Will settled in for the game between The Big City Animals and The Southwest Meanies. His usual chips and picante salsa or a red delicious apple—his favorite—held his appetite at bay until dinner was ready. I didn't mind his Sunday afternoon dates with rich college graduates who tossed and kicked a pig-skin object for hundreds of yards for a living. While dinner was cooking, Will always had a fire burning in the fireplace—that was for me. I sat reading, watching the fire, smelling the wood burning, rubbing Will's head—he sat on the floor beside me.

"Oh, no," Will said. He jumped up to a kneeling position. "Run the ball! What are you doing?"

"Yeah, what are you doing?" I echoed, trying to, as I put it, talk football with the best of them. "They're always passing when they should be running, right, sweetheart?"

"If passing worked, they wouldn't be down by fourteen points in the first quarter."

I respected Will, because although I knew little about football, he always answered any questions I had during the game, no matter how shallow, and responded to my comments as if I had been a head coach. After a few of my comments, though, he looked up, realizing I wasn't totally involved in watching the game, and smiled as if we had said nothing before that point.

On those Sundays, we ate dinner in the living room on trays, our little treat to end the weekend, before starting another workweek. The warmth of the food—Will loved my macaroni and cheese casserole—the coziness of the fireplace, the joy of the love that filled the room, this was it. It just couldn't get any better.

"Are you ready to open your gift?" I asked. "Come, my love. Follow me to my boudoir. Can you believe it's been a whole year?" I caught Will by his shirt and pulled him behind me. "Wait here." I stood on tiptoes and retrieved Will's gift from its hiding place in our closet on the shelf behind a shopping bag filled with boxes of Christmas tree lights, ornaments, and tinsel.

"Open it," I said. I shoved the lime-green, teal, and purple polka-dot wrapped package into his hands before he could object. He shook it, put it to his ear to listen to it, smelled it, and began to open it slowly—too slowly.

"What could this be?" he asked. "By the way, breakfast was delicious. Thanks for making pancakes."

"Just open it, silly. And you're welcome."

"All right, don't rush me. Let me see," he said. He ripped the paper off and opened the box. "Oh, no, you didn't! Honey, I love it." Will held up a Big City Animals football jacket and ski mask. He often had mentioned that his love of football held a third place to his love for God and his love for his wife.

"Thanks, honey," he said, with a look on his face that let me know that he loved and appreciated the gift. "I guess I did get a little into the game last season."

"A little," I said. "Yes, I'd say just a little. Read the card, read the card. "

Will opened the blue envelope and eased out a sheet of blue paper, folded in quarters, with a blue ribbon tied with a bow at the spine of the card. He read aloud:

"I have loved sharing my life with you this year, even though it meant sharing you with football." He looked up at me, winked, opened the card, and continued:

These are the 10 lessons I learned from sharing my life, and football, with you:[1]

(1) Listen to your coach—You're my coach, and Jesus is our Head Coach.

(2) Stay cool under pressure—It hasn't been easy, but we made it through a whole year.

(3) Never give up—Don't you give up on me, and I won't give up on you.

(4) Having a bad game doesn't make you a bad player—Surely goodness and mercy shall follow us all the days of our lives.

(5) Don't leave the game because you made a mistake—We've made mistakes this year, but through them all, we love each other.

(6) Be willing to take a risk—Some say marriage is risky business; with you, it's a sure thing.

(7) Find out in which direction you're supposed to run—With the Lord as our Guide, how can we go wrong?

(8) Make first downs; don't always go for the long yardage—This year is the first in ten, then we'll do it again.

(9) Sometimes you have to play more than one position—My husband, lover, and friend.

(10) Don't celebrate too early—But everyday is a celebration with you!

Praying that we'll have many more anniversaries to celebrate.

Happy First. Your Loving Wife, Patience

"Thank you, Honey," Will said. "The gifts are great, and the card, well, how can I top this?" Will slipped on the jacket and set the ski mask on top of his head. He reached under the mattress on his side and pulled out a small, pink

---

[1]"Ten Lessons Learned from Football," written (without explanations) by Elder Margaret Crosby, TLC Ministries, Rock Hill, S.C.

gift bag and handed it to me. Opening it, I found inside a small, flat box. Inside the box was a delicate gold chain.

"How elegant," I said. "Help me put it on."

"There's more," Will said, reaching in his pants pocket to pull out two small beads. He took the necklace from me.

"This gold bead represents the purity of the love I have for you," he said. He slipped the bead on the chain. "This black onyx represents the purity of your beauty, both inside and out. Each year I will add two more beads to this chain, because each year my love for you will grow, and you will be to me more beautiful than the year before."

I was without words. So instead of saying anything that might have spoiled that precious moment, I leaned over and kissed him. As we held each other, I thanked God for Will. What had I ever done to deserve this man?

For our anniversary, we traveled farther North to Will's family reunion at the house of Will's sister, Faith, one of three sisters, Will being a middle sibling sandwiched between his brothers. His family embraced a lot. It was foreign, but made me understand why Will was such a loving person. Will was closer to his twin cousins, Strength and Courage, whom he had grown up with and lived within walking distance of, than he was to his brothers. Being born only six months before the twins put him in a higher grade than the twins.

Strength and Courage were already situated at the picnic table in Faith's backyard when Will and I arrived and both immediately stood up when we rounded the corner of the house.

"Will," Strength and Courage shouted.

"Hey, you guys. You're here already—at the table feeding your faces."

"When the food is this good, what do you expect?" Strength said.

"Patience, these are my cousins," Will's grin was the widest I'd ever seen on him. "These are the two craziest, yet serious, people I know."

"Crazy," Courage said. "It sure does take one to know one."

The three of them laughed so hard together one would have thought them in pain. Will bore a striking resemblance to his cousins. They could have passed for brothers.

"We go way back," Will said, laughing with one hand on my shoulder and the other holding his stomach.

"Yeah, we moved down the road from you all, what, we were about seven, right Strength?"

Strength nodded his head, still smiling from ear to ear.

"Do you all remember that clubhouse we built in that oak tree in the backyard?" Strength asked. "And what was the name of our club?"

"S-S-S," the three of them said at the same time. More laughter.

"Come on, Patience," Faith said.

"Kiss Mom and Dad for me," Will said. "I'll be in shortly."

I left that trio of Strength, Courage, and Will, started to follow Faith, but stopped in my tracks because the three men together were so fascinating. Will moved between the twins and rested one hand on Strength's shoulder and the other on Courage's shoulder.

"S-S-S? What did that stand for?" I asked, standing a little away from the trio.

"Should we tell her? Keep in mind, Patience, we were just seven years old," Courage said, "and not creative geniuses, to say the least."

"Yeah, yeah, we really had to struggle carrying those huge boards up that big tree, with no ladder."

"You didn't have a ladder?" I asked.

"Ladder? We weren't rich, Patience," Courage said. "No, two of us would climb the tree first, and the other person lifted each board high enough for the two in the tree to reach and pull it up the rest of the way."

"We played up in our clubhouse almost every day during the summer," Will said. "What happened to it?"

"Don't know," Strength said. He leaned against the chain-link fence that bordered the yard. "It must have just fallen apart over the years."

"It sure is good to see you two," Will said, and leaned against the fence with Strength. "You two must have gotten me in more trouble than I care to recall."

"I won't say who got whom into trouble, but those were some good years," Courage said, punching Will in the stomach as he would a punching bag, though not touching him.

"I'll never forget them," said Will.

"All right, all right," Faith interrupted. I hadn't noticed that she had left and was now returning with cold sodas for the four of us. "Patience, don't let them get started talking about their childhood antics. They'll be over here bawling like three babies if you give them half a chance. I can hear them now: 'Will, I'm nothing without you.' 'No, Strength, I don't know what I'd do if you weren't my friend.' 'And, Courage, what would I have done if it wasn't for you helping me talk to my little girlfriend?' You should have seen them up in that so-called clubhouse."

"You! You spied on us! You had no business climbing up," Will said. "We had a big sign that said 'No Girls Allowed!'"

"I had to see what all the S-S-S was about," Faith said. "Patience, they painted S-S-S on a piece of white rag and had it blowing in the wind on a pole like it was Old Glory itself. You see what I had to deal with?"

"I see," I said. "You know, Faith, they changed the subject on me when I asked what S-S-S stood for."

"Oh, I'm sorry, honey," Will said. "It stood for—"

"Secret-Secret-Secret," the three of them said in unison and burst into another bout of laughter.

"Patience. Patience, you've got to see this, you've got to read this." Will ran from his study into our living room holding his Bible. This much excitement meant that he had received new insight into the meaning of a Bible passage.

"What's going on, sweetheart?" I asked. With the edge of the sofa holding my feet in place, I had completed twenty sit-ups, five more than my limit, so I appreciated the interruption.

"It's in John. John, fourteenth chapter, twelfth verse. Sit down, let me start at verse nine. You know, it's when Jesus was talking to Philip, and he was saying that if you've seen me, meaning Jesus, you've seen the Father."

"Yes, what about it?"

"Verse ten says, well, let me just read ten through fourteen: *'Believest thou not that I am in the Father, and the Father in me? The words that I speak unto you I speak not of myself: but the Father that dwelleth in me, He doeth the works. Believe me that I am in the Father, and the Father in me: or else believe me for the very works' sake.'* Remember that part—'the works' sake.'"

Worked up about the Word of God, Will had the unmistakable look that told me that he wasn't seeing his

surrounding. The glow in his eyes let me know he was looking within himself, almost as if he had read the Scripture
and was reading from the pages impressed in his mind, seeing them, looking through me.

"Okay, 'the works' sake.' I'll remember," I said.

"Now verse twelve says, *'Verily, verily, I say unto
you, He that believeth on me, the works that I do'*—see,
works again—*'shall he do also; and greater works than
these shall he do; because I go unto my Father.'*"

"There it is again," I said.

"Now here's the kicker. Verse thirteen and fourteen
say, *'And whatsoever ye shall ask in my name, that will I do,
that the Father may be glorified in the Son. If ye shall ask
any thing in my name, I will do it.'* ... Don't you see?"

"Well, not really. What's your point?"

"My point is that if you're doing the works that
Jesus did, that's when you can ask anything in His name and
He will do it. That's when the Father is glorified in the Son.
Because you're doing His works. Don't you see? So before
we ask anything in the Name of Jesus, we'd better make
sure we're doing the works. The Father is glorified in the
Son if we, His followers, are doing what we have seen the
Son do."

"I see. Wow."

"It's like this. Just imagine if we had a child." Will
caught himself, and sat down at the table beside me. He
knew how much I wanted us to have a baby together.

"Honey, just imagine. If we did our best to teach our
child to do the right thing, and when that child grew up,
made friends, and all his friends behaved as our child
behaved, what greater compliment as parents could we
receive? We would be glorified and would love his friends
who were reflecting our wishes. And those friends wouldn't

do anything our child wouldn't do, or ask anything our child wouldn't ask, but would only ask those things that were necessary to do the right things, as our child did. And we would grant them."

"That's wonderful, sweetheart. You're working tomorrow, aren't you?"

"That's right. I promise I won't leave you alone on too many more Saturdays."

"You'd better not. Come on, let's go upstairs."

"Just time for one last cup of coffee, honey," Will said.

An uncontrollable poutiness took control of my otherwise perky morning mood. I enjoyed our Saturday mornings together, winding down from a week of commuting, students, department heads, and running around.

"How long do you think you'll be?" I asked. The last Saturday Will had worked, he didn't get home until six-thirty.

"Don't know—could be late," he said, and took another drink of coffee. "I don't want you waiting up for me. Sunday morning comes quickly, and you and I both are scheduled to teach Sunday school."

"That's right. And I still have work to do on my lesson."

"I'll call if it gets to be too late." He swallowed his last forkful of pancakes, gulped down the remainder of his coffee, grabbed his briefcase, put on his Animals football jacket and ski mask, which he rolled into a hat instead of pulling over his face, kissed me, and left.

I Am Will

At work, I got a jump start on the Monday's sales meeting scheduled for nine o'clock. My boss didn't listen to excuses, and I liked to have all my figures checked and double-checked. We had a good work relationship. Having majored in marketing in college, I was a natural for my job as assistant vice president of marketing. It was an answer to a prayer: an open-ended job—I wasn't even limited by the sky. I developed a five-year plan to become executive vice president and was well on my way.

"This looks good," I said, while flipping through my report. "I'll have the admin type it up and make it look pretty. I need bar graphs. Not a problem."

I hope Patience gets a chance to cross-reference those Scriptures for me. John 12:14—God is good.

I'd never realized just how much those verses contained.

Keep your mind on the task at hand. What was last year's revenue? The net total for revenue ...

For hours I calculated figures and percentages, column after column, line after line. My eyes grew tired, as it became more difficult for me to concentrate the later it got. I was in all respects a morning person, a difference in Patience's and my personalities that we had to get used to. It was at this time of the evening that my sermons would start to come together during my study time, that is if I were schedule to preach the next day. I looked forward to the time when I could work in ministry full time.

Maybe someday start my own church ...

"Oh no, I fell asleep." Opening and closing my eyes a few times, I forced the sleep to leave. I shuffled papers noisily together, stacking some and filing others in my side desk draw.

"It's past eleven-thirty, and I didn't call Patience. I'll let her sleep. Lord, I take this time to pray for my wife. She's my life, my joy. Next to You, no one means as much to me. Keep her, Lord. Protect her. Give her peace. I thank you for Temperance who means the world to her. Protect and keep her. And Rocky, help me to be an example for him so he will grow up to be an example for other young men. In Jesus' Name. … Oh, Lord. … My heart is heavy."

I prayed in the Spirit—in my personal prayer language—for several minutes until I was peaceful.

"Amen." I looked around my disheveled desk and straightened it. "All right … looks like I'm finished here." I inspected the lobby a final time, opened the door, reset the alarm, and pulled the door shut behind me, making sure it was secure. The bank was deserted, a sharp contrast to how it would become Monday morning.

Outside, dry leaves rustled in the winter breeze. A full moon brightened the gloom and warmed my heart, if not my body. I had almost gotten down the bank's long walkway when I noticed someone crouching on the far side of my truck. It was a man. He stood up.

"Hey, who are you? What are you doing?" The man got into the passenger side of a dark-colored pickup truck with one of its headlights missing. The truck and its passengers squealed across the parking lot, made a screeching sharp right turn, and sped down the street. I heard police sirens. Questions raced through my mind.

What was he doing beside my truck? My tag is loose on one side. I never noticed that before.

A squad car pulled behind my truck, blocking me in and turning on its bright floodlights. One of the police officers walked up to me with one hand on his weapon. The other officer surveyed the lot. I was curious, but otherwise not too concerned about the situation.

"Good evening, sir," First Officer said.

"Good evening," I said. "I think someone tried to steal my license plate. They must have heard your sirens. What's going on?"

"What are you doing here, sir?" First Officer asked.

"I work here. I was just leaving for home."

"Did you see anything suspicious tonight?"

"I've been shut up in my office until now working on a report. But I did see a dark truck speeding—"

"It seems there has been a break-in at The Gun Shop, and several weapons have been stolen and the shop owner killed—"

"Hey, First Officer," Second Officer said. "I think you'd better come over here and take a look at this."

Shop owner killed? What?

The other officer pointed to a rifle in my trunk beside my yard rake and toolbox.

"Who put that gun in my truck?" I asked.

"That's what we would like to know also," First Officer said. "Seems like you forgot this one. Where did you stash the rest of them?"

"Read him his rights," Second Officer said.

"Sir, you have the right to remain silent." He opened the squad car door.

This is ridiculous. Have those police lights been flashing all the time?

Red, blue, red, blue.

"Anything you say can and will be used against you

in a court of law." Second Officer pulled my arms to my back and put handcuffs on me.

Patience. I didn't call Patience. She'll be worried. No, she's probably asleep.

Red, blue, red, blue, red, blue.

"You have the right to speak to an attorney and to have an attorney present during any questioning." Second Officer pushed my head down as he guided me into the squad car.

My God. What is happening? How could this be happening?

The door slammed shut.

Red ... red ... red.

The smell of moldy carpet nudged my dull senses.

"If you cannot afford a lawyer, one will be provided for you at government expense."

The Lord is my shepherd. I shall not want. He maketh me to lie down in green pastures. He leadeth me beside still waters. He restoreth my soul. Yea, though I walk through the valley of the shadow of death, I will fear no evil. For Thou art with me ...

"Get a tow truck out here and impound his vehicle for evidence," First Officer said over his radio.

"That's a ten-four," a dispatcher said through the radio.

The car windows misted. It had started to rain.

... Blue ... blue ... blue.

Patience. ...This is a mess.

I Am Patience; I Am Will

I didn't want to go to Will's trial. Not only did they charge him with armed robbery and possession of a stolen weapon, but with murder. Brother Defence, a new member at Rugged Cross, took Will's case. In the arraignment, he filed a motion that all charges be dropped for lack of a motive, but the judge ruled against his motion. The state prosecutor said that precedence had been set which overturned the need for a motive, giving as an example the case of the wealthy celebrity who shoplifted from exclusive salons for no other reason than she was able and wanted to.

I couldn't bear to see Will in any kind of distress. But I had to go. I had been up since three, had showered and dressed, and had sat reading in the wingback chair in our bedroom. Through the part in the curtains at the window across the room, the clear black sky was brightened by the moon and many stars, their radiance overpowering the streetlight in front of our house.

Temperance, along with Strength and Courage, came over early that morning—it was still dark but I could see them through the window as Courage parked the car. The three of them got out of the car, blurred by the two sources of light that juxtaposed each other—my eyes may have been half-closed—I couldn't tell. I took another sip of the water I had heated earlier, didn't want coffee, didn't want to be stimulated by the caffeine. I set the cup on my nightstand and remembered the time when I had first found those suitcases. The incident seemed so long ago. How silly it had been to keep a pair of old suitcases then. How silly it was to have kept them until now. The doorbell rang.

I'd better let them in. ... Jesus.

"We know we're early," Temperance said. "I knew

143

you'd be up, so I figured you could use some company."

"That's quite all right. Come on in. Can I get you anything?"

"Coffee would be great," Courage said.

"I'll make some."

I was in awe about my emotions. The closest thing I'd come to being in this state was when Mama died. But though I loved Mama, I had not been one with her—body, mind, and spirit—as I was with Will. I had no doubts that my present emotions had a direct bearing on the feelings I was having, or the lack thereof.

What's happening to Will?

The smell of urine kept me awake the night before my trial, along with jail noises—my cell mate's snoring, random sounds in the night that I dare not describe, screams from the cells of one of the other newbies—jail jargon for new inmate—the water dripping from the ceiling in an adjacent cell, the sight of bars. My lawyer, Defence, had assured me that I would be home before Christmas, but it was already April; he had been waiting for a trial date for four months. Defence had also assured me that the jury wouldn't deliberate long and that Prosecutor didn't have a case—that the weapon in my possession was circumstantial evidence.

Now I didn't know what to believe, or whom to trust. Still I trusted God, Who I was confident had matters in control. I had been known to say that no matter how circumstances looked, it was God Who was controlling my life, not the person interviewing me for a job, not the cashier who shortchanged me, not even my wife who loves me more than life, who at one time had complained about my not finishing my master's degree course work.

The police officer on night duty leisurely walked through the cell block twirling his PR-24 baton like an inexperienced majorette.

"Do you have a Bible, officer?" I asked. Slumping on the side of my cot made me look much older than I was.

"A Bible? You one of those religious freaks?" the officer asked.

"I'm a minister of the Gospel of Jesus Christ." I looked up at the officer for the first time. "Is that what you meant?"

"Yeah, that's what I meant. What they get you for? Embezzling church funds? What?" The officer gave his PR-24 another twirl and dropped it. Bending to pick it up, he watched me to see my reaction.

"I'm here because circumstances dictated it. Do you know the Lord?"

"What?"

"I asked you if you know the Lord—in the pardoning of your sins."

Surprised at my question, the police officer became nervous, as if the situation were reversed, as if he were the one behind bars awaiting judgment.

"I go to church. I'm a Christian. Who isn't?" This officer honestly believed that if you weren't a Jew, you were automatically a Christian.

"That's a real good question. Who isn't a Christian?" I contemplated. "If you have a minute, officer, please indulge me. You don't have anywhere to go, and I'm certainly not going anywhere tonight."

The officer looked around a few minutes and pulled up the stool that was in the corner. He listened to me, trusting me, for some unknown reason.

"I'm behind bars—" I said. I stood up and grasped two bars in my hand. "But who isn't? Who isn't guilty?

Who is it who doesn't deserve to be tried, sentenced, and condemned? Who hasn't lied, or stolen, or cheated, or gossiped, or lusted?"

By this time the officer felt rather pleased with himself.

"Yeah, that's the truth," the officer said, and squirmed in his seat.

"Who doesn't deserve to be punished for their guiltiness, for their filthiness?"

"That's right, preacher, who doesn't?"

"The answer is those who not only profess to be Christians, but those who have truly accepted Jesus as their Savior, those who have acknowledged their sins and have repented and have been converted. Those who believe that He died and that God raised Him from the dead. Those people, sir, though their sins are many, their slates are wiped clean by the Blood of Jesus."

The officer stood up, nervously straightened his tie, and hiked up his pants.

"You pray for me, Preacher. I do the best I can."

"I will. I'm Will. What's your name—so I'll know who I'm praying for?"

"My name is Peace Maker."

"It suits you."

"You better get some rest, Preacher. Tomorrow's a big day for you. You still want that Bible?"

"No, thank you. You're right, I'd better get some sleep. Good night, Peace Maker."

Through the sheet I could see the stains on the mattress where I was to lie down. The caseless pillow beckoned to me, and I responded, "Why not? It won't kill me." I closed my eyes while scenes from my past projected on the wide screen behind my eyelids.

A little trouble: Mom had phrased it the way she wanted it to be. In reality, what she thought was a little trouble could have landed me in jail.

It was the spring before God called me into the ministry. All of the fellows whom the girls considered to be "hip" owned at least one of the latest shirts by Elite. Strength, Courage, and I peered through the department store window at the Elite display, dreaming of the colors we wanted to own.

"I can buy two Elites if I wanted to, but I'm waiting," I said. "I don't want to spend fifty dollars apiece for shirts and have to tap into the money I'm saving for a car."

"Yeah, right," Strength said. "Why not buy four or five, you're so rich?"

"You think I'm jiving, don't you?" I asked. An idea fleeted through my mind. Taking hold of and running with the notion, I verbalized it to the others. "Hey. I know how you can get one for free."

"Get one what for free?" Courage asked. He couldn't believe what I was saying. "What are you talking about, Will? Nothing in this world is free."

"It's easy. All you have to do is casually walk through the store and slip the shirt under your jacket."

"That's stealing," Strength said. "You'll get caught, because you're no thief, Mr. Will B. Done."

"You won't get caught, not if you're discreet," I said.

"Discreet. Where did you learn that word?" Courage and Strength laughed.

"Never mind. Just do it."

"I'm not going to do anything. You do it."

"Courage, how about you?"

"I'm not crazy."

147

"All right, all right, I'll do it then. You two pansies need to be renamed."

We tried to be cool, not wanting to appear to the two giggling girls from our high school who walked by us that we weren't used to wearing expensive designer clothes. Strength stretched his arms, flexing his muscles; and Courage looked directly at the girls, smiling until they had passed. But I ignored them all, focusing instead on my plan.

I instructed the twins to act the way they used to when they were much younger; we called it their "cute act." The routine involved mirroring each other's actions. For example, Courage would unbutton his coat and at the same time Strength would unbutton his coat. By age twelve, they had perfected their cute act to the point that family members would be in stitches after watching them only a few minutes.

"That'll draw everyone's attention from me," I told them.

"Why are you doing this anyway, Will?" Courage asked. "You said you had the money."

"Because I can," I replied without giving much thought to my answer. "Besides, it'll be only this one time. ... And I plan to give this store my business when I start making a lot of money; I'll buy all my clothes here." Strength and Courage didn't buy my lame justification. "Do you know how much this store marks up clothes? They make big bucks on us. ... Come on. ... They won't miss one shirt."

"I don't think you'll do it," Strength said.

"Yes, I will."

"No, he won't," Strength said to Courage.

"You two just take care of your part."

Inside the store, we climbed the stairs to the second floor to the men's department. Strength and Courage, each wearing navy blue Peter's jackets and beige gabardine slacks, drew the sales force's and customers' attention by flailing their arms in the air. Soon everyone was watching them, which gave me the perfect opportunity to meander toward the Elite display table. Being careful to choose the right size, I stuffed the shirt under my tan Peter's jacket and walked nonchalantly toward the stairway. At first, it appeared as if I had gotten away with the theft, but as I approached the twins, I looked back at the display and bumped into a man who had blocked my path. He flashed his store detective badge at me and ushered me to the back of the store. The twins saw what was happening but continued their act.

"What do you think you're doing?" he asked, almost whispering.

"What do you mean, sir?" I struggled to keep the bulge under my jacket from falling to the floor. "I was just, I was just, I was just looking for a—"

"Looking for what?"

"For a, for a—"

"Stupid." He spat out the word as if it had a bad taste. "Don't you know you're being watched?" He grabbed me by the shoulders and studied my face. "You're Gall and Chutzpah's boy, aren't you?"

"Yes, sir."

"Umh, umh, umh," he grunted. "You're coming with me."

Pulling me by my arm, the store detective also arrested the attention of Strength and Courage, who faced each other, frozen in a mirror image of utter fright with everybody in the men's department still watching them. The store detective led us to a small, dark, six-by-nine room with dark-red walls; its only furnishings were a desk and two wooden chairs. He sat down while we stood with our backs against the back wall.

"Do you boys know what Black time is?" he asked. He stood up and sat on the desk, dangling one leg over the side, his white sock catching my eye.

We shook our heads, still in shock, not able to say a word.

"It's jail time, but it's different from regular jail time." He stood up. "I'll be back," he said, and left the room."

I didn't know much about jail, much less Black jail time, but I had heard of the Reformatory, where delinquent, bad boys, were locked up until they were old enough to go to a real jail.

I'll rot in the Reformatory until I'm twenty-one. Then they'll send me to jail, and I'll do Black time. I've sinned—stolen—and the wages of sin is death. Death to my college career. Death to any chance of me making a lot of money.

My conscience whipped me, and I was sure Strength and Courage were experiencing the same thing.

Reformatory.

The word sounded dreadful, foreboding.

I need to be reformed. My mind, my thoughts, my actions, all need reformation. I'm saved. How can I be so ungodly? What was I thinking? Mom and Dad will be disappointed in me. Aunt Soul will be disappointed in me, leading her sons astray like I did.

"You're the oldest, you should set the example," I had heard since I was in elementary school.

What will they do to me in jail? Will the police be brutal? God, help me! I'm sorry. I will ... I will turn from my wicked ways. Cleanse me, Lord. Please, God, use me to Your Glory. Reform me so I won't be an embarrassment to the Church—or to You.

After three hours, the store detective returned to find Strength, Courage, and me with our heads down and our mouths moving as if we were praying. He left the door open.

"They're in here," he announced, and motioned to someone—which I was sure was the police—to come in. But instead of police, Mom, Dad, and Aunt Soul entered. Surpassed by our surprise and amazement were the anger, disbelief, and disgust on our parents' faces. Strength, Courage, and I kept our heads down.

"I'll handle it from here," Dad said, and pointed in the direction of the door, our signal to get out. "Thanks, Guardian," Dad told the store detective. "I'll see you at the conference next month?"

"What's wrong with him, Chutzpah?" Aunt Soul asked my mother.

Just inside my bedroom door, Mom stood with a white sheet draped across her arm prepared to cover me quickly, I had supposed, if I were to fall dead. Aunt Soul gripped the base of a tall glass filled with ice water, probably thinking in the state I was in, I would need a drink or pass out and require a splash in the face to revive me. As through a translucent bubble, I saw the two women watching me, and when they talked, what I heard sounded as if they were standing in the wind.

"He's been like this for three days, hardly sleeping and not eating at all," Mom said, blotting perspiration from her neck with the back of her free hand. "He just walks from room to room, back and forth, not saying a word, just staring at nothing in particular." In a synchronized manner,

Mom and Aunt Soul shook their heads, Mom smoothing the sheet and my aunt swishing the ice water, creating a miniature whirlpool in the clear glass.

"How about your doctor, Chutzpah, or your pastor?" Aunt Soul asked. "Can't one of them do something?" Mom shook her head again. "You and Gall must be worried out of your minds."

"Gall believes Will's okay, that he's mulling over his life and the direction it'll take now that he's graduating. Or he's thinking about college and everything that goes along with that … or about the trouble he got into with Strength and Courage." With a barely audible grunt of "umh, umh, umh," both women shook their heads, but this time in opposite directions.

"Will takes after Gall, who knows how strong-willed his son can be," Mom said. Aunt Soul handed the glass to Mom, who gulped the ice water. "We both are proud Will's going to college and majoring in business. Ever since he started walking, he's wanted money in his little pockets—a nickel, penny, whatever, it didn't matter. And he'd ask for your money before he'd spend his own."

"Our boys have always been hard workers," Soul said. "I remember the paper routes Strength and Courage shared with Will."

"Yeah, it was more like your, Gall's, and my paper routes," Mom said. "But always the overachiever, that's my Will. He told Gall and me after working last summer at *The Herald*, 'If you want to make any kind of real money, you have to be in business.' That crushed any prayer of ours for Will to go into the ministry, you know, his being so wise for his years when it comes to spiritual matters." Mom took another drink. "I am a little concerned, though. I guess I should call Gall and let him know how Will's doing."

My parents took pride in not "worrying" about any-thing. For them, to worry meant that they lacked faith in God to handle the situation, so they were careful never to confess that they were worried.

"You don't have to be concerned about one thing, and that's drugs," Aunt Soul said. "Our boys know better. Some of these young people are messing up their minds with that stuff. Not our boys, though."

"Never," Mom agreed. She took a final drink of water and gave the almost empty glass back to Aunt Soul. "Will's been saved since he was ten, just like your boys. They got into a little trouble, that's all. Will learned his les-son, and that's the end of that, thank God. I just don't want him to get sick. Excuse me, Soul. I've got to call Gall." Aunt Soul and my mother left my room, Mom pulling the door shut behind her.

Rising to another level, I couldn't hear Mom or Aunt Soul. With my arms hanging loosely to my sides and head tilted upward, I gazed into a beautiful light. Surprised that it didn't hurt my eyes, I heard the Word of God, not so much with my natural hearing because I wasn't in a natural state, but in my heart—my spirit—I heard Him say:

"Prepare yourself to preach the Good News of My Son, Jesus."

A calmness and peace engulfed me as I looked down from a place I couldn't define or describe, but from which I could see Mom talking on the telephone in the hallway adjacent to the living room, Aunt Soul at her post outside my bedroom fanning with the flap she tore from a cardboard box she had found behind my door, and myself in my bedroom facing the wall where I had hung up a poster of the Meanies' quarterback.

"I thought you weren't drinking coffee this morning," Temperance said.

The four cups, a pot of coffee, cream and sugar, and doughnuts jostled on the tray I brought from the kitchen.

"I couldn't sleep last night," I said.

The three of us talked so long that morning that before we knew it, the sun was up. Strength quoted encouraging Scriptures, Courage held my hand, and Temperance's calm demeanor restrained me from breaking down.

Nervousness threatened to overcome me the closer we came to leaving for the courthouse. Strength put his arm around my waist, Courage took my hand once more, and Temperance gave me a reassuring smile.

"We'd better get going," Courage said.

"I'll get our coats," Temperance said.

"Thanks for taking off today to be with me," I whispered to Temperance.

"You've been there for me many times," she responded. "Rocky says he loves you, he's praying for you and Will, and that he'll meet us at the courthouse later. Patience, I insisted that he not postpone his math test this morning."

"I understand," I said, a little disappointed. "Really. I do."

Strength took my hand in his and squeezed it. "You're family," he said.

When we arrived at the courthouse, the media was setting up both inside and outside. Though not high-profile, Will's case involved the clergy and was therefore newsworthy.

"You don't have to answer any of these turkeys' questions," Strength said.

"Don't worry, she won't." Temperance took my arm and walked close to me.

"Thank you, Temperance, but I can speak for

myself."

"Sorry, Sis. But they make me so sick, no regard for people's feelings. It doesn't take a telepath to know when a person is hurting, but some reporters don't care, they'll stick a camera in your face in a minute and ask stupid questions."

Steep, wide, cement steps ascended before us, reminding us of today's new challenge. In silence we climbed, and at long last Temperance resumed her speech.

"What's more amazing to me is that those hurting, sometimes grief-stricken people actually talk to them," she said. Pausing for a moment to catch our breath gave her the time she needed to finish her speech.

"I was looking at the news the other day, and a woman's house had just burned down. She had jumped out the window holding her three-month-old baby. Miraculously neither of them was injured, but the husband was killed in the flames. What thinking person during a time like that would ask her a question like, 'Tell me, madam, how does this make you feel?' What was the woman thinking? Looking bad, face all torn up, crying on TV. ... It boggles my mind."

At the moment Temperance finished speaking, a reporter approached us.

"Are you Mrs. Done?" she asked, not knowing that she was addressing Temperance. "How do you feel, ma'am, about the predicament your husband is in? Do you think he'll be acquitted?"

We kept walking, looking straight ahead. Courage walked in front of us, Strength behind me, and Temperance was by my side with her arm locked in mine. Another reporter approached.

"Mrs. Done, how did a high-powered weapon end up in your husband's truck? Why was he at work so late that night? Are you having financial problems? Was Mr. Done selling illegal weapons?"

I'd had enough. But before I could lose my temper, Strength pulled me away from Temperance's grip and into the courthouse, and Courage grabbed Temperance before she could say anything.

The courtroom was small and cold, in temperature as well as ambiance. Typical were the gray walls; rows of straight-back, black plastic and metal chairs; two rows of chairs up front for the jury; two tables each with three chairs behind them for the lawyers; the judge's bench; and the witness stand beside it. The scene reminded me of every episode of Perry Mason that I had ever watched. I prayed that the defense would win just as on those shows, with a confession by the guilty party in the end.

The courtroom came alive as members of Rugged Cross began to fill all the seats. Brother Liberty fellowshipped with Sister Wisdom, holding her hand as they talked. Just as he did every Sunday morning before service started, Brother Compromise went up and down the aisle shaking hands with everyone fortunate enough to be sitting close to the aisle, finally removing his raincoat revealing light blue pants, a navy jacket, and a white turtleneck sweater. He neatly tucked his coat around the back of his chair and started talking to the man sitting behind him. Little Jimmy Fulfillment started to leave the room, probably in search of a toilet, but stopped and took a long look at little Janie Wishful, then changed his mind and went back up the aisle, walking up and then back down the aisle. Brother Sower held a piece of paper as he talked to Sister Substance and Brother Evidence. They were clearly working out some ministry business.

Pastor Shepherd's sister, who was in her seventies,

made her courtesy rounds, stopping to speak to a few women and then to Brother Prophecy, who detained her longer than she expected, but there was no getting away from him once the conversation had been launched. Saving her, Sister Discernment stood up and puckered her lips in the general direction of the pastor's sister's cheek. The Minister of Music stopped at an empty row, put down his hat, but then moved to a different row. The pastor's sister had now made her way up to the front row. Brother Fruitful waved across the room to Brother Healing.

Sister Evangelist strolled in, clad in a mink coat and hat. Sister Piety, who had had foot surgery on her left foot, entered dragging it, and took a seat on the end of the row. Commotion to the left turned out to be Brother Zeal, the head usher, shaking a chair that was wobbly. Sister Glamour in orange and white flowered African regalia drew attention as she sat. She needed to get to the other side of the room, so she apologized as she squeezed by Temperance, Strength, Courage, and myself. On her way across, she shook each of our hands and attempted to hug me, but the abundance of material in her dress and the small area in which she had to maneuver hindered her. Long after she arrived where she was going, her heavy perfumed lingered in the air. People who had been trying to give me space and privacy took Sister Glamour's actions as permission to come over and convey their well wishes, and from that time forward, a receiving line of church members passed in the row in front of us, which the occupants kindly cleared.

All over the courtroom, people were settling into their seats, meeting, greeting, hugging, and giving out holy kisses—until it settled into everyone's mind, almost at the same time, why we were here. A hush came over the court- room. Then I heard someone humming a tune. It was

"Amazing Grace," and it was coming from the direction of the Minister of Music. People joined the humming, and soon everyone who knew the tune was humming "Amazing Grace" and swaying from side to side in their seats. Sister Action started singing the words, but the Minister of Music stood and shushed her with a finger to his lips. With my eyes closed and one hand raised at head level, I hummed also, thinking about the goodness of God. The humming suddenly stopped, leaving me as the only person left humming "was blind but now I see." I opened my eyes to see that the jury was in the jury box and the lawyers were entering.

Good. Will has on the blue suit that I sent. He looks so handsome in navy blue.

Will's eyes met mine.

Oh, Patience. My beautiful queen.

"All rise. The court is now in session. The Honorable Judge Frank Candor is presiding," the bailiff announced.

"In this case, Number 541 R294, arising from events which took place at the Commerce Bank on the night of December eighteenth, the night The Gun Shop, located on Shady Street was held up, resulting in the owner's murder, and the theft of twenty-four high-powered rifles, the defendant Will B. Done has been charged in the three indictments, as follows: Count 1, with second degree murder; Count 2, with grand larceny; and Count 3, with possession of an unregistered firearm."

"How do you plea?" Judge Candor asked.

Will's attorney, Defence, stood. Something about him disturbed me. Something, while not wrong, was not quite right. I couldn't place the feeling, except that it reminded me of a feeling I used to get when Mumzy smiled.

"Your Honor. My client, Mr. Done, pleads not

guilty." He sat back down, patted Will's hand, and gave him a nod of reassurance.

"Will the prosecution present its case?"

Prosecutor stood.

"Yes. Your Honor, and ladies and gentlemen of the jury, I intend to prove beyond a shadow of a doubt that Mr. Done, on the night in question, with the help of a yet-unidentified accomplice, broke into The Gun Shop, robbed that said shop, making off with the stolen weapons with the intent to sell them in the black market, and before fleeing the scene, shot and killed the owner." Prosecutor remained standing.

"Call your first witness," Judge Candor said.

"Your honor, I call to the witness stand Mr. First Officer."

First Officer took the stand and was sworn in.

"Do you swear to tell the truth, the whole truth, and nothing but the truth, so help you God?" the bailiff asked.

"I do."

"Mr. First Officer, tell us in your own words what happened on the night of December eighteenth," Prosecutor said.

"At eleven o-five, I received a 911 dispatch inform-ing me and my partner of a break-in at The Gun Shop on Shady Street," First Officer said. "My partner, Second Officer, and I proceeded to the location and found that the shop owner had been shot. I also saw a handgun lying beside the owner, and bloodstains were on the carpet in front of the door as well as outside on the sidewalk directly in front of the door. We, Second Officer and myself, looked around for evidence and observed a truck quickly leaving the scene. It looked suspicious, so we then proceeded to pursue it. The pursuit continued down Deal Boulevard, and that's when we lost them, until we pulled into the parking lot at Commerce Bank. We pulled up behind the vehicle and asked the defendant a few questions, and my partner saw the rifle in the back, and then he saw blood on the back right fender of the truck."

"Your Honor, I would like to submit into evidence as Exhibit A a lab report that confirms that the blood on Mr. Done's truck was the same blood on the rug in the Gun Shop," Prosecutor said.

The bailiff took the report from Prosecutor and handed it to the judge.

"How many people were in the truck you were pursuing?" Prosecutor asked.

"There were two," First Officer said.

"How fast was the truck traveling?"

"The speed was in excess of ninety miles per hour. It's a good thing it was so late and hardly anyone else was on the street or someone could have been hurt."

"Were you able to get the tag number on the truck you were pursuing?"

"No. It was going too fast."

"What made you stop in the bank's parking lot?"

"First of all, there was a truck parked in the lot. Second, standing beside it was a man taking off a ski mask. Third, it was close to midnight, and it was suspicious to see someone in a deserted parking lot at that time."

"What kind of vehicle did you and your partner chase the night in question?" Prosecutor continued.

"A late model Dodge Ram pickup."

"No further questions."

Will looked unsure. I could tell he was concerned. He wrote something on a pad of paper and showed it to Defence, who nodded and then leaned over and whispered something to his assistant.

"Would the defense like to cross-examine?"

"Yes, Your Honor."

Defence walked slowly up to the witness stand.

"Mr. First Officer, you said that Mr. Done was taking off a ski mask. Was it cold that night, cold enough for a hat or a ski mask?"

"Well, yes, it was December."

"Wasn't the defendant in fact putting the mask on, having come out of his place of employment, being cold, when he was interrupted by the commotion of your squad car?"

"Well, I guess that's possible."

"When you confronted Mr. Done, did he offer any type of resistance?"

"No, he didn't. He just acted like we all were getting ready to set up chairs for a parade or something. But then my partner saw the gun in his truck and the blood on the side of the truck." First Officer squirmed in his seat and looked from the judge to Prosecutor.

"Can you beyond a shadow of a doubt say that the truck you were chasing and the truck in the bank's parking lot were the same?"

"Yes, I can."

"How can you be so sure when you testified that there were two men in the truck you were chasing, but in the parking lot there was only one man—Mr. Done? If it were the same truck, what happened to the other man?"

"Objection, Your Honor, calls for speculation," Prosecutor said.

"Sustained. Restate your question."

Regrouping, Defence moved closer to the witness stand.

"Mr. First Officer," he said. "What makes you so positive that Mr. Done's truck was the truck you were chasing, when you testified that you were traveling at a speed in excess of ninety miles an hour?"

"It was the same," First Officer said, leaning forward in his seat.

"No further questions."

"Call your next witness," Judge Candor said.

"Your Honor, the prosecution calls Mr. Homeless."

A respectable-looking man in his sixties took the stand. He wore a tweed overcoat. Appearing from under it was part of his jacket collar, the starched collar of a tailored shirt, and the knot of a purple-and-white striped tie. This man was obviously an upstanding businessman, or a politician, or maybe a shopkeeper from the Avenue.

"Mr. Homeless," Prosecutor said. "Tell us in your own words what you saw in front of The Gun Shop on December eighteenth."

"Yes, sir," he said. Homeless tended to slur his words, especially his *S*'s, which sounded more like *th*'s, making it difficult for the listener to understand whether he had said, for example, the word "street" or the word "sweet."

"I was on my way to my place of abode," Homeless said, "when all of a sudden two men wearing those caps, you know the kind that keep your whole face warm, anyway, they came out of The Gun Shop, and one was bleeding from the shoulder. His right shoulder. No, it was his left."

The second time he said "shoulder," people in the courtroom chuckled. They had held it in through all the "was's," which made him sound like a two-year-old just learning to talk. I didn't think it was funny. Sister had a slight lisp, which I had always secretly envied because people said she sounded so sweet, or "thweet," as she would say.

"Order in the courtroom," Judge Candor said, and pounded his gavel on his desk.

"Continue, Mr. Homeless," Prosecutor said.

"As I was saying," Homeless continued. "One was bleeding. The other fellow helped him in the truck, then got in himself, and they sped away. The police arrived shortly, and I told them which way the truck went."

"Was there anything peculiar about the caps they were wearing?"

"Peculiar. No. Wait a minute. One of them, the driver, had some writing on it. What was it? Oh yes, it said 'The Big City Animals.'"

"What color was the truck?"

"It was dark blue, no, black. Black, definitely black."

"Did you happen to notice the license plate?"

"As a matter of fact I did," Homeless said. He reached inside his overcoat, pulled from his jacket pocket the purple-and-white handkerchief that matched his tie, and wiped his forehead.

"What did the license plate say?" Prosecutor asked.

"The license number of the truck that sped away was J35U5," Homeless said.

"Did you write down the tag number that you remember ... so well?" Prosecutor asked.

"No, I didn't have to."

"Do you make it a habit of remembering tag numbers?"

"Not customarily, but I remembered this particular tag number."

"And what made you remember this particular tag

163

number?"

"Because it offended me," Homeless said.

A dull noise of people whispering to each other disturbed the judge again, but he said nothing.

"It offended me," Homeless continued. "His tag said 'Jesus.'"

"Jesus?" Prosecutor asked.

"Yes, Jesus," Homeless said. "Well, J35U5. At first I thought it said 'JESUS.' Who in his right mind would personalize a license plate like that, is what I thought at the time. I don't believe in Jesus, or anything that those so-called, self-righteous Christians have to say about Him. They're always coming up to me, up to *me*, imagine, asking me have I been born again. I've been ignoring people like that for well over a half century. If there was such a thing as a Son of God, we all would be sons of God." Homeless stood. "The fact is, God does not exist. I am a *self-made* man. I'm glad they caught him. I hope they lock all of 'em up."

Another dull whispering of the courtroom crowd caused the judge to give a look that warned all paying attention to quiet down.

Neither Will nor I had ever made the connection before of the resemblance of his tag number to the Name of Jesus. It was just a state tag number to us. Will looked surprised. Defence's assistant leaned over and whispered something to him.

"Your Honor," Prosecutor said. "I would like to show the tape from The Gun Shop's surveillance video which was recorded on the night in question."

"Granted," Judge Candor said. The bailiff and a helper set up a screen and reel-to-reel movie equipment, dimmed the lights in the courtroom, and started the tape.

"Mr. Homeless," Prosecutor said. "In this video, a truck can be seen through the store window. What kind of vehicle is it parked outside of The Gun Shop?"

"It says Dodge Ram."

"And what is the license plate number?"

"It says J35U5."

"That's all, Your Honor," Prosecutor said. "The bailiff can now turn off the equipment."

"Defence, do you agree?" Judge Candor asked.

"I have no use for the tape equipment, Your Honor," Defence said.

"No further questions for this witness, Your Honor," Prosecutor said.

Prosecutor sat down and conferred with his associate, huddling closely.

"Did you see that?" I whispered to Temperance.

"Yes, I did," Temperance said. "There was a height bar on the door sill."

"The two men leaving the crime scene must have been at least four to six inches shorter than Will," I said.

"How could Defence have missed that?" Temperance asked.

"It looks like my instincts about Defence were right. And I don't think I'm allowed to even tell him about it."

"Defense, cross-examine?"

"Yes. Mr. Homeless," Defence said. "The Animals are having a good season, are they not?"

"Objection, Your Honor," Prosecutor stood up and said. "I don't see the relevance."

"Where are you going with this, Mr. Defence?" Judge Candor asked.

"Your Honor, if you would just allow me a little leeway, it will all come together."

"I'll allow, but get to the point. Objection overruled."

"The Animals are doing pretty well, wouldn't you say?" Defence repeated.

"I certainly would, as would everyone else who calls himself a loyal Big Cityan. It's been a long time since the Animals have won every game they've played."

"And would you agree that just about everywhere you go, you can see people wearing sweatshirts or jackets or caps, or sporting banners on their cars with the Animals' logo?"

"Well, yes," Homeless said. "From time to time even I display the Animals pennant that I found lying on the ground in front of the grocery."

"What about ski masks?" Defence asked.

"Objection, Your Honor," Prosecutor chimed in. "He's leading the witness."

"Sustained."

"How many people on Shady Street did you see wearing Animals ski masks that day?" Defence restated.

"Let me see. There was one man going into the donut shop. Then there was that kid, I mean youngster, coming out of the pharmacy carrying a large drink, who also was wearing one. Oh, everywhere I went I saw them."

"Would you also agree that it's not unusual to see a man in winter, during a winning Animals season, wearing a Big City Animals ski mask?"

"All right, yes."

Defence walked back to his seat, pushed it farther under the table, and folded his arms. From behind his chair, Defence leaned over the chair, and with a calm voice, addressed Homeless.

"Mr. Homeless, what is your address?"

Homeless looked at the judge for help and found neither sympathy nor empathy.

"I see what you're trying to do. So what if I live on the street? So what if that night I was on my way to my grate before anyone else claimed it? And so what if I had had a little to drink? I still saw what I saw. You can't take that away."

"No further questions for Mr. ... Homeless, Your Honor." Defence shook his head as he sat down.

As Homeless took his seat, I saw that his coat was tattered and torn, soiled from the streets, stained from his life, dirtied from his choices. His coat opened, revealing a jacket that was now multiple shades of the street on which he lived. The stripes on his tie were actually rips and tears.

How could I have been deceived? I was so wrong about Homeless. Was Defence deceiving us, too? Who else had I been wrong about? Will? Will. Help me, Lord.

"Your Honor, the prosecution rests."

"Defense, would you call your first witness,"

"I call to the stand the Executive Vice President of Commerce Bank," Defence said.

"Mr. Executive Vice President, what is your relationship with the defendant, Mr. Will B. Done?" Defence asked.

"Mr. Done has worked for Commerce Bank for seven years, and for the last two years, he has reported directly to me in his position as assistant vice president."

"And in those two years, have you ever known Mr. Done to work extra hours?"

"Mr. Done is an exemplary employee. He often does above and beyond what is expected of him. He works on the weekends, prepares special reports to enhance meetings— or just to prove a point—all to make the bank look good. For the past two months, he has put in a lot of hours on the weekend to get ready for a big national meeting, mostly on

Saturdays, but not Sundays because he's a minister."

"So it's not surprising that he worked the Saturday night in question to prepare for a meeting that was scheduled for the next Monday?" Defence asked.

"Objection, Your Honor," Prosecutor said. "The defense has not yet proven that Mr. Done indeed worked that night."

"Sustained."

"I'll rephrase," Defence said. "Would Mr. Done's working on any given weekend be out of character for him?"

"Not at all," Executive Vice President said. "As I mentioned before, he was always a cut above when it came to doing his job."

"No more questions, Your Honor." Defence took his seat.

"Prosecution?"

"Yes, Your Honor," Prosecutor approached the stand. "Mr. Executive Vice President, did you ever know Mr. Done to work so late on a Saturday night?"

"Asked and answered," Defence said.

The judge gave a "you know that's right" nod.

"Your Honor, it's one thing to work on Saturdays during daylight hours and another to work up until midnight," Prosecutor said.

"Overruled," Judge Candor had to agree. "The witness is instructed to answer the question."

"I only know that he said he worked late on Saturday nights," Mr. Executive Vice President said.

"No further questions," Prosecutor said.

"Call your next witness," Judge Candor said.

"I would like to call to the stand Mr. Will B. Done," Defence said.

"Hallelujah, that's what I'm talking about," shouted a spectator behind me. Another person said "Praise the

Lord," and another, clearly not in the spiritual mind-set of the first two, however, just as enthusiastically supportive, shouted "Right on."

"Mr. Done, why were you in the parking lot of the Commerce Bank on the night of December eighteenth?" Defence asked. He remained seated. All eyes were on Will.

"I was leaving work on my way home," Will said.

"What time did you arrive at the bank?"

"I got there around nine-thirty in the morning."

"Did anyone know you were working that day?"

"Yes, my wife."

"Was anyone else in the building while you were there?"

"No. The bank doesn't open on Saturdays. I was the only person there."

"What time did you leave work?"

"It was going on midnight."

"When you got to your vehicle, what transpired?"

"As I approached my truck, someone stood up. I noticed that he put his right hand on his left shoulder as he got in on the passenger side of another truck. Then the truck left the parking lot, traveling very fast, so fast, they left tread marks on the cement. Shortly afterwards, a squad car pulled behind my truck. I had noticed my license plate was loose on one end, hanging off. I mentioned it to First Officer, but nothing more was made of it. Then Second Officer saw the rifle in my truck's bed and pointed out some blood on my back fender. Then they arrested me."

"Was that license plate secure when you left your truck in the parking lot that morning?" Defence asked.

"Objection, Your Honor," Prosecutor said. "What person checks his license plate before getting in his vehicle?"

"I'll allow. Answer the question, Mr. Done."

"Yes, it was in place," Will said.

"First Officer testified that there was nothing distinctive about your truck, that it was just a black Dodge Ram. Is there anything you can think of that would distinguish your truck from another?"

"Yes, sir. My truck has a horse painted on each door."

"How large are these figures on each door?"

"The two figures each take up most of the door, from the bottom edge to the windows. They're so large that at first I wasn't going to buy the truck, but then I convinced myself that maybe the horses could represent one of those in the book of Revelation, so I bought it."

"Revelation. Revelation." Throughout the crowd, heads turned from side to side as people whispered the word.

"No further questions, Your Honor," Defence said.

"What?" somebody shouted.

"Order!" A pound from Judge Candor's gavel broke up the din. "Prosecutor, cross-examine!"

"Yes, Your Honor."

"Mr. Done. I'm a little familiar with the book of Revelation, though not an expert," Prosecutor said. "Help me out a little. Are not the horses distinguished by color?"

"Yes, they are."

"What colors are the horses that you refer to in Revelation?" Prosecutor asked. He squeezed his chin.

"They are white, red, black, and what the Bible calls pale."

"Let's just eliminate black right away. That leaves white, red, and pale. White would definitely stand out on a dark night, and maybe even pale. Are the paintings on your truck either of those colors?"

"No, they are red," Will said.

"Would you say they are bright red?"

"No sir, just red."

"No further questions," Prosecutor said.

"Your Honor, the defense rests," Defence said.

"There will be a short recess. We will adjourn and reconvene after lunch to hear closing arguments." The almost deafening sound of Judge Candor's gavel against his desk echoed throughout the courtroom. The officer led Will out of the courtroom. He turned and reassured me with a look that said "I'm okay." Temperance tightened the hug around my shoulders. Strength held my hand.

"Prosecution, present your closing argument," Judge Candor said.

Slow and methodical was Prosecutor's walk around his table to the front of the twelve jurors, twelve people who held the fate of my husband in their hands.

No. What was I saying? Will's destiny lies in God's hands.

I couldn't read too much from the jurors' body language. One woman in her thirties nervously played with the hem of her black sweater. In the second row, a salt-and-pepper-haired man nodded off to sleep and then jerked himself awake again when his chin reached his neck. A woman fumbled in her bottomless purse in search of an item that never surfaced. Every sixty seconds or so, a man cleared his throat. A woman hurriedly scribbled notes on a pad, but then put the pad away after the bailiff said something to her. Two men chatted, without looking at each other. Three other men just stared straight ahead, as if into space.

"Your Honor and ladies and gentlemen of the jury," Prosecutor said. He had taken his place in front of the jury. "The defendant, Will B. Done, on the night of December eighteenth, willfully and with malice of forethought robbed The Gun Shop and after doing so, shot and killed the owner.

171

The defense would have us believe that Mr. Done was working that day up until close to midnight preparing a report, because he, after all, was a good worker and liked to make his employer look good. The facts are that an eyewitness saw a truck matching the description of a truck registered in the defendant's name at the scene of a crime, a crime that resulted in the death of the shopkeeper.

"Furthermore, ladies and gentlemen, the truck's license plate number was positively identified by a witness who remembered the number because he felt so impassioned about what the number reminded him of, that is, the Name of Jesus. Please bear in mind that this testimony, coming from a witness who has a background of staunch anti-Christian sympathy, is solid. But beyond that, Mr. Done was caught with one of the stolen weapons in his possession, and the blood on his truck matched the blood found at the scene of the crime. Ladies and gentlemen, I strongly recommend that you find Mr. Will B. Done guilty on all counts charged. Thank you."

Widened eyes and clenched teeth could not stop the hurt that was making my eyes blur with tears. Strength held my hand, gently stroking the back of it with his thumb. Courage passed me his handkerchief. Temperance eyed both Prosecutor and Defence with a mixture of distrust and disillusionment.

"Will the defense make its closing argument," Judge Candor said.

"Your Honor and ladies and gentlemen of the jury, many questions pertaining to the prosecution's case remain unanswered. Allow me to list them. Question number one: Why did the officers omit from their report the *small* detail about Mr. Done's tag being loose? Question number two: If these officers could leave out such a pertinent fact, what

172

other facts have they omitted? Question number three: Where is the second perpetrator of the crimes? Question number four: Why would Mr. Done remove his ski mask, as the officers suggest, when they arrived? And lastly: Where are the other weapons that were stolen?"

The body of people in the courtroom moved like ripples on a pond, baited by Defence's questions. I nervously pondered where he was going.

"A key element in this case is the truck involved in the crime," Defence continued. "Mr. Done testified that he told the officers of a person beside his truck when he came out of the bank that night. This person was kneeling, then he stood up. Kneeling because he was returning Mr. Done's tag after putting it on the vehicle that was driven to The Gun Shop, the truck that was truly at the scene of the crime. The tag was loose because Mr. Done interrupted the culprit before he could secure the tag to Mr. Done's vehicle. Again, the officers left this fact out of their report.

"The fact is that Mr. Done's truck had painted on it horses that the eyewitness did not, could not, testify as seeing, because he saw a different truck. A truck with, yes, Mr. Done's stolen tags on it. The guilty parties saw a lone truck in a parking lot late at night, stole the tag, committed a crime, came back to the truck, switched the tag back but were interrupted by Mr. Done, the truck's owner, then sped away, leaving blood from the wound one of them received at the crime, and leaving the tag loose. Ladies and gentlemen, you *must* find Mr. Done innocent of all counts. Thank you."

"Jury, you're dismissed for deliberation," Judge Candor said. "This court is in recess." He pounded his gavel on his bench for the final time.

Both rows of jurors arose from their seats, each row filing out in turn. While people casually dispersed from the courtroom, the bailiff turned out the lights. Members of Rugged Cross lingered outside the double doors. Brother Fervent raised his hand, lifted his head, and prayed. A few of the church stewards talked to the media in the hall and kept them away from me. The reporters finally gave up, attracted to Prosecutor, who swelled with a predetermined pride of an anticipated victory.

"I'm confident justice will be served today," he seemed to be saying.

Sister Purpose and Sister Focus approached me and embraced me, offering words of encouragement. All of us who were still in the darkened courtroom moved closer to the glass French doors to take advantage of the light from the hallway.

"It's in God's hands now," Strength said. "Do you want to go down to the cafeteria and get something to eat? … Patience?"

"I'm sorry. I'm not really hungry," I said. "I don't know how I feel. It's like something's leaving, like I'm emptying out. I want to cry, but I refuse to give in to it. Defence did a good job, but was it enough? He didn't even mention the bank's alarm. Wouldn't the time it was set prove that Will was there?"

"No, that wouldn't have proven anything," Courage said.

"Why not?"

"Think about it," Strength said. "When Will arrived at the bank, he probably turned off the alarm, then he reset it while he was working. And when he got ready to leave, he turned it off again so he could open the door without its going off. Then he reset it, and closed the door behind him—"

"I see what you're saying," Temperance said. "He could have done the same thing, arrived at the bank after robbing The Gun Shop, turned off the alarm, and reset it without going in."

"Prosecutor would have punched holes in that defense," Courage said.

"Well even I noticed the height bar by the door in The Gun Shop," I said. "He didn't even bring that up."

Temperance, Courage, and Strength looked at me, and at each other, not having the right words to say that would have made me feel better.

"Looks like the courtroom has just about cleared out," Courage said. "Why don't we pray. And then let's get out of here and get some fresh air. Come on. Let's hold hands and take turns. I'll start. ..."

The sunlight from the hallway reflected on Courage's face. He paused, eyes staring into nowhere, smiled, and began his prayer.

"Dear Heavenly Father. You know all, You see all. We need you now in this hour, and Will and Patience need you the most. I pray that Will's heart has been lifted after seeing how we, his brethren, support him. Bring to the forefront of his mind Scriptures that will encourage him at this time. In Jesus' Name."

Next, Temperance prayed. Her deep alto voice was bold and strong.

"My Lord, and My God. I know that whatever the outcome of the trial may be, you are in control. Lord, we rest in the knowledge that the fruit of the Spirit which Will boldly exhibits, there is no law against such. In the Name of Jesus, I pray."

Then Strength prayed, lifting up his brother's hand on his right and my hand on his left. Soon all hands in our prayer circle were raised, clasped together in solidarity.

"Our Father, Who art in Heaven. Strengthen Will and Patience, and all who love him, by Your might in their inner parts, in their spirits. Let them know there's joy in the deepest sorrow. There's a sorrow upon my sister Patience, and I'm sure upon my brother Will. Uphold them by the seed of your Word that's planted deep within them. Thank you, God, Who gives us the victory through our Lord and Savior Jesus Christ."

Finally I prayed, unable to hold back the tears, which Temperance blotted with a tissue for me. Then she rejoined hands with us.

"Abba Father, Daddy, I pray for the jury. Open their hearts to the truth. Give them wisdom that only comes from You. Slow them down when they may want to rush through this, Lord. Give them peace of mind about their families and loved ones waiting for them. My Will is in Your hands. My Will is Yours. Keep him. ..." Sobbing I continued. "He has heard ... and ... and he knows Your word, and keeps it. Let him bring forth fruit, no matter what happens. Lord, You know my heart, You always have. Keep it ... keep it from breaking. ..." I thought I might faint, but Strength and Courage upheld me. When I composed myself, I continued. "I thank you for my family who is such a support for me. Bless them. In Jesus' Name. Amen."

"Amen," the brothers and sisters from the church said, standing around us, forming an outer circle without our having noticed that they had been praying with us. Brothers Togetherness and Involvement stood directly behind me, and their Amens resonated through my ears to the depths of my spirit. Next to them, Sister Fulfillment was praying in the Spirit.

Hope, a teenage girl from our church, handed me what I had initially thought to be another tissue, but was in fact a lace-trimmed handkerchief, reminding me of Miss Grace and of my father. How I needed a father's love at that moment.

"I love you and Brother Will, Sister Patience," she said as though she were responding to my thought. Hope became the point of contact and recipient of the emotions inside me, as I embraced her, not wanting to let go. At that moment she reminded me of myself when I first came to The Big City, innocent, not knowing where to turn for help, yet determined to make it on my own.

"I love you, too," I said. "Hey, why aren't you in school today?" Without thinking, I blew my nose on the handkerchief.

"Dad told me I could come. Besides, I got my schoolwork from my teachers. Mom and Dad said they'll call you later to check on you."

During the hours that the jury deliberated, most of us waited in the cafeteria and read, taking our minds temporarily off the grave situation at hand. Temperance made some headway through *East of Eden*. Strength and Courage leafed through their Bibles. I tried in vain to read the home and garden magazine I brought with me, but my mind kept wandering to Will's and my home.

"Rock, my man," Courage said. He and Strength stood and hugged him, patting his back. The sight of Rock walking through the courtroom door lifted my heart.

"Sorry I'm late, Big Ma. How are you doing, what's happening with the case, how's everything going?"

"You made it," I said. "I'm so glad. The jury's in deliberation." I was surprised how my despondency had vanished when Rock arrived. My prayers were being answered. "They've been out for about four hours. I can't speak for Will, but knowing him, he's making the best of the situation."

"You need anything?" Rock asked. "Do you want me to go out and get you all something to eat? How was the trial?"

"Settle down, honey," Temperance said. "We're fine. We all prayed together, and now we wait, with patience, strength, and courage."

Rocky sat down beside his mother. She pinched a piece of lint off his chin.

"He's a fine young man," Strength said. "What is he, in high school now?"

"Yes," I said. "You and your brother should come up and visit more often. Rock needs good examples of Christian men in his life, especially now."

"We'll try to do that," Courage said.

"The jury has reached a verdict," Brother Fruitful said, sticking his head through the cafeteria door. "Sister Patience, we'd better get back."

The bailiff announced the return of the judge with his traditional "All rise." We all stood and then sat at the bailiff's signal.

"Jury, have you reached a verdict?" Judge Candor asked.

"Yes, Your Honor, we have," the foreman said.

"Would the defendant rise," Judge Candor said.

Will stood with dignity. His lips were moving, indistinguishably. I knew he was praying in the Spirit.

"Your Honor, we find the defendant, Will B. Done, in Count 1, second degree murder—guilty; Count 2, grand larceny—guilty; and Count 3, possession of an illegal weapon—guilty."

Judge Candor addressed Will.

"Mr. Done, a jury of your peers has found you guilty as charged in all three counts. The sentencing hearing will take place in three days in this same courtroom at nine a.m. This court is adjourned."

"All rise."

I didn't want Will to see me in a discouraged and weakened state. I smiled at him and nodded my headed to assure him that it would be all right. ... It. ... What was that rhetorical "it" that would be "all," not partially, not somewhat, but *all* right? What was right about any of this?

He looked over his shoulder as they led him away handcuffed and nodded back at me, looking as if over the top of glasses, as if warning me that I had better keep the faith and be strong. I forced another smile that let him know I understood.

"I'll see you in the back," I finally called out to him.

My heart leapt inside my chest.

"My Will," I said.

"My Patience," he mouthed back to me.

"You are hereby sentenced to thirty years in Parable State Penitentiary. This court is adjourned."

Jail officials forbade me from seeing Will that day. I talked by phone to him from the other side of a thick glass barrier. When he saw me, anguish changed to instant, fleeting joy. The mixed emotions of love, melancholy, righteous indignation, all masked with concern, contorted my face, but soon the wrinkles above my brow turned to the love he was accustomed to seeing on my countenance. I spread my arms wide, embraced myself, then pressed one of my hands against the cold glass. He couldn't return the gesture, his wrists still incarcerated in metal cuffs.

No words—what could I say? Could I make small talk and ask this man how he was doing? He was doing time for a crime he didn't—couldn't have—committed. Could I ask him, "How's it going?" "It"—meaning injustice—wasn't going away. What would be his answer to, "What's going on?" I'm sure he'd say, "Going on will soon be a prison uniform and a number instead of a name." And to the question Rock liked to ask, "What's up?" What was up was time for the life we had hoped to live together and had planned for.

My heart beat, not to its normal rhythm, but to a painful tempo that served as a background cadence for the truth: I was soon to be parted from my husband for the first time in our short marriage.

"Only for a while," I mouthed, not wanting the officer to share what I was feeling at that moment.

His mouth shaped the words, "I know."

How could he have known what I was feeling? How could he have not known? In a little more than a year of marriage we had truly become one.

"Is there anything special I should do?"

"Pray," he said.

"Every day. Always."

"And stay in touch with Defence. He could have news of an appeal at any time."

"I have his number, and I'll see him at church when he comes. Your cousins are waiting outside to see you. You're blessed to have cousins who are such good friends. Only one visitor is allowed in at a time."

"I know. They told me."

Will bowed his head, and I silently prayed for him.

"Don't worry about me," he said. "He promised never to leave me or forsake me." I knew the "He" Will referred to was Jesus.

"Don't you worry about me either, and I mean it, Mr. Done."

At that, Will smiled, almost laughing, remembering that he once had told me if I ever had to stand toe to toe with a bear, he would worry about the bear.

"And remember my fourth lesson learned from football: Having a bad game doesn't make you a bad player." I may have gone too far in trying to cheer him up. He laughed and then leaned forward so his forehead touched the thick glass. With closed eyes, he prayed. I touched where his head was with my head and prayed in the Spirit.

We remained in this position until we felt a release to move. After several minutes, we sat back in our seats, with tear-glazed eyes. And then our strength returned, and with it came our joy.

"All things work together—" He carefully formed the words so I would be sure to get their meaning.

"For good." I had used Romans 8:28 on many occasions when the outcome of a situation looked bleak for us. Will and I practiced seeing the good in all situations. "Don't look at the circumstances," he always told me.

This is hard, Lord.

Behold the State I'm In

... I Am,
ThereWith ...

Behold the State I'm In

.

My Will

May 16, 1985

Dear Patience,

Just writing your name reminds me of how dear you are to me, and how much I wish I was there with you. The prison administrator finally got around to giving me paper and pen so I can write to you. Before I forget, you can write to me now, but you have to address the envelopes exactly like this: Will B. Done, #7117117, Cellblock E, Parable State Prison, I'm-In, State 66600. When you write me, tell me everything and anything that's going on with you. To me, everything is important there, and nothing here is of interest to me. That is, except the inmates—or should I say, my fellow inmates. Most of them have given up on life. Pray for me that I'll never lose faith, in God or in my fellow man.

It's been hard, but I don't want you to worry about me. God is with me. ~~The bed that I sleep on~~, well, I don't want to take up my letter complaining. The Bible says in all things give thanks. I'm thankful that I have a bed to sleep on.

On my first day here, it became real to me that I was in prison. During processing, a correctional officer took away my wedding band. You should be receiving it in the mail soon. There's one particular tower officer named Buck Intimidator who gives all the new inmates a really rough time, ~~especially if you're Black or Latino~~. In fact, from what I can see, Intimidator gives everybody a hard time.

"What are you looking at?" Intimidator asked the new inmate standing next to me.

"Nothing," the inmate said with a scowl on his face

and spat on the floor.

Intimidator grabbed him in the chest by his shirt, threw him on the floor, and kicked him in the back of his head. The scene made all of us restless. Intimidator then pulled the inmate back up to his feet and grabbed his shirt at the neck.

"You got a problem?" Intimidator asked. "I don't like problems."

Pray for Intimidator—call him by name. I heard two inmates plotting to kill him.

When the other new inmates heard the officers call out my number (that I gave you above), some of them started calling me "Lucky" because my number was seven-eleven, seven-eleven, seven. The officers said that that number hadn't come up since they had worked at the prison, and for one of them that had been twenty-two years. I corrected those inmates and told them I don't believe in luck, that my name was Will.

No orientation prepared me for my daily routine. I've almost got it memorized now: At 7:00 a.m., a bell rings. Everybody stands up and turns on their lights for a head count. At 7:30, another bell rings, and we assemble for breakfast in the dining room, or should I say, mess hall. Between 8:00 and 8:30, inmates go to their various workplaces. Because of my white-collar background, I've been assigned to help the prison administrator. At 9:30 the cell block yards are open, and recreation lasts for about an hour. At 10:00, anyone who is sick can be seen by the prison doctor. I think the doctors are volunteers. It's lunch from 11:30 to 12:30, which is announced by a bell. At 2:30, the yards reopen, but then close again at 3:30. We eat our evening meal at 4:30. At 5:15 a bell rings letting everyone know that cell lights should be on for the evening head count. And it sort of goes downhill after that. It's pretty *much the same as it is on the outside—but without the free-dom to come and go as you please.*

Come and go as you please—that always sounded so cliché to me, until I came here. Now I realize what a blessing it is to come and go as you please. I have to ask permission to do everything, even going to the lavatory and speaking. My cell is small, to say the least, about nine feet by nine feet. The back wall is made of some type of sheet metal and the other two are made of cinderblocks, which the last tenants painted bright green. I'm told that to get better living conditions, meaning a one-man cell, or even a two-man cell with a steel door that closes, you have to keep your cell clean. And that means painting it from time to time. The floors are black-and-white tile. And the cell faces a cement wall.

There's always lots of commotion. You can imagine two to three hundred men in the same building, the noise, shouts, sometimes screams, singing, moaning, complaining, pounding on the walls with open hands, arguments through the bars with the officers or with each other.

Don't confuse my wordiness for excitement. ... I say again, honey, don't worry. I know you. I've known you inti-mately since we received our prayer language together, when we became one in the Spirit. Right about now, you're in tears, but you just turn those tears into tears of joy. If God is for me, He's more than the world against me. I'm just telling you what it's like and what's going on because we've never kept anything from each other, whether good or not so good. Remember when you told me how it was with Mumzy? State prison can't compare with an unkind stepmother, but I'm sure at times you felt like you were in jail. That's it ... go ahead and smile ... for me.

Pretty soon I'll be able to call you. We have to sign

up to call out, but you won't be able to call me at all. I'll call you as soon as I can. To hear your voice right now would really be good.

One last thing. I must tell you about Fire. The day after I was processed in, during recreation, the guys started calling me Lucky again. I told them again that I didn't believe in luck.

"Your name is Lucky," a hard-looking, tough inmate repeated. "And you'd better get used to it, because that's all you'll be getting from my boys."

"My name is Will," I said again in defiance and frustration.

"Well, Will, my name is Fire, and from now on you're Lucky." Fire was just as stubborn as I was. A couple of inmates moved toward me, but Fire gave them a look and they moved back.

"You know what, boys, I like him, Lucky isn't afraid. Most fishes would've peed in their pants by now. But no, not old Lucky. Leave him alone, boys, let him get settled in. And don't forget ... he's mine."

A fish is what the veteran prisoners call new inmates. I've read and heard about prison life and had an idea what Fire might have meant by "he's mine." But I kept repeating under my breath: "God has not given me a spirit of fear, but of love and of power and of a sound mind." Fire heard me.

"What did you say?" he asked.

I didn't answer him at first.

"I don't think he heard me," Fire said. "Snake, can you help Lucky with his hearing?"

Patience, this guy Snake's whole body must have been covered with tattoos—serpents and crosses, naked women and men, stars, lightning bolts, a rose, you name it.

He worked in the laundry, and his uniform, compared to some of ours, was impeccable. Despite his tattoos, some of the inmates called him Pretty Boy, howbeit behind his back. He wore his black wavy hair slicked back and neat, and his salt-and-pepper mustache was always trimmed. But for a scar that reached from the corner of his left eyebrow, around his cheekbone, to the corner of his mouth, Snake's appearance was flawless.

Since the Bible teaches to be wise as a serpent, I spoke up.

"I said God has not given me a spirit of fear, but of love and of power and of a sound mind."

"Are you a preacher or something, Lucky? A man of God, per se?" Fire asked. He spat on the floor when he said "man of God."

"I am."

"You am what?" Fire asked. All of his gang members roared with laughter at Fire's ungrammatical question.

"I am called by God to preach the gospel of His Son Jesus Christ and licensed by the state."

"So you know a lot of Bible verses, do you, Lucky?" Fire asked. He moved a little closer to me. "The man I killed knew Bible verses, too. But most of his was in Latin. I grew up around men of God—priests. One of them liked me a little too much. And when I got old enough, I wasted him. He was quoting Bible verses when I sent him to hell. Now, Lucky, let me see if you're true to your name, if you're Lucky enough to make it past your second day in the can. Quote me a verse—preach to me—save your life."

Now Fire's face was an inch from mine when he finished talking. His breath smelled rotten, like decaying food. The situation looked threatening. I felt like Daniel must have felt, and I knew the only thing that could close this lion's mouth was the Word of God. But what to say? The first Scripture that came to mind was the one I had meditated on while awaiting my trial date, and throughout the trial, and during the bus trip here, and in the holding cell, and at my job at the bank, and before God gave you to me. So up and out came the Word, bold as David facing the bear.

"Not that I speak in respect of want, for I have learned, in whatsoever state I am, therewith to be content."

The anger on Fire's face softened, the frown lines smoothed, the scowl on his lips turned into a smile. The smile turned into a laugh. Pretty soon all his boys were laughing also.

"Whatsoever state you're in?" Fire asked still howling. "The state you're in is prison." Still laughing. "You're in a pen. ... Just behold the state thou art inneth."

His boys had stopped laughing, but Fire still thought my verse was the funniest thing.

"Let's go boys, leave the preacher alone. He's all right with me. Somebody, find him a Bible. If he's going to be preaching around here, he'll need a Bible, a real one. Let's go. You need anything else, preacher man, let me know. Me and my boys have stockpiled a few necessities." He hunched Snake with an elbow. "You know, in case of an emergency." It must have been an inside joke.

Needless to say, Patience, I was relieved that my one-verse sermon went over so well. Snake, however, wasn't so easily won over. He was the last person to walk away from me, turning slowly, looking at me from head to foot.

"We don't have to take being preached to against our will, Lucky," Snake said. "We have rights, even in prison." Snake and fourteen gang members had recently gotten out of disciplinary lockup for beating up an officer. There's something strange going on, but I can't pinpoint exactly what—nor do I really care to.

But just to show you how God works, the next day when the seven o'clock bell rang, I noticed a brown Bible on the floor next to my cot. Someone had slipped it through the bars during the night. One other thing about Fire. He was convicted without the aid of legal counsel. He wasn't released after the law was changed like almost everyone else in his category. It's funny. He didn't have a lawyer ... I had one ... we both ended up in the same place.

We have a new warden, Warden Vulpine. The old one asked for a transfer, or so I hear. And several correctional officers requested transfers, which is kind of odd. This new one is tough. The inmates used to get more than just one shower a week and one roll of toilet paper a month like is the case now. There's talk that he's thinking about doing away with conjugal visits, well, conjugal visits as the men now know them, and the inmates—or we—will only be able to arrange time in a large area where several inmates at a time can visit with their wives or girlfriends. Also, there's talk that he's thinking about bringing back sweatboxes. Those are wooden structures with no windows, about six-foot by three-foot. When two inmates are put in one sweatbox, they say there's no room to lie down. They give you a half-pound hunk of corn bread and some water to last for the duration of your punishment, usually no more than ten days.

Don't worry about taking the long drive up here to visit. I don't want you to see me in these conditions.

Until next time, my love, be easy.

Will

I could almost understand Will's request that I not come to see him, but at the risk of being an unsubmissive wife, I wrote back and told him point-blank that in no way would I honor his request. Hearing about the prison conditions did make me cry as I read his letter—to think he was feeling my pain as well as his own …

Yes, my Will. I, too, know how to be abased as well as to abound. Just behold the state your wife is in, sweetheart. And neither your pride, nor mine, will keep me away from you.

I refolded the letter and placed it back in its envelope. On my way to our bedroom as I passed through the living room, I noticed a framed picture on the end table we took on our honeymoon. Will and I stood in front of Lake Superior waving in front of the camera. I remembered the breeze against my face and how it blew through my hair that day, and how Will held me tightly around my waist to warm me. I shook my head to disperse the memory, lest I cry.

Arriving in my bedroom, I carefully placed the lamp by my bed on the floor and removed the glass tabletop from my suitcase. Will's slippers were still under the bed on my side. The Saturday he was arrested, we had sat there together and prayed that morning. A dried flower from my wedding corsage, Mama's Bible, her pink pitcher, and the lace-trimmed handkerchief Miss Grace gave me seemed to delight in their newest cohabitant, as I tucked the letter into the pocket on the right side of the suitcase, but not before pressing it against my heart and kissing it. In it was Will's substance—his words.

I stood and looked at myself in the dresser mirror. How different I looked now from the picture on my living room table: no Will, no breeze in my hair. A pair of scissors lay on the dresser. I picked them up, ran my fingers through my hair, and began to cut it. Tears fell from my eyes as black curled tresses fell to the floor like wilted rose petals from a wedding bouquet. Sobs that I couldn't control, and perhaps didn't desire to, filled my empty room, as disconnected locks floated silently downward. When the last strain was cut, the tears stopped. The heaviness left. I stared at my shorn head in the mirror as enlightenment set in. I had escaped the bondage of the South, of a father who had seemingly lost his mind over a woman, of ignorance, of dependence on my sister Goody. My hair had kept me in a different kind of bondage. My hair had said to me that God had made a mistake, a mistake that I had to correct with man-made chemicals.

I finally felt free—free from my last bondage.

"I will keep my head covered until Will is a free man," I said, still teary-eyed. "Even if it means wearing scarves for thirty years."

Opening my bottom, side dresser drawer, I beheld an abundance of scarves—a bright red one, and mauve, gold, paisley, and striped ones—all waiting at the ready to be used to tie up my head.

A knock at the door interrupted me as I tried on the paisley scarf. It was Temperance. She knocked again, then pounded. She was prone to worry about me. When I opened the door, we stared at each other. I was still sniffing from crying. She handed me a tissue from her purse, and we went into the kitchen and sat down at the table.

"Don't worry," Temperance said, stroking the side and back of my head. She looked at me in disbelief. "It'll grow back."

Behold the State I'm In

November 18, 1985

Dear Will,

I just got home about an hour ago. You were right about all the red tape I had to go through. Everything looked so foreboding: the rolled razorwire on top of the stone walls that surrounded the compound; the four guard towers on each corner, manned with guards with rifles; automatic doors closing behind me as I walked so that I was locked in chambers as I went along; and the constant showing of ID. They led us through the Administration Building where I met you. We passed by the canteen, some classrooms, and some offices. On my way inside the building, I got a glimpse of the courtyard where some of the inmates were exercising or just standing around. There was an L-shaped building—that's where the cell blocks are, I was told. The guard standing by the entrance of the cell block building came over to the one standing at the back entryway of the admin offices and gave him a light for his cigarette. In a few seconds, he was back at his post at the door. Everything was so colorless, so drab, that my senses went dim.

But they came alive again when I saw you. Your outer appearance may have been altered slightly by the uniform, the haircut, or lack thereof; you may not have smelled like some store-bought aftershave, but rather like the inside of a forty-five-year-old concrete building, with all of its mold, mildew, and fungi. But when I heard you say my name—Patience—and when I touched your face with my trembling hand, it was all worth it. I didn't mind at all the coarse stubble against my fingertips, against my cheek. To be there with you. To talk to you while looking into your eyes, eyes that revealed the true Will, my Will, a beautiful soul, an untainted spirit, an unchangeable heart despite all that you've been through and continue to endure.

This Thursday, I'm spending Thanksgiving with Temperance and Rock—our first Thanksgiving apart since we were married. If for nothing else, I'm thankful for the hours we spent together today. I love you so much, and I always will.

On the shuttle bus ride between the facilities and the place I had to park, I met someone interesting—Fire's wife. Her name is Passion. It happens that she's a Christian. She sat down next to me so hard it almost made my window seat rise off the floor. She immediately began to talk. I just wanted to rest my eyes and let memories of you impress my mind, but there was no ignoring Passion.

"You're new on this run, aren't you?" she asked. I looked up expecting to see a huge figure of a woman but was surprised. Passion was tall—about six feet—but she had a medium frame. And she was as talkative as she was tall.

"My name is Passion, well Compassion, but I prefer Passion," she said. "I figured I'd sit here since you hardly take up a third of the seat. Don't worry, I'll keep the rest warm for you." Passion's voice was such that whatever she said sounded like she was laughing inside. Such a deep joy she had that I couldn't help but experience her mirth.

"I'm Patience," I said. "It's nice to meet you."

"You don't have to be polite to me, I know I can be kind of pushy at times. Patience, is it? Imagine that. Two women, sitting next to each other, whose names both begin with P. Both our husbands in the slammer. Hey, we're like two peas in a pod, get it? Two P's?" She laughed again with a passionate laugh, a laugh that was the introduction of a story that she would tell me, a laugh that caused me to

laugh also, as well as several others on the bus. I had to admit that she was making me feel a lot better. I was feeling a little down. There, I've admitted it. But, Will, my sadness comes and goes. And it's a condition of my head and not my heart, sweetheart. It was Passion's laughter that reminded me of the talk we had just had less than two hours earlier.

You said: "Patience, we both have the Love of God, which is so great toward us. His Love abides within us, through the Holy Spirit. Nothing can separate us from the Love of God, and therefore nothing can separate us from each other, because we have the Love of God. It's the Love of God that keeps us together, through heights and depths, and despite principalities and powers, and spiritual wickedness in high places. Our Love—the Love of God—God Himself, because God is Love—will keep us."

Talking to Passion was easy.

"My husband's name is Fire."

"My husband's name is Will. I believe he spoke of someone named Fire in his letters."

"Before I go any further," she said, "I'd better let you know that I'm saved sanctified filled with the Holy Ghost there with a mighty burning fire and liable to speak in tongues at any moment. Thought I'd let you know, because some folks don't want to be around born-again people. They call us holy rollers."

"I don't do too much rolling, but I try to live as holy as I can myself," I said. "I am ... all you said, too, I believe, although you say it with so much more ... gusto than I do."

"Well, that's my testimony," she said. With bent elbows, she stretched and rolled her shoulders back. "Would you like to hear the rest of it?" she asked as she settled in her seat.

I nodded. Why not? I liked Passion, and we were

stuck with each other, at least for the duration of the bus ride.

"I wish I could say that I been saved all my life," she said. *"But I haven't. I gave my life to the Lord over fifteen years ago. It was during the first year after Fire was sent to prison."*

Passion's face became somber, with pursed lips and squinting eyes. Her beaded cornrows clicked together as she tilted her head to the side and looked out the window. She grabbed her fingers on her right hand, as if they were cold, and squeezed them together.

"When Fire saw that priest," she said, *"seems like something inside him snapped. One night he came home running and said, 'Baby, I done killed somebody.' He was sweating and excited. I had never seen him that way before. Then he told me how that priest had done him when he was in school. He was just seven years old and for four years that man done all kinds of things to him, things no decent person could even imagine. The anger on his face, his clenched fists, I was almost afraid for myself. But I knew Fire would never hurt me. 'Pack a bag, we're getting out of here, they'll be looking for me,' he said. I hurry-upped and threw some clothes in a suitcase, and Fire did the same. Then we heard a knock at the front door, then banging on the door, then the police busted the door in. I screamed, and Fire tried to escape through the window, but the police was too fast and had him on the floor in cuffs in no time."*

I let Passion talk without interrupting her with questions, figuring eventually she would fill in all the details.

"That's a wonderful testimony," I said, anticipating more. But she didn't continue to talk, and in fact was silent for the rest of the bus ride.

The next time you see Fire, tell him that I met his wife.

I'll write you tomorrow, sweetheart. I'm exhausted.
Good night. I love you.

> *Love,*
> *Patience*

Alone, that night, I searched my soul to sort out my feelings. In bed, I felt alone, having never gotten used to not hearing the sound of Will's breathing, missing having a presence with me even more so than before I got married, when God had kept me, before He allowed me to open my heart to this man, to trust him, and to love him.

And now he's gone?

I had to convince myself Will wasn't gone—he was very much still a part of me. But could my love for him alone be enough to sustain me as I faced thirty years of prison visits, of being alone in body although connected in spirit? When such thoughts came, I stopped them in their tracks.

Casting down imaginations, and every high thing that exalteth itself against the knowledge of God, and bringing into captivity every thought to the obedience of Christ.

This Scripture became my battle cry. It was usually at night when I had the worst battle with my flesh. In my bedroom, I continued to study the Scriptures—passages such as Matthew 6:33, which told me to seek first the Kingdom of God and its righteousness, and all these things will be added.

What things? I need peace, God.

"Take your eyes off your situation."

That was the answer. Strange thoughts—thoughts encouraged by listening to unsupportive coworkers, acquaintances, and church members—occurred to me, thoughts that could jeopardize my relationship, first with God, and second with my husband.

Society had wronged me. An unrighteous judicial system had taken my husband away. My colleagues at the university wronged me by disassociating themselves from me.

Well, let them. I don't need them anyway.

"You had better get your hand off me ... now!"

A recent mandate by Warden Vulpine, who succeeded also in abolishing conjugal visits, allowed me to visit Will only once every two weeks. Just seeing and talking to him, along with the letters I received at least twice a week from him, were enough for me. We were one in the Spirit of the Lord. So, I let nothing hinder me from my biweekly visits to see him, which meant that I regularly encountered Passion. Such a free spirit, she was easy to talk to. During our bus rides, she spoke candidly about her and Fire's strained relationship because she was saved and he wasn't.

"We just sit there, and don't say much," she said. "We used to say sweet things to each other and hold each other in our arms, that is before Warden Vulpine. After the new warden took over, I can't make contact with Fire."

"But a husband and wife can express their love for each other in so many ways," I said.

"I suppose so," she said. "He needs prayer. He needs to be saved, but he won't hear me."

"Maybe Will can reach him," I suggested. "Passion, what are you doing next Saturday?" I tilted my bag of corn chips toward her, and she reached in and took out a few.

"Nothing after twelve, that's when I get back from my sick and shut-in visits."

"Ooh, that sounds wonderful. Can I come along?" I asked, impressed that Passion was involved in such outreach. "I've been a little down lately, and ministering to others may be what I need to lift my spirits."

"Sounds like you going through what I went through with Fire." She took out a few more chips and munched them, making a crunching sound that annoyed a woman in the seat in front of us who was reading. She turned around and gave Passion and me a look that said, "You all are getting on my nerves." The woman turned back around, and Passion continued.

"After they sent Fire to prison, I went into a depression stage myself," she said, munching. "I cried all the time. Then one day this woman knocked on my door. I opened it, and the first thing she asked me was did I know the Lord. I didn't want to hear nothing about no Jesus, but she could see that I was hurting. So she kept on. 'Honey, the Lord has revealed to me that you need a comforter.' She told me that Jesus knows all about what I was going through and that I needed to be saved for Him to come and abide in me. Since I was feeling so empty, with my Fire gone and all, I told her to come on in. We talked and talked, and she finally led me to the Lord. I joined her church and tarried for the Holy Ghost, and I been testifying for Him ever since."

"I was baptized in the Spirit, too," I assured her.

"But do you take full advantage?" she asked.

"What do you mean?"

"I'm not one for explaining things. If you took full advantage, you'd know."

"Tell me more about your depression," I said, changing the subject. She was right. I should be the one explaining Biblical concepts to her. I was the educator, the experienced Bible scholar.

"You see, this was not the first time Fire had went to jail. I called myself being a good church-going woman, but I hated my husband. I would pray, 'God take him away from me.' Because I felt I didn't deserve what he did to me. Here I was trying to be the best wife I could be, and for him to do me like he did. It's like he left me stranded, he didn't care about me. Like he deserted me."

"I'm not proud to admit it," I said. "But you're expressing some of my exact feelings. You said he did something to you."

"Yes, and it didn't start the day he was locked up. It started the day he decided he wasn't going to be a husband. And he might not have thought, you know, consciously to do it. He was being selfish and only thinking about him-self—that caused him to do the things that just made him feel good." Passion drew in a deep breath. "I'm talking about taking and selling drugs.

"I'd approach Fire about the drugs and he'd lie to me. So, every night I watched the news looking to see if any of the bodies found dead or killed was his. I knew from the life he was living that he could come back that way—dead. That's what he did to me. He made me always scared, feel-ing I was out here by myself. It hurt, and it made me mad that he put me in the position I was in, to feel the way I felt. So I hated him."

After that, we traveled the remainder of our trip in silence.

Performing like angels of mercy, Passion and the other women from her church not only took their sick and shut-in members food, but they read from the Bible to them, prayed with them, washed and braided one woman's hair, and cleaned and straightened up everywhere they went. As a result of that day, I spearheaded Rugged Cross' own sick and shut-in ministry. This ministry changed my life, occupying most of my time on the weekends when I wasn't at church or the prison.

January 17, 1986

My dearest Patience,

I miss you. I miss our life together. I love you so much. And I'm very proud of you for being so strong during our tribulation. I can't help but believe that God has a reason for me being here.

I was glad to hear that Sister was able to spend some time with you. I know yours and Temperance's love for her is deep.

Work keeps me occupied making the time seem to go faster. But not fast enough. In addition to working in the Administration Building helping with the paperwork involved with processing new inmates, they also use me when new inmates need counseling from time to time. I seem to have adjusted to prison life. That's a laugh. But I'm thankful to have a job, because there just aren't enough prison jobs to go around. In fact, there doesn't seem to be enough of anything. Not enough food, not enough supplies, not even enough staff. They're either on leave or have resigned. And those who are here constantly complain about not being paid enough. Some officers have even requested to be transferred. I don't think that's the answer. Tax dollars for prisons just don't go very far. But there I go again, complaining. At least I get to leave my cell for five hours a day to go to work. That's something. And for every day I work, my sentence is reduced by one day. How about that for an incentive to work for free? One more perk: I can use the prison postage machine to mail my letters to you. There's a mail chute right outside the main admin office, and the mail is picked up every day.

Defence came by this morning. He didn't have any good news. My case was denied appeal again. That hit hard. But my hope is not in the judicial system, it's in the Lord. I'll keep you informed as I hear more.

I mentioned that it was hard. Well, Patience, one day I almost lost it. I can laugh about it now, but it was rough for a while, for my body, mind, and spirit. My body has gone into a survival mode as far as my appetite goes. Yes, I get three squares a day, but there's not one inmate who doesn't leave the mess hall still hungry. I guess that's why some of the inmates have taken to hoarding food. The shelves in the commissary are always bare. My senses took a beating too. Old mattresses and bed linen that smell like a john that's been sprinkled with Ajax, at least to me they do, on top of body odor, including my own, from lack of soap and deodorant. Food and drink that would have to improve to taste as good as water. The constant site of gray uniforms and of officers holding rifles, and hopeless faces and helpless postures. The feel of metal bars and concrete floors and wooden benches and cold sticky toilet seats. It was too much to bear.

My mind and my spirit were forced to team together to support the shock to my physical systems. But in my mind I had to deal with the fact that I was absent from you. I couldn't stop thinking about you, and with every thought of you, also came self-condemnation and self-doubt—if I weren't so ambitious I would have been at home with you that night ... maybe I didn't love you enough to want to stay home on Saturdays (ridiculous thoughts, I know), ... I fell *asleep while I was at the office working the Saturday I was arrested—maybe somehow I managed to sleepwalk or something like that, and actually did commit those crimes. My spirit, though not malnourished for lack of the Word, was definitely in a fasting mode, what with no church, no preachers, no volunteers for church service, few Bibles. I thought I would lose my mind.*

But I had a sound mind, I told myself. So I did what God had put in me to do. While out in the yard, with a couple hundred men as my captured audience, I preached. With all that was within me, honey, I preached. No frill, no introduction, no exegeses, just the pure, rich, straight-from-the-Bible Word. It seemed every Scripture that was in me came out that afternoon in a way that was disjointed yet connected. First, John 3:16 came out of me, strong and pure.

"For God so loved the world, that He gave his only begotten Son, that whosoever believeth in him should not perish, but have everlasting life,*" I said with no hesitation in my voice. And the next Scripture was louder.*

"Take no thought for your life, *what ye shall eat, or what ye shall drink; nor yet for your* body, *what ye shall put on." Style-barren gray uniforms worn by faceless men of every color moved toward me from across the yard, their forms taking shape as they drew closer. "Is not the life more than meat, and the body more than raiment?" Some of my prison brothers looked at me curiously, while others ignored my ranting and others snickered.*

"I beseech you therefore, brethren, by the mercies of God, that ye present your bodies *as a living sacrifice, holy, acceptable unto God, which is your reasonable* service. *... No man can* serve *two masters: for either he will hate the one, and love the other; or else he will hold to the one, and despise the other. Ye cannot serve God and* mammon.*" At*

204

the mention of mammon, those inmates who had drawn closest had on their faces expressions of bewilderment. But as they used to say in the old church, I could feel my Help now. All fear or nervousness or apprehension had left, as the Holy Spirit continued to feed me Scriptures.

"For the love of money is the root of all evil: which while some coveted after, they have erred from the faith, and pierced themselves through with many sorrows. Let not your heart be troubled: ye believe in God, believe also in me." I felt that the Word was accomplishing what it was intended to accomplish. I could see by the look on the faces of some that their hearts were beginning to soften.

"He that believeth and is baptized shall be saved; but he that believeth not shall be damned." Snake was one of the people who had pushed his way up to the closest circle around me. Then out it came.

"Ye serpents, ye generation of vipers, how can ye escape the damnation of hell?" Oh, God. What are you doing to me? My using the word "serpents" was more than a coincidence.

"Are you talking to me, man?" Snake asked. "You better watch it. I don't like people preaching at me, and I don't like people calling me names. And I don't like you."

I continued, empowered by the Holy Spirit.

"But I say unto you, that whosoever is angry with his brother without a cause shall be in danger of the judgment: and whosoever shall say to his brother, Raca, shall be in danger of the council: but whosoever shall say, Thou fool, shall be in danger of hellfire."

With that, Snake, with anger-ridden face, moved one layer back, almost involuntarily. But not before saying, "Careful how you preach, preacher. You might just get bit by a snake."

Snake's threat didn't move me from the Word. I noticed that Fire had also moved up front. I was pleased and surprised to hear what he said.

"Therefore if thine enemy hunger, feed him," Fire said. "If he thirst, give him drink: for in so doing thou shalt heap coals of fire on his head."

It was as if we had connected in some way. I can't explain it. Then the Scriptures stopped coming.

"Not too bad, huh Lucky?" he asked. "Don't look so surprised. I know the Scriptures too. Had to read them for myself when I was in school, since I kind of rebelled against learning Latin."

Frustration left me. Anger had ceased. My heart beat a calmer rhythm. And Fire smiled at me like a child waiting for approval for a job well done. After a few minutes, he shook his head, returned to his Fire persona, turned and looked at Snake, and said: "If Snake bite preacher man, Fire burn snake."

Two yard officers, hearing the din and noticing the excited men, came and dispersed the crowd. But Fire lingered awhile near me to show off the Scriptures he had memorized as a boy. Honey, it was amazing!

"Don't worry about Snake," Fire said. "There's not much around here that he doesn't gripe about. Since Warden Vulpine cut out conjugal visits for sex, him and his crew been trying to get everybody to protest. He's kind of teed off right now. Hasn't been with his woman Amnesty in a while."

It's almost time for lights-out, so until next time, be easy.

Your preacher man (smile),
Will

206

Passion and I grew closer together, the common bond being our husbands and their incarceration, and our love of the Lord. To and from the prison complex, every other week, we talked. Without hesitation—although she tended to ramble on—she opened up her past to me; however, it was becoming clear to me, as well as to Passion, that she was carrying most of the conversations. Temperance continued to be an outlet for my internal struggles, but even with my dear sister, I talked little. With Passion, who never ceased to astound me, I listened, and she was content to share her thoughts and feelings with me.

"When I went to church," Passion said, "seemed like my pastor would just be talking to me from the pulpit: 'You gotta love them who despitefully use you.' I thought of Fire, but how was I supposed to love Fire?' I would say, 'Lord I can't love him. You're going to have to love him through me, 'cause I can't do it.' And God did it. Now I can say I love my husband until this day, whereas I couldn't say it before—wouldn't say it. I wouldn't lie before God.

"But I love him today because of who God wants him to be. I love him because I see him as God sees him. I had to learn to love him, you know, unconditionally. And whereas I didn't respect him before, now I do. I had to learn to respect him for who he was and not look at him for who I wanted him to be. He was my husband. He was in God's eyes the head of my family.

"Jail was the best place for Fire because it spared his life. Knowing that helped change my attitude.

"And it's not over yet. Because when it's all over, those who be watching me will see God, through me and through my husband."

Remarkable. What conviction.

July 11, 1987

Patience, my Love,

I constantly pray that all is well with you. I trust God that he is taking care of you and regret so much that I could not have been there with you when your sister Goody passed. Your family is so close in some ways and so distant in others. Glad that Temperance and Rock were able to help you care for Goody during those last weeks of her life. Cancer is such a weapon of the enemy and I believe it's OK for me to hate it so much. Goody is the only person I've known personally to die of lung cancer. Be encouraged, sweetheart, you did all you could have done for her. Your life was substance of things that I'm certain she unknowingly hoped for. Your life was evidence to her that God, Whom no one has seen, does exist.

Right now, I can imagine your mother's spirit, her essence, smiling down on you, Temperance, Sister, and Soldier from the foot of Jesus' throne. She's kinda nudging His leg with her elbow saying, "Those are my dear, devoted, beloved children."

I'm praying that all of you will be comforted by His Holy Spirit during this time of bereavement.

I know you, honey. Even surrounded by all your family, you're feeling alone because I'm not there. I am there with you. It's strange, because even though we are so many miles apart, we are one. Cheer up my love. I have a feeling that something good will happen soon.

And tell Rock I said I hope his birthday was a blessed one!

Be easy,
Will

That Saturday after visiting with Will, I didn't feel much like carrying on a conversation with Passion or anyone else on the shuttle bus. I felt an anger that I couldn't place its source—and an unfounded nervousness. I wanted to be alone with my thoughts of Will and our visit. But I wouldn't deny her the opportunity to vent if she felt she needed to.

"I told you how I hated Fire, well, he hated me too, probably, still do." Passion began to reveal to me a page out of her life that would last for the duration of the shuttle ride. She didn't look at me when she talked. It was as if she were reading or repeating what she was hearing.

"I was a dream-buster. Fire had big dreams, and the way he wanted to go about, you know, fulfilling his dreams, I didn't agree. And because I didn't agree with him, he didn't do anything but turn back to what he was comfortable doing. What I should have done was to let him carry out his plans, and if they failed, then he would learn for himself. I had to learn to let him be him—let a man be a man. Sometimes we don't know what will or won't work.

"Good ideas come from God. Edison tried and failed with the light bulb hundreds of times before he invented one that worked. But in my mind Fire was going from A to Z, and I wanted him to go A then B then C, on down the line. I should have just supported him and let him be the one who made the decision that this is not going to work. When I backed off, it freed me up to be me and to concentrate on me.

"I knew that God wanted to prepare me for His use. He had to prepare me for my marriage and let me know that my husband wasn't the only problem." She turned toward me and looked into my eyes. "I had issues too."

June 2, 1989

Dear Will,

I apologize that I missed our last visit.

Before I forget. Rocky's getting married. His fiancé's name is Talent. Can you believe it? Temperance is excited and very involved in the wedding plans, that is, as much as Talent will let her. It turns out that her parents are also from The Sticks. Talent attends the university with Rock. Temperance and I both tried to talk them into waiting until they finished college, but neither he nor she wants to wait.

"It's better to marry than to burn," Rocky told Temperance and me.

"But it's only two years, Baby," Temperance reminded him. "You and Talent can get your degrees first. Things will be much easier for the two of you after you both find good jobs."

"God will provide. You taught me that," Rocky said. "And I've seen how He has provided for you, Big Ma, and me. I'm just naïve enough to believe that He will do the same for me and Talent."

Temperance thought about it, and knowing Rock, that he was going to do what he wanted to despite our objections, she gave in and told them that the two of them could move in with her until they got settled.

"No, Ma," he said. "We've already looked at a little apartment not too far from campus, and both our part-time jobs are nearby, so there won't be a problem. We have a place, we have jobs, we can catch the bus anywhere we want to go. And that includes coming by to see you, often."

Temperance dropped her head and shook it slowly.

"Don't worry about your little boy, Ma," Rock assured her. "He's grown into quite a man, if I have to say

210

so myself." Rock took Temperance's chin in his hand and looked her squarely in the eyes.

"I appreciate all the sacrifices you've made for me, and I'll make you proud of me. I promise. You're my main woman, right?" They both laughed and then hugged.

After that, Temperance dove head first into helping Talent make wedding preparations. We must remember to keep them in our prayers. Rock has grown up so fast, and into such a wonderful young man. I know—I'm kind of biased.

I love you!!!

Patience

July 30, 1989

Dearest Patience,

I love you—overused words that hardly express how I feel about you. For now, they'll have to suffice. I Love You! Please know that I am fine. Fine—another word that doesn't really tell you much. What I want you to do is feel my heart, and know that I am safe, that I'm in God's hands.

I don't know what rumors may have made their way to you yet. I don't know why family members of inmates have been calling the warden's office demanding that their relatives be protected. Against what? I don't know. What are they so scared of? I don't know that either. I do know that no weapon formed against me will prosper. Why? Because the Word says so.

Although I try to keep my eyes and ears open, a lot of the scuttlebutt gets past me. I spend my time either working or reading. And lately, I've been ministering in the courtyard to those who insist that I teach them about God. It's really unfortunate that I can only preach to the Black

211

inmates. Fire won't allow any of the Whites, Hispanics, Asians, or Muslims to join my sessions. Segregation—this is the last place I thought I'd see it. I thank God that He has kept me throughout my imprisonment, and I believe that somehow Fire's being here is working together for good, both his and mine. Fire tries to keep me in the loop.

There was talk today about an inmate on death row who got the chair today. No one attended the execution, no family, no friends, just the prison chaplain. They found this writing, a poem, I guess, in his cell, and we've been sort of passing it around. We think it was written to his father. I copied it down so I could share it someday.

"You Were There When I Needed You"

It's late. My journey's ended now in strife.
The tender years of youth have wasted now—
No father talked about this thing called life,
Of his mistakes, of failing love and power.

My rocky road was filled with pain and lies.
No words of comfort from a father's voice—
Instructions plain on how to live and die:
Examples, laws, commandments taught to boys.

My heart is cold, and yet I hunger still
For rules on how to be a son complete.
My hand in his I'd learn "Thou shalt not kill."
(Soon current flowing through this awesome seat.)

Alone, I watch the switch and fight the tears.
As in the past you're there and never here.

If I'm not mistaken, this poem is written in the form of a sonnet, maybe Shakespearean. I'm not quite sure. Such feeling and depth.

Something has to be done for these inmates—these men—before they get to this state. I'm convinced that the cure for cancer is being put to death in prisons like this one, that the answers to world problems are being put to death. I don't believe killing them—us—is the answer. My heart breaks at the thought of a death row, men lined up to be put down like stray mongrels. Sorry about that, my love. I'll write again soon.

Will

I intentionally busied myself so I wouldn't have time to deal with negative people and negative thoughts, standing guard like members of the Corps over every thought, over every word that entered my ear gates, including those coming from Passion. I found myself tuning her out more and more.

The traffic to the prison that Saturday had been horrendous because of the rain and an overturned tractor-trailer truck blocking traffic on the highway that led to the lot where the shuttle buses parked. Even so, I made it there on time. Beside the bus by the door was Passion, waving at me.

"Hurry, Sister Patience," she said. "Just a few more minutes, Buddy," she told the driver.

"You had me worried for a minute there," she said.

"Traffic problems," I responded, and boarded the bus. The bus carried only ten women, all of whom I recognized as regulars.

"Look, Passion," I said. "I'm kind of tired. I just want to close my eyes a bit before we get to Parable. Is that okay?"

"Sure, whatever you say," she replied. Passion

pulled out her Bible, opened it, and began to read. It was the first time in nearly five years that we hadn't chatted on the bus about our husbands, our ministries, the prison system, why I always tied my hair in scarves, or whatever came to mind.

"I'm not going in," I announced to Passion when we arrived at the prison's parking lot.

"I see," she said, looking at me from over her reading glasses. "I'll tell Fire to tell Will you got sick ... or something."

"Thank you."

January 1, 1990[2]

Dear Patience,

Happy New Year! Did Rugged Cross have Watch-Night Service, and did you go? Other than missing you so much ... all the time ... I miss church life. Because my life is, *or was, the church. Last night I thought about what sermon I would have preached for Watch-Night Service. You know how all the sons of the church try to come up with a clever title for our ten-minute sermons on New Year's Eve leading up to midnight. I think mine would have been, "God is Mighty in 1990."*

While in the courtyard today, I ministered to a group of inmates awaiting parole. They were apprehensive about what awaited them on the outside. Some of them had been in prison for twenty years and had only worked at cleaning up interstate highways or some other prison-appointed job.

---

[2]Portions of this letter were adapted by permission from a sermon delivered on March 7, 2004, by Reverend John A. Cherry, II, Assistant Pastor of From the Heart Church Ministries, Temple Hills, Md.

There are limited places to sit in the courtyard, so we sat on the ground. The inmates listened and asked questions as I read from the Bible and talked about the Kingdom of Heaven. Remove from your mind images of the pictures you've seen in Bibles or museums of Jesus surrounded by his disciples. It was nothing like that. Just a group of men struggling with boredom, discouragement, curiosity, or any combination of the same, listening to someone who would explode if he didn't have an outlet for the Word that's in him.

I pray that God will keep this door opened. They need so much in the way of teaching. Some would say it's more on the order of preaching, but what can I say—I am what I am. I read them Ephesians 2:1–10.

"Before you were even born there was a job that was created for you to do," I said. I wanted to address their worldly issues, but I desired more to speak to their need for a Savior. The sun blazed down on us, warming us from its light if not from its heat. A calm wind blew, momentarily distracting me from the cold hard cement that we sat on. Forty degrees seemed warm in this climate, and being outside in the winter was a treat. I rubbed my hands together to warm them, having forgotten my gloves. This weather was confusing, but my mission was clear.

"And on the job description, there are only two words: your first name and your last name. All other applicants need not apply. Because God specifically reserved the job just for you, before time and space were time and space. You are the only one qualified to do what God desires for you to do. Nobody else can fit that spot, nobody else can fill that bill, nobody else can do that thing the way God created you to do it."

In my heart I hoped I wasn't getting too "out there," after all, many of the close to thirty inmates listening to me

215

had not grown up in church, and some had just learned of Jesus since I had started preaching to them.

"And you don't become eligible for employment until you get in Christ," I said. "It's a position created in the Body of Christ. That why the Bible says when we get saved we become new creatures in Christ. It says that old things pass away and, behold, all things become new."

I was disturbed, but only slightly, when an inmate got up and walked away. The others were intent on hearing all I had to say, and my Help had arrived, making me intent on saying it. A cloud passed overhead, and the day turned gray. Everyone seemed to look up at the cloud at the same time.

"When you were born, you were born outside your ability to do your job. When you were born out of your Mama's womb, you were born to cheat, born to lie, born with a propensity to sleep with someone you weren't married to, born to try to use drugs and alcohol. You were born without peace inside. That's why Jesus said you must be born again."

"Born again, born again," Fear said. "That's all I hear. You must be born again. Sounds stupid to me." Fear, whose last name is Not (can you believe it?), is one of Fire's gang members.

"I'm glad you asked, man," I said. "Being born again means that all of the things from the first birth have passed away. You're born into being a new creature." I realized that I was repeating myself, but it didn't matter. I had been taught when I went into ministry that repetition was a good way to reinforce key points.

"You were insufficient to do what God called you to do before Jesus," I said. "After Jesus, you're overqualified. Because once you give your life to the Lord and you are born again, and you become a new creature, old things are *passed away. Meaning all the things you used to do, all the things you used to think about, all the things you may have craved before, all of that stuff is passed away. And behold, not some things, not most things, not almost everything, but all things become new. You're a whole new person.*

"And not only do you become new, but God measured out grace. And he said that His grace is sufficient for you. So where you were underqualified to do a work for the Lord when you came out of your mother's womb by the first birth, when you give your life to the Lord and make a decision to turn your life around, all of a sudden you're overqualified." The look on Fear's face was still a grimace.

"You mean to tell me that all I need is the grace of God and I won't end up back in here for a third time?" Doubt said. He scratched his head and laughed. "I wish it was that easy, man."

"But it is that easy," I said. "The word 'sufficiency' doesn't mean His grace is just barely enough, it means that you have enough grace that even if you mess up, you can still get there. ... Let me put it this way: It's like an airplane. They always put twice as much in the airplane than they actually need to reach their destination. Therefore, in an emergency, they can still make it safely to where they intend to go. That's how God's grace is. God's grace is not just one engine, it's two. Just in case you do something to mess up the first engine, you're going to keep right on flying because He says His grace is sufficient for you."

"Face it, Will," Frustration said. He stood up as if to walk away, but instead he stretched his legs, arms, and rolled his head from side to side to get rid of the stiffness from sitting so long. "The deck is stacked against ex-cons. No decent employer will hire us. There are no good jobs. As soon as they find out about your record, man, you can for-

get about working."

"You got that right," Dejection said from the back of the crowd.

"Yeah," echoed Hardness and Melancholy. They affirmed each other's opinion on the matter with nodding heads.

The men were hearing me and not hearing me at the same time. I realized I was not qualified to explain the ills of our society, nor could I predict their lot on the outside. So I gave them what I had.

"What we have to realize is that we were created in Christ to do good works. With our first creation by Mama and Daddy, we were full of shortcomings. We were full of problems, full of mistakes. But that's okay. Now we can be born again. The first time was by water. The second time it's going to be by His Spirit. The first time came through the pain and suffering of our mothers. The second time comes through the pain and suffering of Jesus Christ.

"When I got born again, not only did He save me and clean me up, but He justified me. He made it just-as-if I wasn't that old person. He made it just-as-if that old stuff didn't happen. So when people see me now, it's the same body, but with different uses. Some ask how can you be so different now than from how I used to know you? It's because the person that you used to know, I had a funeral for him. He died. But I didn't die. I got born again. What a wonderful thing: You crucify your flesh and you get born again, all in one motion. When you come to the altar, as much dies as comes to life. Because all the old you dies, and all the new you comes to life. And just in that moment, you become eligible to step into a created position."

"My old man raped my mama," Bitterness said. He spat something out of his mouth. "So much for my first cre-

ation, as you put it. Talk about cards stacked against you."

"It is irrelevant who your mama and daddy are. You have a job that's created in the Body that's not dependent on your natural genealogy. It's dependent on your being an heir of God, a joint heir with Jesus Christ, a son of God. Changing your parents wouldn't change who you are, because God created you. And he created you with strengths, weaknesses, and problems. But that's all right, because you can be born again. Some people who were born in so-called bad families are doing great, and some people born in good families are doing bad. So it's not the condition of your birth, it's the choices you make once you're here."

Some of the inmates nodded in agreement, talking among themselves.

"Once you get saved," I continued, "you don't have to qualify, you don't have to apply, you don't have to get more training. The Bible says you were created to walk in the job God creates for you. You can't be denied. You can't be turned down. You can't be put out. He created a spot just for you. God before you were born created a job for you and then brought you here. How can you think that you were an accident or a mistake? You weren't born and then God said: 'I need something for him to do.' No, He said 'I got some-thing for him to do, let me get him in here.' Before your mama and daddy knew that they could be a mama and daddy, God had a job for you. And He gave you all the qual-ifications necessary to walk in what He called you to do."

"How do I do it?" Melancholy asked. Fire had joined us. I could tell he was troubled.

"You get God's grace and salvation by accepting Jesus as your Savior," I said.

"I want to do it," Melancholy said. "Come on, let's do it."

"I'll do it too," Frustration said. He stood and moved to the front.

"Me too," Dejection said. Clearly Melancholy's coming forth had encouraged the others. Many came forward to pray with me, but others turned and walked away.

"Repeat after me, and really believe what you are saying," I told them. As I prayed, they repeated each phrase:

"Father, I come to you unashamedly in the name of Jesus. I ask that You forgive me of my sins and cleanse me from all unrighteousness. I repent of not giving You full authority in my life and for disobeying Your Word.

"I believe what Your Word says: that everyone who calls on the Name of Jesus shall be saved. So, Lord Jesus, I ask you to come into my heart and establish Your Kingdom. I know that You are the Way, the Truth, and the Life, and I choose you today. Your Word also says that if I shall confess the Lord Jesus and believe in my heart that God raised Him from the dead, I shall be saved. With all my heart I make this confession and believe it. I thank You that I am saved and that my name is now written in the Lamb's Book of Life. Amen."

"Now go, and think of the goodness of Jesus," I said. "I'll answer your questions at our next session."

As usual, Fire stayed behind.

"My mother died," Fire said. "She's been dead and buried for two weeks. Mail was slow getting to me, and what with no visitation from my wife, I just found out."

Patience, Fire broke down and cried like a baby. I stood in front of him to make sure no one saw him.

Until next time,

Love,
Will

"Where you supposed to be? ... Know your purpose ... find your place ..."

"Mama?" I would have sworn that I heard Mama's voice as I closed up the suitcase after taking a final look at the contents inside.

I read the inscription in Mama's Bible, "To Heart from Grace," and reflected on the two women who had inspired me the most in my life: Mama, the life and spirit of the Christianson family, and Miss Grace, on whose land we sowed and reaped. From my face I wiped tears I had shed more than an hour earlier with the lace-trimmed hanky Miss Grace gave me. I handled Mama's pink pitcher and the hundreds of letters Will had written me, which occupied most of the space in the suitcase and provided cushion for the pitcher. I ran my fingers over the letters, remembering their content: his victories, his questions, and most of all, the love he expressed to me.

"These will have to go now," I said, still crying, agonizing about my decision. I closed the suitcase, snapping the latch, picked it up, and carried it out of the house to the curb.

"Will's gone, Mama's gone, and Miss Grace is far away."

No reason to keep this old stuff.

"Do the right thing ..."

"Mama? Paw? ... Paw." I thought the tears would never stop flowing, the pain, despair, and loneliness I felt being so great. I thought it strange to shed such an abundance of tears without making a sound. I set the pregnant suitcase down at the curb for the trash collectors to pick up the following day and heaved a sigh of relief—empty relief.

When the shuttle arrived at the prison, I couldn't muster up the strength to go in. I didn't feel like dealing with the guards. I didn't want to have to blink to suppress the reality of razorwire fences or automatic doors opening, then shutting me in locked chambers as I passed blurred hallways on the way to the waiting room where I would meet Will; my stomach hurt from the stress of the long, tedious journey to the holding room where I would see my husband.

"We're here," Passion said. She tucked her Bible into a shopping bag, slid it under the seat, and was halfway up the aisle. Out of respect for my feelings, she hadn't attempted to talk to me on the shuttle since I put her off weeks before. That being the case, I believed that our friendship was still viable.

"I'm not going in," I said. The smell of cold fried chicken, which the woman who sat behind me left on her seat, made me remember that I hadn't eaten since delivering a meal to Sister Lovely who was recovering from heart surgery. The red-delicious apple in my purse would have to suffice for a meal until I got home. I pulled it out and took a bite.

"Sister Patience, what's going on?" Passion implored. She sat down again, but this time on the seat in front of me in a kneeling-sitting position.

"I don't want to go in today," I said.

"Why not today?" Passion asked.

"Go on in, without me, and if you see him, or Fire, or anybody, tell them … whatever. I just don't want to go in. I don't want to see Will today."

"Don't you think Will will want to see you?" she asked. She rested her head on the back of the seat.

"Probably."

"Don't you think Will looks forward to your visits?"

"Well, sure. We look forward to seeing each other. We love each other."

"So why don't you want to see him today?" Passion was relentless in her questioning, and something compelled me to answer each of them, as she delivered them in rapid-fire fashion. Her interrogation was unsettling, reminding me of Defence and Prosecutor at Will's trial.

"I don't know," I said, getting irritated. "I just don't feel good today. Isn't that reason enough?"

"Do you think not seeing Will will make you feel better?"

"Better? No ... no. Not seeing him won't make me feel better. Seeing him won't make me feel better either."

"So maybe the problem isn't Will."

"Right. I know it's me. I just told you it's me. I don't feel like it today." I took another bite from my apple and rolled my eyes at Passion.

"That's a nice attitude," she teased. "All I'm trying to get at is why, Patience. Why?"

I pondered her one-word question and couldn't think of a reasonable answer.

"Passion. Every time I go in there, it's like ... I mean ... I've got twenty-five more years of this ahead of me. ... A break ... I need a break. I shouldn't have come today."

"Why?"

"Look, Passion. You're not an unintelligent person. I know you hear what I'm saying."

Passion turned from me and looked out of the bus's window, counting to ten, I supposed, under her breath.

"Yes. I hear what you're saying," she said, facing me again, "and I know where you're coming from, because I've been there myself. I also know that you're not telling yourself the truth. Something you're not telling me."

Passion sat up a little. "What happened?"

I shook my head from despair, starting to experience again some of the feelings I had the night before.

"We got married and now he's gone. I mean, he went to work and he was arrested, and now he's gone. He's in my life, and now he's out of my life. It was the same thing with Paw, Paw was in my life, and now he's out of my life. My brother Soldier … the same thing. It seems as though, … he's a man … it seems like every man, something always happens. Elder Rector, I respected him."

"Every man you respect—you love—something happens to that respect and love to make it go away?"

"Yes."

"Do you feel it's your fault?"

"Well, maybe. If Soldier didn't have to make more money for the family because Paw wasn't acting like a real man or a real father should because of Mumzy, if I hadn't gone out to dinner with Elder …, if I had said 'no' to Will when he proposed to me … maybe everything is my fault."

"Are you in jail?"

"No, I'm not in jail. What kind of question is that?"

"It seems to me like if it's your fault, you would be in jail too."

"I'm not saying it's my fault. If it's anybody's fault it's … it's God's fault." *What am I saying?* "Oh, God forgive me, I didn't mean it."

"Isn't God your protector? Wasn't He supposed to keep you from all that's happened to you?"

"Yes, He was … He was supposed to prevent all of this from happening to me." I covered my face with my hands, ashamed of what I was confessing, hiding from God, sobbing. "Yes, He was. He was supposed to prevent all of this. … He was supposed to keep me. … My Baby's

Father—Oh, God. ... Oh, no!" Passion allowed me to get the crying out of my system before she resumed her questioning. She seemed to be empowered, energized in her interrogation.

"Did God let you down? Is God a man also?" she asked with a matter-of-fact tone in her voice.

"No," I responded. "I mean, no, God never lets me down." Passion reached for my hands, taking them both in hers, and I could then feel her compassion. "God is the Father, the Holy Father. So, yes, in one sense, He is a Man."

"Did Will disappoint you?"

Would Passion's examination end? But with each question and answer, I felt healing of my soul. The pain was ebbing like the ocean's tide at midnight—my personal midnight.

"No, Will didn't disappoint me. My Will was taken away from me. And God didn't leave me. And Soldier didn't leave me. Soldier did what he felt he had to do."

"And Soldier still loves you, don't he?"

"Yes. He'll always be my big brother." My joy was returning. The thought of Soldier's protective, brotherly love brought a faint smile to my countenance.

"So, God, Will, your brother, all of them still love you, right?"

"Yes, they do." More joy returned.

"Men. You've had a problem with them for a long time. What do you think you need to do?"

Men. Could Passion be right?

"You're right. This is definitely something I need to pray about and work out. I can't make a general judgment about all men. Elder Rector was one man. Paw, he's my father, but he's just one man. We're all human and subject to making mistakes."

"If your Paw was here right now, what would you say to him?" Passion still held my hands in hers. I imagined that it was my father—my Father—holding them. I could feel God's love through Passion—through Compassion.

"I'd say, 'Paw, I regret what happened the day before I left home. And I forgive you. And, yes, I'm ready for you to be a part of my life again.'"

"Good. Now what do you think Paw would say to you?"

"You know. I always thought I was Paw's favorite child, whether I was or not. So, if he were here now, I believe he would say something like, 'Baby girl, I'm sorry, too.'"

"Good. Let's talk about Elder Rector."

"You had better get your hand off me ... and now!"

Passion lifted my chin, and I opened my still tearing eyes.

"He touched me," I whispered. "Why did he ... he ... have to touch me?" I finally blurted out. Passion cocked her head, again struggling to understand what I was saying through my uncontrollable sobs. "He didn't have to touch me. And I let Will touch me and now he's gone. Can I trust anybody, I mean, any man? You said you've been through this. You tell me. What's going on, Passion? Why does it hurt so much after all these years?"

"Hush ... hush," Passion said. "I'm Elder Rector. What would you say to him?" Passion let go of my hand, and I faced the unexpressed anger I had toward Elder Rector.

"You took something away from me," I said, almost shouting at Passion. "You took control. And I want it back.

226

Now I realize I can't get back control of my life until I forgive, really forgive you. Not from my lips, or from my head, but from my heart. And I do, I do forgive you. I hope you have changed. But whether you have or not, I take back the control you stole from me."

"And what would you want to hear him say to you?"

"There's nothing he could say to me, Passion."

"How about if he said 'I'm sorry,' and meant it?"

"He never said he was sorry. If he had only said he was sorry." I composed myself. "But I'm a better person now than he was then. I can truthfully say that I forgive him."

"Good. Let's go visit with our husbands."

February 25, 1990

Dear Patience,

Good news! I'm coming home, Baby. Defence was here today and told me the good news. I'll call you in a few days with the details. I'll be there with you very soon—not soon enough for me, though. Until then, be easy.

Love,
Will

"He's coming home!" I shouted up to the heavens. I danced around on the sidewalk, with my hands raised in praise to a faithful God, not caring whether the neighbors or passersby saw me. The Big City air smelled as sweet as the scent of roses to me. With my face toward the sky, I drank in the sunshine like a thirsty man lapping water at an oasis in the desert. A thousand thoughts darted through my soul, but the only words that came out of my mouth were,

"Hallelujah, praise the Lord, thank you Jesus!"

In the spirit of the moment, Temperance danced and praised God with me. "Hallelujah, praise the Lord, thank you, Jesus! Will's coming home!" I locked arms with her and swung her around, and together we shouted: "Hallelujah, praise the Lord, thank you Jesus. Will's coming home!" When I became exhausted, we got in the car. My neighbor and his wife across the street waved at us, and I returned their greeting.

"Will's coming home," I shouted across Temperance through the window on the driver's side.

"You're suffocating me, woman," Temperance said. Then her mouth dropped open as she shook her head in disbelief. "What happened?"

"They caught the real criminals," I explained.

"Wait a minute. Hold that thought. I forgot my Sunday School book. I'll be right back. Don't go anywhere."

Temperance got back in the car stuffing her book in her handbag.

"They caught the real criminals? Where? How? Give me details."

"He said that two men tried to commit a similar crime by switching the tags of another Dodge Ram and using it on their truck to commit a robbery. This time, the investigators matched the tread marks left at the crime scene to the real criminals' truck. And it so happened that the truck the crooks took the tags off belonged to the Chief of Police."

"What?"

"They caught the two men in the act of robbing a gun shop in Suburban City, ran the tags, found out that they belonged to the Chief of Police, and locked up the two men. On a plea bargain, the men confessed to the crimes Will was charged for, and they're releasing Will."

"When will he be home?"

"Week after next," I said.

"Let's invite the whole family."

"I don't need the whole family here. I just need Will." That idea hadn't once occurred to me, and the look on my face let Temperance know how ridiculous I thought it to be.

"Come on. We'll let you two be alone. We'll give you some space."

"No. Maybe after a week or two, or a month. I want Will all to myself."

"Look. It's the perfect time to get the family together. We have the perfect excuse. And you said yourself that we need to have a family reunion. Come on, Sis."

When was the last time the entire family had been together? She's right. I need to see Paw, and Soldier— everybody.

"Well, perhaps. It would be good to see Sister, and Soldier, and Paw."

"And don't forget Will's cousins. Soldier could probably swing by and get Paw." Temperance became reflective, as did I. "It will be wonderful to see everybody," Temperance said. Temperance pulled up at the stoplight.

A couple with a child in the backseat in the car beside us turned toward each other and touched lips. Temperance and I both said, "Ah."

"Maybe Rock can bring Talent," I said. "Let's fill the house with joy and laughter." A fire truck's siren interrupted our conversation long enough for it to go through a red light, which made Temperance miss her light.

"I want to do some redecorating—with bright colors—reds and greens and oranges."

"Don't get carried away," Temperance said. "Will you have enough space for everyone, that is, sleeping accommodations, chairs, tables?"

"I'll figure something out," I said. "But who cares? We'll all sleep on the floor if necessary. Will is coming home!" I grabbed Temperance's hand and raised it in victory.

... To Be Content.

Behold the State I'm In

Hustling and bustling—that's how I would describe that March ninth, the day before Will was to come home. Hammering, bags rustling, and the chittering chatter of Temperance and Rocky enlivened the living room as it had never been before. On the floor, Temperance supervised Rocky on a stepladder in how to put up new living room drapes.

"Will won't care about new curtains, especially fuchsia ones," Rocky said. "I hope you aren't doing this for his sake."

"Will? You call him Will now, do you?" Temperance asked. "You need to be a little more respectful."

"I have the highest respect for Will," Rocky said. "Will and I are cool."

"You watch your step around me and Patience," she said. Rocky's foot slipped, but he recovered quickly before falling off the stepladder.

"I didn't mean for you to literally watch your step, but do that too," Temperance said. She stood up and steadied the stepladder while Rocky fastened the last drapery hook to the traverse rod.

"Don't worry about me falling," Rocky said. "My middle name is Graceful."

"I can see that," she said. Remembering that his middle name was really Ernest made her look forward to seeing Paw again.

What has it been? Over thirty years? Unbelievable.

"Hurry up," she said. "Before our company gets here."

Rocky got down off the stepladder.

"Oh, I'm not company any more?" he asked.

"You never were," Temperance replied and gave him a mock punch in the stomach. Since Rocky moved out, the two of them seemed to have more of a sibling relationship than that of parent and child. And since Rocky and Talent still hadn't set a wedding date, choosing rather to finish college, pay off outstanding debts, and generally learn all they needed to know about being single before they entered the state of matrimony, Temperance didn't have a reason to dote over him.

"What do you want me to do next?" Rocky asked. He rubbed his hands together like a miser over stacks of gold coins. "I've devoted my whole Saturday to helping Big Ma."

"Check in the kitchen and see if there's anything that needs to be done in there."

"Okay, Ma," Rocky said, and walked toward the kitchen. Since he was a baby and spoke the word for the first time, Temperance turned to mush whenever she heard him say "Ma."

"Rocky?"

"Yes, Mother?"

"There's a bed frame in the spare room. Would you put it together so we can set up another bed?"

"Check and double-check," Rocky yelled back, and headed to the bedroom whistling a tune that, at first, sounded a lot like "Going Up Yonder," but turned out to be the theme from the movie *Rocky*.

"Strength and Courage are here," Temperance shouted. She ran to the door before they could ring the bell.

"If it isn't my favorite pair of twin cousins—in-law—kind of," Temperance said. "Come on in. It's so good to see you."

Probably looking quite alien to the twins, judging from the expressions on their faces, I also ran to the door, having with my hair tied up, howbeit not in a fashionable silk scarf, but in a grayish elasticized cloth cap that I donned only when I dusted or did other odd jobs around the house. My housedress was more akin to the old sacks I wore as a young girl. I had made it from a piece of thick navy-blue paisley material that I was saving to make a tablecloth, or some curtains, or something else domestic. Instead, I was overtaken by a sewing spell and designed and created a moo-moo with big pockets, which resembled those on an electrician's or carpenter's apron, to hold my supply of household cleaning and polishing products, a feather duster, extra sponges, and the like. Red fuzzy bedroom shoes, a gift from Rocky from a Christmas long past, were on my feet. With toilet brush in hand, I waved to Strength and Courage.

"Good morning, you're early," I said.

"She takes her cleaning very seriously, doesn't she?" Strength asked Temperance in a tone just above a whisper.

"You don't know the half of it," Temperance whispered back.

"Guys. I can hear you. And don't you dare tell them about the time I cleaned the—"

"You're about to tell on yourself," Temperance interrupted.

"Cleaned what?" Courage asked.

"Naw, naw, it's too early for this," I said. I threw my arms around each of them and kissed them on the cheek.

"I apologize for smelling like industrial-strength cleanser," I said. "You two make yourselves at home. On second thought, make yourselves useful and see if Rock needs help putting that bed frame together."

"Where's your luggage?" Temperance asked. "Aren't you staying here tonight, and I have room to put up a couple of people at my place also."

"Do what you want to do," I said. "Everyone's doing too much talking for me. I have to go get dressed. It's almost lunchtime and I still look like this."

"Bye, Patience," Temperance said. "She's as excited and nervous as I've ever seen her. This house is as sanitary as a hospital's operating room, and she's still cleaning."

"We checked into a hotel not too far away," Strength said. "We didn't want to be any trouble. We got a room for Faith, too."

"What was that?" I called from the bedroom. "A room for Faith. Cancel it. Faith is staying right here. End of subject. Really. A hotel? City folks."

"All right, Cousin Patience," Courage yelled back. "We brought you a ham. Knew you were having lots of family in. It's in the car. I'll go get it."

"I'll go help Rock, then," Strength said. He took off his jacket and flung it on the sofa.

I'm behind schedule and don't have time to entertain. Thank God for Temperance. Let's see. Sister and Faith in the guest room, and Paw in the spare room. Ooh, lot's of people in the house. It'll be fun, and it's just for a couple of nights.

The doorbell rang. It rang again. Courage had forgotten to take the lock off.

"I'll get it," I said.

What was that smell? A fresh pot of coffee.

Its aroma intermingled with the leftover smell of fried sausage from breakfast, a smell that always immediately took me home in my mind, to The Sticks.

In my bathrobe with a towel wrapped around my wet hair, I opened the door to a sight that was not only balm for tired eyes, but a helium balloon for my heart, though it sank again when painful memories turned down the fire that fueled the helium. When I saw Paw, feelings, some related to Paw and some not, feelings that I had buried, deep, mixing and colliding with each other, threatened a resurrection, or rather an insurrection. My mother's death, Goody's lifestyle and death, Paw's harsh treatment of all of us after Mumzy's arrival, Soldier's leaving home because of it, my desperate attempt to protect Temperance, our leaving home—my home—in fear that we were no longer safe. All these thoughts, and the circumstances surrounding them, sprinted through my mind.

But I was reminded that this was a new day. I had ended ungodly relationships; had changed my mind, mortified my flesh, and renewed my spirit; implicitly accepted God's guidance, wisdom, and will; engaged myself in God's service; submitted to God's plan for my life; and had made an effort, thanks to God and Compassion, to reprogram pain-filled memories of my past. I was okay.

I could open this door, or any other door that God led me to, with love, joy, and forgiveness. I had forgiven Paw. What's more, I had forgiven myself for leaving him. I once told Paw that if a man hit me, I would hit him back. I learned that I didn't need to worry about such a scenario because I was married to Will, and I had verified him—set him up against a standard—based on the Word of God.

"Paw! Soldier!" I said. "Come in, you two. Just look at you both!"

Courage came up the front walkway carrying the ham. Paw was limping; Soldier had to help him to the sofa. I sat down beside him and caressed his head, knocking his hat to the side.

"What's wrong, Paw?" I asked. "Why are you limping?"

He drew in a deep breath and coughed as he let it out.

"It's just old age, baby girl," Paw said. "Old Arthur

done crept into my joints."

Paw coughed again, almost uncontrollably, taking a long time to recover. He didn't look well, and he sounded even worse. Rocky and the twins joined us in the living room and sat down, Rocky sitting on the floor in front of the coffee table with his legs crossed under him.

"Paw, this is Strength and Courage, Will's cousins," I said.

"It's a pleasure to meet you, Mr. Christianson," Courage said. He shook Paw's hand.

Paw nodded to him.

"The same here," Strength said, also shaking his hand. Strength sat down on the other side of Paw, who took in another deep breath. This time, though, he let it out slowly, and his cough was more like a clearing of his throat.

"And sitting in front of you," Temperance said, moving toward Paw, "is your grandson, Rock ... Rock Ernest Christianson. ... I named him after you, Paw."
Paw looked curiously at Rocky and smiled.

"He has your mama's eyes," Paw said. "Yes, sir, there's a lot of Heart in that boy. I can see that even with these old dim eyes of mine."

Rock stood up and came around the table to hug his frail and aging grandfather.

"Nice to finally meet you, Grandpaw," Rocky said, and took his seat again on the floor in front of the table.

I slid over to give Temperance some space beside Paw. She embraced him around his shoulder and leaned her head against him.

"Oh, Paw," she said, crying. "I'm sorry I didn't come see you and bring Rocky. I'm sorry, Paw."

"I can't help but forgive you, baby girl," he said, and patted her knee stiffly. "I'm sorry about a lot of things myself that I can't change now." He cleared his throat again, pulled out his handkerchief, and blew his nose.

"How's your wife?" Courage asked.

At the mention of "your wife," which in my mind translated to Mumzy, I looked away.

"Excuse me, everybody," Soldier said, and stood up to leave. At the kitchen doorway, he stopped. "Patience, you got any beer in the house?"

"We don't drink in this house," I said. "Soldier, please stay in here with us. It's been a long time since our family has been together. Please."

He sat back down, bent forward with hands together, and looked at Paw sideways.

"Why did you do it, Paw?" I asked. I looked around at Soldier and my sisters, and by the looks on their faces, they wanted answers also.

"Do what, baby girl? You mean marry Mumzy? Take her side against you all?" Paw coughed and scratched his head. "I've had a lot of time to think about it. And I reckon I can boil the reason down to one word. Fear."

Fear? I had never known Paw to fear anything.

"I feared losing her like I lost your mama." He blew his nose again into his handkerchief. "I blamed myself a long time for Heart's death. Having five children on top of working. A lot of women didn't work back in them days. Before she took sick, she didn't seem too happy either. I blamed myself for that, too. It's a man's job to make his woman happy."

Paw coughed feebly again and pulled up his knee to straighten out his leg.

"So I guess I got a little carried away dealing with Mumzy. Anyway, to answer the young man's earlier question, she's dead and gone now. Got too riled up about something or other and had a stroke shortly after Patience moved away with Temperance. Then she lost her mind completely. I came home from town one evening and found her in the backyard walking around naked and talking to herself. She said that the devil was in her mouth and was cutting through her face with a butcher knife. I told her that it was just that old rotten tooth she had been complaining about, but Mumzy insisted it was the devil himself in her mouth trying to cut open her pretty face from the inside out. I contacted her brother. He checked her into the state insane asylum. I didn't try to contact anybody. Figured you all wouldn't care. But I want you children to forgive me. And Patience, she wanted me to give you something. But before I do, let me tell you all a little about Mumzy."

Curiosity drew all of us, including Soldier, a little closer to listen to Paw as he told us about Mumzy.

It was 1939. Mumzy was eighteen years old and had a job working at The Café, made famous in The Sticks by Miss Jewel's chitterlings and pig's feet sandwiches. She had been working since she was old enough to count money—always wanting to keep money in her pocketbook. When she wasn't washing and ironing clothes for the White people, which accounted for most of the money she had, Mumzy swept the floor, washed dishes, counted money, and sometimes helped with the cooking at The Café.

She had been working since sunup that Friday. By eight o'clock that night, payday for most of the people, The Café's jukebox was wailing "See See Rider" and "The Midnight Special," filling the room with rhythm and sound, making some of the people's hearts long for good times to be had or past times to be relived, and took the minds of others off the fact that they couldn't afford to buy just one of Miss Jewel's "chit'lin'" sandwiches.

Mumzy was so tired, she felt as though she had been whipped.

"Stop your sweeping and socializing with the customers," Miss Jewel said verbally, but more so with a single motion of her hand, "and come and help me with the food."

Leaning her broom up against the wall and wiping her hands on her apron that could have wiped back for its being so soiled with blood from the meat, she ended her conversation with Breach, one of the local fellows. He gave her a knowing pat on the rear end, and she went behind the counter and started serving up chitterlings sandwiches.

Miss Jewel didn't trust too many people with counting the money she was responsible for. But this Friday night had been unusually busy at The Café, so around eleven o'clock she asked Mumzy to get a head start on the money counting, since people had stopped ordering food. Mumzy took the money box to the back room, behind the kitchen.

Old ledgers, clothes, and extra pots and pans decorated the small counting room in a sort of all-purpose fashion. You had to go through the kitchen to get to it. One small window, about two feet by three feet, stared at Mumzy sitting at the counting table in the corner. Something peaked from beneath a sheet and took hold of her attention. She lifted the sheet and saw two pieces of luggage—a medium-size piece that couldn't contain any more than two of Mr. Pride's suits and maybe a shirt or two, and a smaller piece for cosmetics and such things.

She stacked the paper currency and coins by denomination as her mind drifted to what she would do if all the money and the suitcases belonged to her. She would take a trip like the Prides take and visit some far-off land and talk to people she didn't know and couldn't understand. Caught up in her daydreams, she didn't realize that she had been in the counting room for nearly an hour and hadn't totaled the money for Miss Jewel. Licking her thumb after every few bills, she finished counting the paper money and had started to divide the quarters into stacks of four, when Miss Jewel poked her head through the door.

"It's almost quitting time," Miss Jewel announced. "You almost finished?"

"Yes, ma'am," Mumzy said.

Mumzy was surprised at the night's take—fifty-seven dollars and seventy-nine cents. She tied a string around the bills, put the loose coins in a small sack, and left the money on the table, but then remembered the money box kept under the table. The suitcases made her wonder, so much that she, as an added safety factor and to prolong her dreams of travel, opened the small overnight case.

Money—seven hundred dollars in tens and twenties. This must be the new place she keeps the money.

She added the night's take to the money in the overnight case, got her coat and pocketbook, and was home in about twenty minutes.

The next morning she got to The Café and was surprised to see the owner, Mr. Miller, there talking with Miss Jewel.

"There she is," Miss Jewel said.

What's wrong with her?

"Where's that money and the suitcases, you little wench!"

"What?" Mumzy asked. "I put the money in the little suitcase with the other money!"

"What? ..." Miss Jewel asked, taken off guard.

"What other money? ... Besides, them suitcases been stole, too. And you stole 'em!"

"No, I didn't. You's a lie, Miss Jewel. I never stole no money, and I left them suitcases in the corner where I found them."

"How dare you call me a lie. You're the liar, you're the liar. Call the police on her, Mr. Miller, call the police on her!"

"Well, Mumzy, I hate to do it," Mr. Miller said. He seized Mumzy's forearm. "But Jewel's been working for me for nigh on to fifteen years, and we ain't had no trouble out of her before in the matter of money. She says you were the last one to have your hands on the money. Now it's missing and so are the suitcases that Jewel says have been back there in that room since she started working here. I hate to call the police on you, and I won't if you just bring back the stolen items."

"I can't bring back what I don't have," Mumzy said. Anger and fear dominated Mumzy. Anger at Miss Jewel and fear of going to Women's Detention.

"Then I'm afraid you're in a lot of trouble, gal," Mr. Miller said.

Mumzy stomped down hard on Mr. Miller's foot, causing him to cry out for the pain and let go of her arm. She burst through The Café door and ran toward home.

"Now there's no use in running, gal," Mr. Miller yelled out through the door to Mumzy, his foot still in pain. "You won't get away with this!"

Mumzy arrived home and threw some clothes into a suitcase and an overnight case. She met Breach at his house, and the two of them left town in his ten-year-old Big Car that his father had paid a White man to purchase for him before the car company decided to sell Big Cars to

Coloreds, and they headed for Sin City with the intention of getting married. They never did, though.

"How did you find out about this, Paw?" Soldier asked.

"Mumzy told me before she died," Paw said. "Patience, you still have that big suitcase you found?"

"No, Paw," I said. "I threw it out. I was depressed over Will's being in prison, and I guess I had a lot on my mind. But it's gone, and so are all the letters Will wrote me, Mama's Bible, and that little pitcher of hers. They were all in the suitcase, and so was the handkerchief Miss Grace gave me. I hope Will can forgive me for not keeping his letters. I regret I got rid of such precious—"

"You don't have to regret anything," Temperance said, "and Will won't have to forgive you." She left the room and returned carrying my suitcase. "I drove up when you were putting this out for the trash. I figured whatever you were going through, it wouldn't last, and you would want these back." She handed me the suitcase, and I hugged her tightly and kissed her on her cheek.

Opening it revealed five years' of letters from Will, which burst forth in neatly rubber-banded packs.

"Amazing," Temperance said. "I hadn't realized there are so many."

"If you think about it, Will wrote me two or three times a week, faithfully," I said. "You do the math."

"Take all of 'em out," Paw said. Each letter was so dear to me, that to touch them was almost like Will was near.

"Now get some scissors and cut out the lining behind the left side pocket," he said. Again I did what Paw asked.

"Cut near the top edge so you don't damage what's back there," Paw said.

"What is it?" Rock asked.

"Wait a minute," I said. I carefully felt behind the lining and at first didn't feel anything unusual. I made a bigger rip in the satin cloth and felt around.

"It's a document of some kind," I said. I pulled out a brown envelope and opened it.

"What is it?" Rocky asked again.

"It's a U.S. Savings Bond with a face value of one thousand dollars. Soldier, you know about these things. How much do you think this is worth today?"

Soldier took the bond from me and examined it.

"Hmhh ... It's in excellent condition," Soldier said, "A Series E bond. Issued May 1941. Must have cost ... hmhh ... probably around seven hundred and fifty dollars or so. Today it's worth close to maybe twenty-five hundred," Soldier said, and handed me the bond, "and that's probably on the low side."

"But how ... where—" I couldn't get the words out of my mouth before Paw intervened.

"Turns out Mumzy did steal the money from The Café that night and used Breach to get her out of town," Paw said. "At least that's what I think. She never said she did, but when I asked her, she didn't say she didn't do it either."

I hadn't realized how late it had gotten. I could tell Paw was getting tired now. He slumped more in his seat and talked slower than when he started. His coughing started again. Strength covered Paw's hand with his. Temperance and I had prepared dinner the night before—all of Will's favorites, and some of Paw's, too, as much as we could remember. In fact, still lingering in the air were traces of the aroma of the feast: candied yams; fried chicken; fresh kale cooked with ham hocks, onions, and a dash of vinegar; potato salad—that was Temperance's specialty—macaroni and cheese; and apple and sweet potato pies.

"Rocky, would you get Paw some water, please," I said, "and bring out that platter of chicken wings on the stove."

"Make that hot tea, if you don't mind, son," Paw said.

"It's in the cupboard on the right, sweetie," I said.

"When the relationship didn't work, they went their separate ways," Paw continued. "I want to believe that she didn't steal the money, that she earned it. But where would a woman of color get that much money back then? I would like to believe that if she stole it, she was planning to return it someday. She told me she wanted Patience to have it."

"And you know I can't keep it, Paw," I said, "not unless it was rightfully hers. And why me?"

"I don't know. Maybe because you stood up to her. But I wanted you … wanted you all to know that Mumzy wasn't all bad." Rocky came in with the hot tea, and Paw sipped it slowly, blowing into the cup before each sip—the way he used to.

As we sat thinking about Paw's story and about the bond, Sister came through the door with a weekender garment bag folded over her arm.

"Hey, everybody," she said. "You're not in the country, girl. Don't you know to lock your door?" She saw the somber mood that Paw's story had put us all in. Soldier had slipped away to the spare room and turned on the TV to catch the evening news.

"Did somebody die?" she asked, then dropped her bag on the floor and greeted everyone around the room with a wave. "Paw. Patience. Temperance. Rock old man, how are you? Are you married yet? And I don't believe I've had the pleasure of meeting these two gentlemen. Patience, are these Will's good-looking cousins you wrote me about?"

"Yes. Sister, this is Strength and this is Courage," I said. "I don't know how I could have made it without them."

"Quick. Turn the TV on in there," Soldier shouted from the bedroom. "Hurry up. Channel 13."

Temperance, sitting closest to the television turned it on to channel 13. A special report was already in progress. The headline flashed in the top left corner of the screen in a box that was overlaid with bars: "Parable Under Siege." A woman reporter, well-dressed in a gray business suit and red scarf tied around her neck, spoke quickly, precisely.

"For those just tuning in, I'm Sunny Sun, broadcasting live from Parable State Prison where a riot broke out around three o'clock this afternoon. Four inmates are holding three people hostage, one of whom is the acclaimed news anchor/reporter Dan Sooner. A camerawoman and Correctional Officer Buck Intimidator are also being held hostage. Inmates currently have control of Cell Block E and the adjacent guard tower."

Gripping shock would describe the state I was in. I sank to the floor, weak from what I had just heard, my will to do anything threatening to leave me, save sitting and staring at the images flashing before us on the picture tube.

"Isn't that the prison where Will is at?" Paw whispered to Strength, who nodded in disbelief, almost robotically.

"This is a mess," Paw said with a phlegm-ridden voice that screamed to be cleared. Sunny Sun continued.

"Dan Sooner and his camera crew were visiting the

prison today after receiving mail from the mother of one of the inmates complaining about unsettling conditions there. For the past year, Sooner has been investigating prison conditions all over the country. Although Parable was in a heightened state of security given the fact that a high-profile visitor was touring it, inmates succeeded in overtaking all correctional officers in Cell Block E, which is now in a state of riot. The commotion drew enough attention away from the guards' tower, making it possible for an inmate, who is as yet unidentified, to overtake the tower guard, seize his weapon, and use it to force Mr. Sooner and the other two hostages into the Administration Building, where they are being held at this moment.

"A confidential source at the prison told Channel 13 News that certain inmates had been planning a riot for years, and that Dan Sooner's visit gave riot operatives the right opportunity to carry out their plans.

"This just in: Channel 13 News has just learned the name of the hostage-taker and the riot's mastermind: Fire Stalwart, a convicted murderer of a priest, who is currently serving consecutive life sentences without the possibility of parole. Channel 13 News has also learned that he and his gang members prevented a scheduled lockdown by gaining access to an electrical room in the facility. They cut the wires that fed into the gate, making it possible for gang members to overpower the correctional officers on duty in that cell block and seize their weapons. Then gang members in each of Cell Block E's cells physically held the cell doors open after power was shut down. Cell Block E houses more than 200 inmates. There has been no word from Warden Vulpine yet as to his plans to retake Cell Block E or to free the hostages. Over to you, Mike."

"This is Mike Buzz at broadcast house. State troopers are working tirelessly to keep people safe and away from the prison's parking lot, as spectators, thrill seekers, and family and friends of the convicts, after hearing news of the riot and hostage situation, have been gathering for hours. A candlelight vigil is being planned for dusk tonight for the release of the hostages. Dan Sooner's father is flying in for that vigil.

"More breaking news. Warden Vulpine at Parable State Prison has stated that he will discuss the riot and hostage situation with Channel 13 News anchors tonight on 13 News at Eleven. Tune in at eleven for this exclusive interview. Back to you, Sunny."

"Thanks, Mike. Once again, just hours ago here at Parable State Prison, inmates, led by Fire Stalwart, a convicted murderer, took hostage news anchor/reporter Dan Sooner, camerawoman Pat Black, and Correctional Officer Buck Intimidator. Their demands have not yet been made known. Stay tuned as Warden Vulpine at the prison speaks to Channel 13 News in an exclusive interview. Also, tune in tonight at eleven for Channel 13 News' special report 'Imprisoned Shame,' an exposé on prison conditions across the country."

Click. Soldier switched off the television, sending the screen into blankness, as blank as the expressions on our faces. He stood in front of the TV. We all stared at him, until I spoke up.

"Well I'm not going to sit around here, complacent, content to do nothing," I said. I rushed to the door and flung it open, the knob making a thud as it hit the wall. "I'm going up there."

"Are you sure that's the right thing to do?" Temperance asked, joining me at the door. "Never mind, let's do it. Do you have any candles for the vigil?"

"I'll drive you," Soldier said. "Wait a minute, let me get my jacket from the bedroom."

"Wait a minute, everybody," Sister said. She came and stood close to us. "Patience, Temperance. Come on, now." She looked at Soldier. "Soldier. Be sensible. Suppose someone tries to contact you, Patience. You know, as Will's next of kin. I mean, his wife needs to be home. And the whole family is here with you." She turned to Paw. "And look at Paw. You don't want to leave him here. And he's in no condition to do unnecessary traveling."

Paw had nodded off to sleep for a few moments and woke to hear Sister's plea.

"What you all doing?" he asked. "Planning a jail break? Count me out. I'm too tired."

Picturing Paw and my family storming Parable State Prison and breaking Will out of jail caused me to lose control. It started in my mouth—I parted my upper and lower teeth without parting my lips and moved my bottom jaw from side to side. As the corners of my mouth upturned, my diaphragm contracted a few times and sent spurts of carbon dioxide from my nostrils. Then out it came—laughter. Soon, we all were laughing. After several minutes when the laughter petered out, I was left crying in the middle of my siblings who engaged me in a group hug, instigated by Sister.

"I know—we've never done this before," Sister said, "but it's about time."

The Christiansons were not given to bouts of mushiness, at least not outwardly. Breaking it up, Paw asked Rock to go out to the car and bring in the grocery bag he had put in the trunk of Soldier's car. It was not quite time for the eleven o'clock news, so we all settled back down in our seats. Rock brought in the bag and handed it to Paw, who reached in, brought out a handful of roasted peanuts, then cast them on the coffee table. At first nothing happened; there was no reaction from us. Then Soldier reached over and picked up a couple, cracked them, and ate them. Paw threw out a few more. Soldier reached for a couple more.

"Not so fast," Sister said, and raked the rest of them toward her. Then we all dropped to our knees around the table, including Strength and Courage. With the news of Will, I had forgotten about dinner. The platter of chicken wings was long gone and forgotten. Paw came through for me.

At eleven, Rock turned the television in the living room back on. Two stiff and serious-looking newscasters sat behind the anchor desk.

"Thank you for tuning in to Channel 13 News' special report on the riot and hostage situation at Parable State Prison. I'm Mike Buzz, along with Sunny Sun. Sunny, let's go right to our live interview with Warden Vulpine at Parable."

The television screen divided so both Mike Buzz and Warden Vulpine could be seen simultaneously.

"Good evening, Warden Vulpine, and thank you for joining us tonight," Mike said. "Has the situation escalated at Parable, and what is your plan of action to deal with it?"

The warden looked to be in his late fifties, with graying hair and mustache, and deep wrinkles under his eyes and around his mouth. He wore a dark gray tweed jacket and a blue, green, and black diagonally striped tie.

"There has been no change in the situation," Warden Vulpine said. "Cell Block E and the adjacent guard tower are still under inmate control. As soon as a line of communication can be established, prison officials as well as members of state law enforcement, and myself will attempt to ascertain what the inmates' demands are, and as much as possible, try to negotiate a peaceful settlement of this situation. Until then, we'll just wait it out."

"Has there been any word on the condition of the hostages?"

"No, none yet." The warden tugged at his ear. "My prayers are with the hostages and their families, that they will be released, and that there won't be any bloodshed."

"Speaking of bloodshed," Sunny cut in. "How many weapons do the hostage takers have access to, and do the inmates in Cell Block E have weapons also?"

"I'm not at liberty to divulge that kind of information, especially while the lives of the hostages are at jeopardy." Warden Vulpine pointed at the camera accusatorily with his left index finger and tugged at his right ear with his right hand, probably a habit he picked up while conducting parole board meetings throughout his career.

"What do you make of accusations of mistreatment of prisoners?"

"This interview is over." He blocked his face from the camera with his palm turned outward, got up, and exited the scene.

"That was Warden Vulpine from the warden's home right outside Parable State Prison," Mike said. "As you've just heard, Warden Vulpine and other prison officials plan to wait it out, that is, wait and see what the inmates' demands are and wait for negotiators to take over and do their jobs. Now to other news ..."

Click.

"Wait it out?" I asked in disbelief. I'd never felt so helpless and not in control in my life. "Lord, give me strength."

"All right. Let's all wait it out here and get some

rest," Sister said.

"Soldier, can you help Paw to the guest room and show him where the bathroom is?" Temperance asked. She and I went into the kitchen to put the food away. It seemed we had all lost our appetites.

"Patience, Temperance, do you need anything before Courage and I leave?" Strength asked.

"Forgive me, Strength," I said. "I apologize for my manners tonight." I got their coats from the hall closet and kissed them. "We'll be fine. I'll see you tomorrow?"

"First thing," Courage said. "Faith's arriving early, so we'll pick her up from the train station and bring her with us."

Wonderful. I missed Faith.

My Will—Too

March 10, 1990

Dear Patience,

Although you may never get this letter, I must write you anyway. I'll get right to the point. I love you, I believe I have since I first met you. The time we have spent together, well, I wouldn't take anything for it. My life is complete because of you, and my life means nothing without you.

My love, these are dangerous times, and I'm in a dangerous situation now. If anything happens to me, please be assured that I'm resting with the Lord. Please feel free to distribute my personal belongings as you see fit. I have only one special request, and that's that you make sure Rock gets my Bible. My father gave it to me, and Rock is like a son to me. Tell Mom and Dad and the rest of my family that I love them. *Their visits have meant to me more than I can tell you. And tell my sister Faith and my cousins Courage and Strength that, like you, they have held special places in my heart. I couldn't have made it through these five years without the four of you on my side.*

Temperance and you have always been inseparable, and I know your relationship will continue to thrive and endure. Give her, Sister, and Soldier big hugs and lots of kisses for me. For my sisters and brothers in Christ at Rugged Cross, tell them that I have reaped the benefits of their prayers. Exhort them to do good, eschew evil, and love each other.

It's my prayer that if after a time you get lonely, that God will put another man in your life—that your second marriage will truly be as blessed as ours has been.

God has blessed and prospered me throughout these years. I believe James 1:2, which says: "Blessed is the man who perseveres under trial, because when he has stood the test, he will receive the crown of life that God has promised to those who love him."

Don't take this letter as a sign that I've given up or that I'm defeated. I just want you to be prepared for whatever happens.

I love you.

                    Will

March 11, 1990

My dearest Patience,

Yesterday, I wrote you and dropped it down the mail shoot in the Administration Building where I am. I pray that you'll get it.

I'm writing this letter to chronicle what I'm witnessing here. Dan Sooner lies on the floor unconscious. I fear he may have a concussion. Intimidator and a female are bound, though not gagged, and have been huddled together face down on the floor here in Warden Vulpine's office. I had gotten special permission from the prison administrator to be excused from head count yesterday to work on some filing in the warden's office when Fire, Snake, and Fear burst in dragging Dan Sooner and otherwise coercing the other two hostages. As I'm writing, I'm also keeping watch over what's going on. This office has French doors, and through the three-quarter-inch space between them, all I can see in the hallway is darkness. All electricity has been turned off. Snake broke into the vending machines right outside the office, so we've had enough to eat, namely candy bars, crackers, chips, and soda.

Here's what happened. As Dan Sooner and his woman cameraman toured the facilities, the lockdown of Cell Block E was somehow thwarted. I suspect Fire and his gang had something to do with it. When the head correctional officer shouted, "Manual lockdown, manual lockdown—secure Administration—sound alarm," Fire and Snake, who had alluded the prior head count check because of all the commotion caused by Dan Sooner and his crew's visit, hid in the electrical switch closet. They burst from the closet. Fire kicked the officer hard in his back and took his shotgun. Snake knocked Dan Sooner to the concrete floor, and Fear grabbed the woman, managing to overpower her even though she was about the same size and build as he.

The warden's office is large, about twelve feet by twelve feet. It has its own restroom with a sink and toilet. There's no window in the toilet, so Fire let's everyone go in alone to use it. The desk, cluttered with papers, envelopes, and manila folders, sits in front of a standard-sized window that's shaded by venetian blinds. Behind the desk is an executive-type brown leather chair. Directly in front of the desk are the French doors, and beside the doors is a dark-green five-drawer file cabinet, which is kept locked with a chain and padlock. The toilet is to the left of the file cabinet. To the right of the desk is a black three-draw file cabinet, where records on prisoners who are up for parole are kept. The warden must like horses, because on the walls are framed pictures of horses with jockeys posing next to them or sitting on them.

"What's this guy writing over there, Fire?" Fear asked. He came from across the room and grabbed my arm and shook it, knocking my pencil to the floor. "You writing about me?" I brushed his hand off my arm, pushing him off balance.

"Leave him alone," Fire said. "Let him write his old lady. Let him write whoever he wants. What can they do to us now?" He pointed his shotgun at Sooner's head.

"That's right, Fire, that's right," Fear said. "What can they do to us now?" He laughed and snorted.

Short in stature and small-framed, with a goatee and shaggy hair, Fear sat down on the hard linoleum floor beside the female. He stroked her hair, and she jerked involuntarily, which caused Fear to jump back almost a foot. Kneeling beside the woman, looking to Fire and Snake for instructions, breathing through his mouth because of his cold, and wiping his nose on his shirt sleeve, Fear reminded me of a lost puppy—powerless, hopeless, weak. What possible use to Fire was he?

"Come on, man," I said to Fire. I eyed the shotgun in his hand. "What is this proving? So you got a few hostages. Have you looked out the window lately? Can't you see the sharpshooters? If Dan Sooner dies, it's the chair for you."

"Shut up," Snake said. Through the space between the French doors, I saw something move. A shadow. But how could that be? There was only darkness out there. A shadow in darkness? A reverse shadow, maybe—one formed when darkness is blocked by something lighter? I let it go. Suddenly drawn to the window which provided a modicum of light to the room, as all power had been shut off in that part of the prison, Snake lifted a blind and peaked out.

"Yeah, shooters in the two towers," he said. That's when I noticed that he had a handgun in his pocket. Pulling it out, he cursed. "Crud. This crap is useless against what they have. But I'll waste whoever tries to take back this building, if my boys downstairs don't get 'em first."

"What are your demands?" I asked, looking up from my writing, appearing to be disinterested in all that was transpiring, venturing a question in hopes of distracting him from his plans. Then I continued writing.

"That's right, we need demands," Snake said. He opened the desk drawer and took out a pencil and a yellow legal pad.

"You mean to tell me you don't have your demands already laid out?" I asked.

"Listen, Jesus-boy," Snake said. He reached in his pocket and pulled out the handgun. "I'm about sick of you and your I'm-better-and-smarter-than-all-y'all attitude. Now sit down and keep your trap shut." Wisdom took control of me as usual, and I backed off.

"Will," Fire said. He shook his head, regretting the display of weakness by showing me respect in using my real name, instead of Lucky, in front of Snake and Fear. "Get over here and write down what I say."

I'll get back to you in a while, sweetheart.

The doorbell rang louder than usual the next morning, or so it seemed. Eight-three-zero—eight-thirty—shone brightly from my digital clock. Yawning, I saw my reflection in the dresser mirror and realized that I had fallen asleep in my clothes, on top of my comforter. Fortunately, my red double-knit suit was resistant to wrinkling. I needed coffee. I needed a bath, but showering would have to wait.

Faith, Strength, and Courage had arrived early.

Thank God.

The house, resurrected, showing signs of life after only a few hours of being in the grip of captivity's darkness. Temperance, who had fallen asleep beside me, stretched, energizing her being, and Paw, clad in his faded black flannel pajamas, hobbled out of the spare room into the bathroom.

It seems all Fire wants from authorities is better food and for the warden to abolish the use of the lash and sweatboxes as punishment. Snake wants conjugal visits to be reinstated, in the pure sense of the term. He wants Amnesty, his lady friend. I've never seen her, Patience, but according to other inmates, Amnesty is so beautiful, that to look at her is to desire her.

"Did you put Amnesty at the top of the list, Lucky?" Snake asked.

"And Leniency," Fear said. "That's my woman. But, yeah, Amnesty, that's right, Amnesty."

"Yes," I said. "You saw me write it, didn't you?" Snake went back to the window and peaked out again. He sat on the corner of the desk, with the butt of the shotgun he carried on the floor, and bit his bottom lip so hard that I thought it would draw blood. His eyes took on a sinister look.

"I want Amnesty," he repeated. "Everybody wants her, but she's mine."

"I don't need Amnesty," I said. "I have Patience."

"You have nothing," Snake said in a furious whisper. For every hour we were shut up in that office, anger was building in him.

"I will kill you and your Patience," Snake said. He lean in to me and held some sort of makeshift knife to my throat.

Between the doors, something moved in the hallway again, making me turn away from Snake suddenly and look to see what it was. No one else seemed to notice, neither the hostages nor the hostage takers. Something made Snake drop his weapon. He bent to pick it up.

"You can threaten me, Snake," I said, in the same tone he had used with me, "but you can't kill me. And you can't touch Patience." Where was this boldness coming from—and with such power? "Go ahead, try. Just try to kill me."

Despite the low volume at which we spoke to each other, the hostages heard our exchange. The woman turned her face to the wall, but Intimidator looked right at us. Snake rested the tip of his weapon at my jugular vein. More movement in the hall—Snake's hand opened—involuntarily—and the weapon fell to the floor again.

Fear, who was oblivious to what was transpiring between Snake and me, started to chant.

"Amnesty, Amnesty," Fear chanted.

"Amnesty," Fire and Snake joined in, chanting, Fire pounding his fist into his palm, Snake looking at me and Sooner as a lion looks at dead meat.

"Amnesty ... Amnesty ... Amnesty," they chanted.

I knelt down beside Sooner, attending to his head

wound, and prayed as the three desperate men's chanting grew louder. Fear knelt on the other side of Sooner, keeping a close watch on me. Fire unlocked the French doors and went out into the hallway, still chanting.

"Amnesty ... Amnesty ... Amnesty," he shouted. Soon throughout Cell Block E, inmates intensely, passionately, determinedly chanted her name—it was the desire of their hearts, a desire so great that most of them no longer thought clearly, for Amnesty was on their minds. They would kill for her if given a chance.

Fire returned to the warden's office, pleased with himself. Snake locked the double doors behind him, still stirred up by the commotion Fire had started.

"You don't need Amnesty," I said to the hostage takers. "You need Jesus! Amnesty can only free your body, but Jesus can truly make you free—body, mind, and spirit. Surrender to Jesus before it's too late. Let Him come in. Let Him have free rein. Confess that Jesus is the Son of God, that God raised Him from the dead, and believe it in your hearts."

"I said shut up!" Fire said. "I don't want to hear it—not today. I'm too close."

Too close to what? Standing between the two men, I wanted to shout to them (as if they would hear) that they were close, close to freedom. But not as the world describes freedom. To be outside of these stone walls, outside of these iron bars, didn't necessarily mean they were outside of prison. They were still in prison to sin, to the love of money, to all the lusts of this world. Only Jesus could free them, and they were too blind to see it.

To my surprise and delight, Dan Sooner revived and looked up at me, at first afraid because of my prison uniform and the hard outer appearance that five years of imprisonment had forced on me. But then he looked deeply into my eyes. I smiled and nodded to him, and peace enveloped him.

"My head, ooh," Sooner said, and tried to lift his hand to rub it, but the duct tape around his wrists stopped him.

"You'll be all right," I told him, still emboldened by an unseen, yet not unknown power. "Lie still." But he didn't—he sat up. His weak voice drew Fear's attention.

"I know how you can get your demands heard," Sooner said, still groggy from his head injury. His statement immediately caught the attention of Fear, who was the only hostage taker who heard him.

"Fire, Snake, listen," Fear shouted. "Say it again, say it again," he said to Sooner. The four of us in our gray uniforms fixed our eyes on Sooner, as he collected his thoughts and stretched his neck, rolling his head to the side.

"I said I know how you can get your demands heard, and maybe get some satisfaction in the process," Sooner said.

"All right, let's hear it," Fire said.

Sooner, determined to stand, went from sitting to kneeling, and with my help, knelt on one knee and finally stood. It was a tedious success. And with his wooziness and hands bound behind him, his balance was off-centered, causing him to almost fall backwards. Quick thinking on my part made me slide the rolling executive chair behind him in time to catch his weakened body.

"My cam ... ooh ... my camera is right ... downstairs ... where we came in," Sooner said. Closing his eyes, he rolled his head around again to stretch his neck. "If I'm not mistaken, this is Warden Vulpine's office. Right?"

"Yeah, yeah, go on," Fire said. He rechecked the

ammunition in the barrel of the shotgun and set the safety.

"You may know that I came here to do an exposé on the conditions in this prison," Sooner said. "What better way to expose Warden Vulpine than right here in his own office? Do you think he has anything to hide?"

"I believe he does," I said. About a week ago, when working special duty in this office, some figures on some invoices and receipts drew my attention away from the tedium of the job I was doing. Seeing the numbers reminded me of the work I had left behind at the bank. I was sickened at what the numbers meant, and I filed the papers away in the drawer where I did my regular filing. I found the invoices and receipts and showed them to Sooner.

"Take a look at these," I said. "And cut him loose, Fire. He's no threat to you."

At Fire's signal, Snake used his weapon to cut the duct tape around Sooner's wrists.

Sooner examined the papers closely.

"Uhmm. Seems like the warden has been greasing his pocket."

"What do you mean, what does he mean, Fire?" Fear asked, shining the floodlight in the face of Fire, who jerked his hand up to protect his eyes from the blinding light.

"Look at this," Sooner said, handing the invoice to Fire. "Notice that last month Warden Vulpine billed the state for four hundred pounds of potatoes, a thousand rolls of toilet tissue, five hundred bars of soap, and so on."

"Yeah, and on the receipt, he actually paid for two hundred pounds of potatoes, five hundred rolls of toilet tissue, and 250 bars of soap. And on dozens of other items, he paid less than half the amount he billed for," Fire said. "That low-down dirty piece of sewer scum."

"He's pocketing that money while we suffer," Snake said. Snake overturned the file cabinet next to the door in anger, surprising Intimidator and the woman, who squealed.

"To keep this kind of operation quiet for so long," I said, "he's got to be making payoffs. Somebody's got to be helping him. I'll bet he keeps a record somewhere in this office."

"That wouldn't be too smart," Sooner said. "But we're not saying Warden Vulpine is the smartest person in this state."

"I'm going to tear this office apart," Fire said, and cocked his gun to shoot off the padlock on a file cabinet.

"No, wait," Sooner said. "That's part of my plan. You can do it, but let's do it live, on camera."

"What's in it for me?" Snake asked. He walked over to the window, lit a cigarette, and peaked out.

"I told you, you get your demands heard, and we take down Vulpine," Sooner said.

"I like it," Fire said. "The warden won't be able to easily lie his way out of it when millions of people are watching him on TV."

"I like it too, Fire," Fear said.

"Fear, you and Snake, go down and bring up the camera. How you going to operate a camera without electricity?"

"Don't worry about that," Sooner said.

"Can they show the warden on TV at the same time you're doing your ... interview?" I asked.

"Yes, I'll insist on it," Sooner said. "I'll need to use the phone to call the station, though."

"I'll do the calling," Fire said.

Sooner's camera was a new battery-operated HL-79A. The camera reception was made possible through an

263

uplink to satellite receivers. Sooner would interview Fire, who would outline his demands. He would then ask about prison conditions and direct specific questions to Warden Vulpine on live television.

In the excitement of this live exclusive, Sooner over-looked his weakened state. He gave Fire the telephone numbers he needed to the station, and I found the number to the warden's home in his Rolodex. Fire called Channel 13, and the station manager and producer called Warden Vulpine. The interview is set up to take place at noon tomorrow.

"Let's set up early," Sooner said. "I want to make sure everything is working right."

March 12, 1990, the third day of not knowing whether Will would live or die, I was glad I would be able at least to see him on television. Two days earlier, it had rained all day, which did nothing to elevate my spirits. My family had remained with me, a good thing for them and for me. Decades-old wounds were being healed, and unworthy memories were being buried, never to rise again.

Today, out in my front yard, the sun had come out, and it was warmer than a mid-March day should be—around sixty degrees. Yellow pansies, planted last fall, opened up with fresh blossoms. Dried blood from the hardware store around the corner, which I sprinkled gingerly around the flowerbed, had succeeded in warding off any small animals that might attempt to munch the inviting blooms. I breathed in the fresh air and lifted my head toward Heaven, thanking God for another day He had kept me, for family who, though not as perfect as ones in books or on television, kept watch with me, and for my husband, whom I was certain would be home soon.

"Let's go in, Patience," Temperance said. "Honey, it's time. It's twelve o'clock."

Her voice and the distant sound of an airplane in the sky brought me back down to Earth. I braced myself, prepared myself, for what I was about to see, then relaxed myself and let the Holy Spirit take control of my thoughts through the Word.

"Whatsoever things are true, honest, just, pure, lovely, of good report, think on these things," I said. Temperance smiled. I smiled. I reached out for her hand. She tucked my scarf under on the right side of my face. We went in.

As expected, everyone had assembled in the living room. Over the past few days, they had become accustomed to making themselves at home and pitching in wherever and whenever necessary. Last night, Soldier had made chili, his specialty. And although the weather was warm and not conducive for the meal, Paw, Rock, Sister, Faith, Strength, Courage, and I ate chili as we waited to see Will.

"Good afternoon, and thank you for tuning in to Channel 13 Noontime News. I'm Mike Buzz. Today, in our live coverage of the hostage situation and the takeover of Cell Block E at Parable State Prison, we will bring to you another exclusive story. From inside Warden Vulpine's office, Dan Sooner, one of the hostages, will interview the hostage takers live, along with Warden Vulpine from his home. Are you ready, Dan?"

"Yes, thank you, Mike. This is Dan Sooner, sitting at the desk of Warden Vulpine in his office at Parable. Standing to my left, holding a shotgun as you can see, is Fire Stalwart. To his left is Snake Torrid. On my right is Fear Not, and on his right is Will Done. Camerawoman Pat Black is behind the camera, and Officer Buck Intimidator sits on the floor, still bound at the wrists with duct tape.

"Let me just say this. Inmate Done was not party to the riot or taking of the hostages. He was caught in the proverbial wrong place at the wrong time. Because of his care for my head wound, I am probably alive today. Thank you, Mr. Done." Will nodded and gave a half smile. He looked good, despite his weight loss since I had last seen him and his longer hair.

"The situation here is intense, to say the least, Mike. The inmates have agreed to this interview as an attempt to make their demands known and to communicate with Warden Vulpine. Are you there, Warden?"

Warden Vulpine's image appeared on a split screen. Dark circles under the warden's eyes made him look tired or sickly. His furrowed forehead gave him a sinister air—the camera was not kind to him at all.

"Good afternoon, Dan," the warden said. "I and all who are viewing this broadcast are concerned about your welfare. I only hope this ordeal can be remedied quickly, without violence or bloodshed. History has shown that negotiations with terrorists seldom succeed. True, this situation is unique in that a news reporter is a hostage. However, I would like to go on record and say that—"

"Warden Vulpine," Sooner interrupted. "Is it true your office bills the state for supplies that aren't ordered?"

"Why you ... What are you trying to pull, Sooner?"

"These inmates, though in a compromised situation here, are prepared to testify that your administration has brutally and illegally punished inmates and has withheld basic sustenance of food and hygiene supplies from them."

"They're prisoners," Vulpine said. He wiped his forehead with a handkerchief. "They have no rights."

"What are you hiding in that locked file cabinet,

Warden?" Fire asked. "Suppose I just shoot off the lock. What would I find?"

"This is outrageous," Vulpine said. "This is supposed to be an interview, not a sideshow."

Fire rolled the chair with Dan Sooner it in from behind the desk and stood in his place directly in front of the camera.

"Would I find evidence of the sweatboxes and the lash?" Fire asked. "Would I find names of the guards you pay off to beat up me and my boys? Would I find names of those who suddenly, without cause turn up dead? Have you been paying Intimidator? It's all so clear now."

Fire pointed the shotgun toward the file cabinet. We all scattered like roaches in a lighted kitchen, not knowing what Fire would do in the angered frame of mind he was in. Pat stayed her course and panned in on the file cabinet, the gun, Will's and Sooner's shock, Fear's passiveness, and Snake's anger.

"This is ridiculous, this is ridiculous," Vulpine said. "Isn't somebody going to stop this? He's standing in front of the window." Vulpine stood, agitated. "He's standing in front of the window."

Crash. Shattering glass. The force of the bullet coming through the window dislodged the venetian blinds and sent them to the floor. Fire had been shot. Dead television air for two or three seconds. Then Mike Buzz came back on.

Shock waves, emanating from the TV around my living room, forced our mouths open and widened our eyes. Three days of this madness had conditioned us to pray at the drop of a hat. If only it had been the drop of a hat instead of the firing of a high-powered rifle through a window.

Patience, I don't know how much of this ordeal you've been watching on the news, but I'm OK. Fire was shot, the force of which knocked him down. He's losing a lot of blood.

"It was a setup," Snake said. He picked up the shotgun that lay at Fire's side. "You set us up. This was your plan all along. Wasn't it?"

"No, no, I assure you," Sooner said. "It was the warden. He must have given some sort of signal to one of the sharpshooters in the towers."

"Turn that camera off and get over here," Snake said. With renewed trembling, Pat obeyed.

"Snake, you're making a mistake," Sooner said.

"Tie them up again and line them up over there beside Intimidator," Snake said. Fear obeyed.

"What are you doing, Snake?" I asked.

"Will ...Will." It was Fire. I bent closer to hear what he was saying.

"What's that prayer?" He asked.

"That prayer? What do you mean?"

"That prayer that gets you into Heaven," Fire said.

I knelt over Fire and prayed for him and with him. There, on the floor in the warden's office, in a pool of blood, Fire gave his life to Christ and accepted Him as his Lord and Savior. I cried with him as he wept as he did when he learned his mother died.

"And Will," he said. "It's On-Fire."

"What's on fire?" I asked.

"No. My name. My parents named me On-Fire."

"If we get out of this mess alive," I said, "promise me that you'll be On-Fire for the Lord."

"Lucky," Snake shouted. "You get over there too. You're all getting it, so say your prayers." He put the shot-

gun to Intimidator's head. "You first," he said.

Through the crack between the French doors, dark light flashed again. No sooner than it did, the doors crashed open. Into the office stormed three men dressed in all black riot gear: helmets with opaque face masks, heavy breastplates, thick leather boots, and loin protection. On their backs were the words "H.I.S. Force." Name patches on each of their breastplates told who they were. H.I.S. Power snatched the gun away from Snake before he could react. H.I.S. Presence unbound everyone's wrists and single-handedly put Fire on a gurney. And H.I.S. Peace wiped my face with a moist white towel.

"Well done," H.I.S. Peace said. "Prepare to go home. People who love you await your return."

It won't be long now, sweetheart. Be easy. Will

Although Will was not charged in any way as having anything to do with the riot and taking of the hostages at Parable, he couldn't be discharged until the completion of a full investigation. In the last in the series "Imprisoned Shame," Dan Sooner revisited Parable and interviewed Will.

"This is Dan Sooner, here with Will B. Done. Warden Vulpine's personal assets have been frozen after evidence found in his office was seized as state's evidence against him and his accomplices, including Officer Buck Intimidator. They both have been put on administrative leave with pay, pending the outcome of the investigation.

"Fire, Snake, and Fear have been put on restriction, and their yard, television, library, and other privileges have been revoked.

"Will, Fire has asked you to return to Parable on a

regular basis as part of a prison ministry. Do you think that's in the future for you?"

"I certainly hope so," Will said. "Fire made a promise to me and, more importantly, to God when he was lying on that floor bleeding, and I believe he'll keep his promise."

"I've arranged a surprise for you, Will."

"Mrs. Done," the news producer said. "On five. Four, three, two, one." He pointed to me, my cue to speak.

"Hi, sweetheart," I said. Dan Sooner had called me the night before and asked my permission to have a camera crew at my house that day. On such short notice, I didn't want to agree at first. Passion was there having tea with me when the call came in and persuaded me to appear on TV and talk to Will. Because of the investigation that could last for weeks, this may be my only opportunity in a long while to speak with him.

"I love you, honey," I said, and waved to him.
Will was speechless. He remembered that in his letter, he was prepared never to see me again. With his elbow on the arm of his chair and his semi-clenched fist under his chin, he watched me with intensity in his eyes—controlled excitement—and a half smile.

"Mrs. Done," Sooner said. "In the past five years, what have you gained most from your experience?"

"During these five years, God has shown me a lot of things, Dan, one of which is that I have a knack for ministering to the sick and shut-in, especially the elderly. I visit them at least once a week." I paused a moment, reflecting on the men and women I visited, almost seeing their beautiful, radiant smiles.

"Other than that, I've been standing on what's been taught at Rugged Cross through Pastor Shepherd. Will and I have been taught that at each stage—or level—of our lives, there are different *states*—or conditions—that we must *contend* with. I believe that because of our latest state—Will's being in prison and my having to *contend* with his being there—I have advanced to my next stage.

"During these five years, God has also prepared me for Will, for the Will who's coming home to me in a couple of weeks. I'm sure this ordeal has changed both of us, and I'm trusting that it's for the better. I've had time to deal with ... well, let's just say some internal issues. I've had to get rid of a lot of unnecessary baggage I've been carrying and nursing for too long. I've gained a lot, but I've gotten rid of a lot also, Dan. I'm sure this emptying out of what has served only to hinder God's plan for my life and God's filling me back up with what I need to carry out His plan will allow me to be a better helper in my husband's ministry.

"This growth was made possible through forgiveness: my forgiveness of others and God's forgiveness of me." I swallowed hard. Although I was used to public speaking, being on live television invoked a different kind of exhilaration and nervousness.

"The Word of God says that for God so loved the world that He gave .... One could almost interpret that as 'for God so *forgave* that He gave .... And Psalms thirty and five says: 'For His anger endures but for a moment; in His favour is life: Weeping may endure for a night, but joy comes in the morning.' And today I'm joyful, that is, teeming with joy! I'm full of joy—my cup runs over with joy! Forgive me, Dan, but I can't help myself!" .

"Are you an ordained minister, Mrs. Done?" Sooner interrupted. "You speak with such power and conviction."

"No, I'm not, Dan."

"Patience, Sister Done," Will said."

"Thank you, Mrs. Done," Sooner said.

"Bye, Sweetheart." I waved again at Will and blew him a kiss.

"And cut," the producer said.

"Will," Sooner continued. "You were in prison for five years, innocent of the charges against you. What did *you* learn in those five years?"

"The greatest thing I've learned, Dan, is how to be content," Will said. "Let me explain. The only way you can be content in a situation such as the one I've endured here at Parable is to be *in* Jesus. That is, to be contained *in* Him—to move, to live, to have your being *in* Him. The last five years were only one chapter in my life, and in my wife's life. It's like a book, having a table of contents."

Dan sat nodding as Will shifted to the side, leaned on the right arm of his chair, and pointed and shook his right hand. His state of mind was moving from being interviewed to ministering.

"Now, depending on the story, those contents can end with that book, or there can be many sequels," Will said. "I believe God has many sequels planned for me and my wife, and my family. Because when you're contained *in* Jesus, that is, moving and living and having your being *in* Him, you know that every place He takes you is for a purpose—His purpose. In His contents, He's the Author and Finisher of your faith—you can rest in that knowledge. You see, this is not the first time I've been a prisoner. When I was called into the ministry, I became, like Paul, a prisoner of Christ, sold out. My employer may not have known it when he hired me. My wife may not have known it when she married me. I, myself, may not even have realized it. The fact is that I was 'contained' in these walls, but I was 'content' in something much larger.

"This experience have changed me—changed my

focus. When I get out of here, my focus will be to seek god-liness, not worldly gain. That's what true contentment is."

"What do you most look forward to when you're released?" Sooner asked.

Soldier, Sister, and Paw had been with me since the ordeal began to see me through to the end. Strength and Courage had to return home to their jobs. Soldier picked up Will from Parable that morning. We waited on the front porch, watching for Soldier's car turning onto my street. Finally, it did. I stood in front as Soldier parked the car. Will got out. I untied my scarf, ran my fingers through my shoulder-length natural hair, combing it out with my fingers into a full Afro. Like the petals of a daisy, it fluffed in the gentle breeze, as if it would blow away if I turned into the wind.

Will's smile was back, in full force. We applauded as he ascended the steps. He grabbed me and we must have hugged and kissed until everyone got embarrassed and went into the house.

"Your hair," Will said. "It's like a halo." He held me tightly again. "My Patience," he said, as we held each other.

"Patience Done," I whispered in his ear.

Behold the State I'm In

Postscript

Behold the State I'm In

"Big Ma," Rock said. "You've been telling me those stories all my life. You and Will need to write a book. You never know, somebody might benefit from it."

Patience-Temperance didn't say anything at first, and Rocky knew why. It was because he had called her Big Ma.

"What's going on with you?" she asked. "Every time you call me Big Ma I know you're overly concerned about something or the other. What is it, Rocky."

"Am I that transparent?" Rock asked. "Sorry, Ma."

"I must admit, kid, I sort of like it when you call me Big Ma. Ma is nice, too. Ma was the first word you ever spoke, you know." She pinched Rock's jaw. "Ooh, you need a shave. I think you're on to something, though, about the book. I'll definitely think about it. I know Will will have a lot to contribute to it if I do write one."

"I'll see it when I believe it," Rock said. Patience-Temperance laughed.

"What was that?"

"I mean, I'll believe it when I see it. You knew what I meant, Ma."

"Yes, I did. See ya, kid."

"If you decide to write, you can use my computer. Bye, Ma." Rock picked up his coat from the floor beside the coat rack next to the kitchen door, not realizing until that moment that he had missed the hook earlier. "Tell Will I'll be over Sunday to watch the game with him."

"I will. Bye."

Patience-Temperance went into her bedroom sat down in her wing-back chair, opened her Bible, and read out loud, displacing with the Word the silence and stillness that Rock always left behind after one of his visits.

"And beside this, giving all diligence, add to your

faith virtue; and to virtue knowledge; And to knowledge temperance; and to temperance patience; and to patience godliness; And to godliness brotherly kindness; and to brotherly kindness charity. For if these things be in you, and abound, they make you that ye shall neither be barren nor unfruitful in the knowledge of our Lord Jesus Christ. Second Peter one, five through eight. That's why Mama named me Patience-Temperance. Because of this Scripture."

From a corner in the room, under a plastic cover, her old Underwood called out to her. It had been five years since Will had been released from prison; what better time than now to start a new project. She sat down in front of it and pondered how she should begin, almost changing her mind, but the Holy Spirit nudged her to begin to type. So she did.

"Computers." She almost spat out the word. "I'm sick of computers. Why do they try to force on the professors every new thing that comes out?"

Patience-Temperance removed the plastic cover and exercised her fingers, extending and bending them.

"No. My typewriter will do just fine," she said, and typed a few words. Soon she was up to her old typing speed, her creative juices flowing as steadily as the spring water behind the old house where she lived back in The Sticks.

She was hot, she was cold. Mama's shallow breaths tickled my ears. Mama shivered, Mama shook. It was a noisy kind of shaking, I heard a dull rumbling deep inside Mama's chest. I felt special getting all of Mama's attention that day.

. . .

278

About the Author

Born in Gaffney, South Carolina, B. (Bunni) Graham Simpson and her family migrated to the Washington, D.C., area in the 1960s. She was baptized at the age of nine, and as an adult she rededicated her life to the service of our Lord and Savior Jesus Christ.

From Memphis to California, she and her husband, Eugene C. Simpson, Sr., a retired Marine, have served in church administration, Christian education, the music ministry, and wherever a need existed in their local church. Her relationship with her husband holds a place that is second only to her relationship with God. Her spiritual gifts are exhortation (according to Romans 12) and teaching (according to Ephesians 4).

Since before the publication of her first book, Simpson has given book presentations and addressed women's groups in the Metropolitan Washington area. She earned her Bachelor of Arts degree in English from Howard University, Washington, D.C., and Master of Arts degrees in management and in business from Webster University, St. Louis, Missouri.

Behold the State I'm In is the second in B. Graham Simpson's series of seven *Behold* books.

Behold, the Bridegroom Cometh, the first in the series, is centered in the Scriptures and effectively marries nonfiction with fiction to create a work of art that will encourage, exhort, and instruct the single Christian woman who wants someday to be married.

The reader will examine overcoming experiences from the author's life: from childhood to recovery from being a widow at the age of 19, to emotional and spiritual growth, to God's uniting her with her husband.

Lisa and Vernetta, fictitious characters, will journey with you through the book. Their comments and questions to the author and to Biblical personalities will help the reader come to grips with issues and concerns facing today's single Christian woman.

To order, visit:
www.BeholdBooks.com